Paladin

The Welsh Guard Mysteries:
Crouchback
Chevalier
Paladin

The Gareth and Gwen Medieval Mysteries:
The Bard's Daughter (prequel)
The Good Knight
The Uninvited Guest
The Fourth Horseman
The Fallen Princess
The Unlikely Spy
The Lost Brother
The Renegade Merchant
The Unexpected Ally
The Worthy Soldier
The Favored Son
The Viking Prince
The Irish Bride
The Prince's Man
The Faithless Fool

The Welsh Guard Mysteries

PALADIN

by

SARAH WOODBURY

To Carew

Cast of Characters

Catrin – lady-in-waiting to Queen Eleanor
Rhys – kingsman to King Edward
Justin – Catrin's son
Edward – King of England
Eleanor – Queen of England
Edmund – Earl of Lancaster, Edward's younger brother
William de Valence – Earl of Pembroke
Vincent de Lusignan—William's relation
Gilbert de Clare – Earl of Gloucester
Humphrey de Bohun – Earl of Hereford
Miles de Bohun – Humphrey's uncle
James – Windsor's butler
Geoffrey Pickford – Windsor's constable
Fernando de Galicia – Alfonso's steward (see below)
Charles – Alfonso's tutor (see below)
Thaddeus – captain of the Windsor's garrison
Father Giles – Windsor's priest
Mildrith – Elizabeth's nanny (see below)

<u>Edward and Eleanor's Children</u>
Daughter b. 1255 – deceased
Katherine b. 1264 – deceased
Joanna b. 1265 – deceased
John b. 1266 – deceased
Henry b. 1268 – deceased
Eleanor b. 1269
Juliana b. 1271 – deceased
Joan b. 1272
Alfonso b. 1273
Margaret b. 1275
Berengaria b. 1276 – deceased
Daughter b. 1277 – deceased
Mary b. 1278
Son b. 1280 – deceased
Elizabeth b. 1282
Edward II b. 1284

A Note on *Paladin*

In the courtly literature of the medieval world, a *paladin* was one of the twelve heroic knights of Charlemagne, equivalent in many ways to King Arthur's *Knights of the Round Table*. Stories of the twelve paladins were as much a part of popular culture in the thirteenth century as Arthur's knights, and included *The Song of Roland*, which tells the story of the paladins' defense of Charlemagne's army against the Saracens and their subsequent deaths. Other stories describe their pilgrimage to Rome and their retrieval of holy relics stolen by the Saracens.

One scholarly theory is that the *Historia Caroli Magni*, a twelfth century pseudo-history of Charlemagne, written under the patronage of Alfonso VI of Spain, doesn't chronicle Charlemagne's activities so much as Alfonso's. In fact, the story conflates the two rulers in much the same way that Geoffrey of Monmouth's *History of the Kings of Britain*, from which the legend of King Arthur in large part derives and which was written under the patronage of Robert of Gloucester, conflates King Arthur with William the Conqueror and justifies the Norman conquest of Britain.

1

Gwynedd

22 August 1284

Catrin

"My king! My king!" The unmistakable relief in the messenger's voice at reaching the royal party carried all the way to where Catrin and Rhys were riding at the rear of the company.

For the journey from Caernarfon to Bangor, Queen Eleanor had given Catrin a reprieve as her lady-in-waiting, and Rhys's task was far less momentous than usual, in that he was charged merely with keeping an eye on the left side of the road, which at the moment wasn't much more than the Menai Strait and hardly worth the attention of a king's guardsman, quaestor, and spymaster. They were within sight of Bangor Cathedral, having traveled ten miles that day, which was something of a miracle given the sodden state of the road and the unrelenting rain.

Edmund, King Edward's younger brother and the Earl of Lancaster, known to all and sundry as *Crouchback*, had been riding towards the front of the company, so he was the first to hear what the messenger had to say. The moniker was a remnant of Edmund's participation in the ninth crusade. Rhys had participated in that crusade too, but for over a year after King Edward's conquest of Wales, he had hidden himself in Caernarfon. But these days he was out in the world again, married to Catrin, and serving the King of England. He could no longer deny who he'd been then and who he was now.

So he wore the cross on his left shoulder too. It was a necessary concession now that he was a member of the royal court again. To all in that court but Catrin and Rhys, the conquest of Wales was a triumphant victory, not to be questioned. Wearing the cross mitigated the extent to which others looked upon him with suspicion.

"Rhys—" Catrin put out a hand, bringing both their horses to a halt, which was just as well since the entire company was also stopping.

Rhys gripped her hand. "Perhaps it's just another message like Cole was carrying and nothing to concern us."

He was referring to the first investigation he'd conducted for the king, in which a messenger from Gilbert de Clare had brought news from the French court. That news had been important to King Edward but not worth dying over. But Catrin and Rhys had heard bad news so many times in the last few years, from so many different directions, that Catrin couldn't stop her heart from constricting to think what could unsettle the king so completely that he'd keep the entire company standing in the rain.

And then Simon, Rhys's commander and closest friend, reined in at the edge of the road and spoke in the coldest voice Catrin had ever heard him use, "You need to come right now. You too, Catrin. The queen needs you. Alfonso is dead."

For a moment, Catrin refused to believe it, and then a wail of horror began rising in the back of her mind, made worse with every heartbeat by Simon's hurried explanation of what had happened. They arrived at the queen's carriage to find it stopped in the middle of the road, and the queen herself pale as new snow. She clutched baby Edward to her, even as her cousin Margaret begged to take him from her, since he was crying at being held so close. King Edward stood next to the open door of the carriage, bowed in grief and heedless of the rain falling on the back of his bared head.

Rhys and Catrin dismounted to one side, not wanting to intrude by approaching too closely. "I'm so sorry, my lord," Rhys said.

There was nothing else to say when faced with such grief. Catrin wasn't able to speak at all. Alfonso had been the eldest son, though really just the surviving son, since his older brothers had died before him. And now, as Simon had hastily explained on the short ride to the queen's carriage, he too was dead of an illness that had killed him with unexpected rapidity.

At Rhys's words, however, the king's head came up, and although tears streamed without shame down his cheeks, when he spoke his voice was steady. "You will go, you and Catrin, right now. Rhys as my representative and Catrin as the queen's." He swung around to look at his brother. "Edmund will go as well. Through him, you will have all the authority you need."

Catrin knew without asking that the only reason the king was sending his brother with them was because he couldn't go himself.

"Of course, my lord," Rhys said, as if he could have said anything else in this moment. "Where are we going?"

It appeared from the outside that the king's grief was already further along than that of his wife, whose face remained white enough to indicate shock. But then, how does one ever encompass the sudden death of a beloved son? The king wanted action, and he had the power to make other people do his bidding, whether or not what he wanted made sense. It was enough that, in his grief, he wanted it.

"To Windsor."

That was where the royal children were being raised while the king and queen toured their newly conquered territory. In order to reach their party on that windy and rainy road near Bangor, the news had traveled first to Chester by pigeon, and then the horseman would have been sent racing across Gwynedd to Caernarfon in hopes of reaching the king before many more days had passed.

As it was, by the time the king heard the news, Alfonso had been dead three days, and would soon be buried at Westminster Abbey. The boy had died exactly ten years to the day after the king himself had been crowned in the same spot. Having served two years at Queen Eleanor's side, Catrin herself had known the boy. He'd been clever and even-natured, and the devastation to his parents at his death could not be underestimated. Even Catrin, who so despised what King Edward had done to her country, could not rejoice at the loss of his son.

Simon, who'd dismounted too and remained nearby, stepped closer at the king's words. "My lord, if I may, what are you hoping to achieve by sending Rhys and Catrin all that way?"

"Answers."

None of their previous investigations had carried the heavy weight of the king's own expectations. The news the messenger had brought in that hour—the very day the king's entourage had set out from Caernarfon heading east—was the worst and most terrible that parents could ever hear.

Appropriately, as they stood on the windswept road from Caernarfon with the ruin of all the king's hopes and plans in the muck at their feet, the rain started coming down hard enough to make none of them sure what were raindrops and what were tears.

In utter silence, the party made its way into Bangor, where they'd planned to spend the night in the cathedral guesthouse. The king and queen chose to forgo all sleep, in favor of standing vigil from afar over their dead son. Catrin and Rhys spent a restless night, rising early with the intent to leave at first light.

That made it very early indeed when Simon sought them out with their last instructions, making clear what he had to tell them came directly from the king. "Queen Eleanor has birthed sixteen children. Ten are dead. Only five daughters and baby Edward survive. At ten years old, Alfonso was long past the age where he should have been felled by disease."

"The king truly suspects he was murdered?" Catrin asked warily.

It wasn't that the idea was new. She and Rhys had lain awake most of the night discussing the possibility and its ramifications. How could they not? As the king's quaestor, or *one who asks questions*, it was Rhys's job to investigate unexplained death. He would be the first to admit, however, that not all unexplained deaths were murder.

"He does. I might even say that he hopes for it." Simon lowered his voice, even though they were alone in the guesthouse common room at the monastery. "If God ordained him to be king, why has He given him such fragile sons? Is he being punished for his misdeeds?" Even as he spoke, Simon threw out a hand to stop either Rhys or Catrin from making the obvious observation that the brutality of Edward's conquest of Wales was worthy of divine retribution. "He needs to know if his son was struck down by God's wrath, punishment for the sins of the father visited on the son, or if a human hand was involved."

"Just because a human hand was involved doesn't mean it wasn't God's Will." Catrin couldn't help pointing out the obvious omission in the reasoning. "The world is always as God ordains. The difference is if He actually sent the hand that felled Alfonso or if He simply allowed it to happen."

"The theology of men's free will is not our concern today," Simon said grimly. "It is Edward who rules by God's Will. It is between him and his priest to determine why God would allow him to keep his throne and yet send him so much grief. But if someone murdered his son, he needs to know. And—" Simon paused in a way that had both Rhys and Catrin watching him carefully.

The pause was long enough for Catrin to prompt him. "What is it, Simon?"

"If Alfonso was murdered, then we have to consider the possibility that his other sons were too."

It was a fearsome idea. Catrin could well imagine the anguish and guilt wracking the king for him to look back at those other deaths, long accepted as natural and put to rest, and question them too. It also made the task with which Edward had charged them all the more momentous, as if it wasn't great enough already.

"If someone did murder Alfonso, we will do our best to find out who," Rhys said.

"The king knows you will."

"But how are we to manage this?" Catrin spoke with a tinge of despair in her voice. "There will be no physical evidence left by the time we arrive. All we'll have to go on is what people say or don't say, and even with the help of Prince Edmund, nobody at Windsor is going to want to talk to us. We are Welsh, Simon!"

"Didn't I mention this already? The king knows the nature of the royal court as well as anyone. He is sending for some friends to assist you."

"What friends?" Rhys looked hard at Simon. "His or ours?"

"I suppose that's a matter of perspective. Anyway, riders have already been sent to summon Vincent de Lusignan and Miles de Bohun. This was at my recommendation, you understand." Simon gave them a small, sad smile. "It will be just like old times."

Catrin begged to differ. Not only were they being sent to Windsor to investigate the death of Prince Alfonso, but they were now to do it with two men they couldn't trust: Vincent had left Rhys for dead at Cilmeri less than two years ago; and Miles was their chief suspect in an act of sabotage that might have ended the king's life only three weeks ago at Nefyn.

It wasn't going to be *like old times* at all.

2

Windsor Castle

1 September 1284

Rhys

*T**en days later …*

"Vincent really did come." Catrin squinted across the upper bailey of Windsor Castle as a figure strode towards them, having exited the great hall. There were two great halls at Windsor: one in the lower bailey, which was for the majority of the retainers and workers at the castle, and a second, smaller one, here in the upper bailey, intended for the use of everyone who catered specifically to the royal family.

"And he beat us here." Rhys found himself glaring at the newcomer until Catrin poked him, and he subsided.

"Of course he came," Prince Edmund said. "The king himself summoned him."

And that was all one needed to say about the power of the King of England and those who served him.

Since the king had ordered them to Windsor, Rhys and Catrin had done nothing except ride across England and plan for their approach to the investigation of Alfonso's death. They had decided to begin in Alfonso's quarters, progressing to interviewing residents of the castle and then the citizens of Windsor, if that became necessary. It would be a matter of starting with a single moment, Alfonso's death, and working inward (rather than outward) from there, almost like walking the spiral of a snail's shell, circling ever closer to their central objective: namely, the truth. Hopefully, they also wouldn't be working at a snail's pace.

Getting the residents of Windsor Castle to talk, and even more to tell the truth, had to be done, and done thoroughly, if they were to assuage the fears of their grieving king. And although Rhys wanted answers, the first moments of their arrival were a time for observation, not questions. His first observation was that it felt odd—given that everyone in their party was still suffering some degree of shock at Alfonso's death—to see everyone here going about their usual business. At least at first glance.

The guards at the main gate had been respectful and well-organized, the stable boys had taken charge of the horses with minimal fuss, and the garrison captain, a man named Thaddeus, had himself come to greet them. The prince's men had then dispersed to their various duties, with one running ahead to the upper bailey to inform the constable, Geoffrey Pickford, that Prince Edmund had arrived.

Rhys remembered Captain Thaddeus from the Holy Land, which was likely how he'd achieved his present position. (Not so different, in a way, from Rhys himself.) Thaddeus would have escorted them to the upper bailey if Prince Edmund hadn't dismissed him, telling him he wanted to stretch his legs with only Rhys and Catrin as company. Edmund was a prince, the king's brother, so of course the captain gave way with a bow and the repeated assurance that if he needed *anything* he had only to ask.

Vincent had been on crusade too. At first, he had been friends with Rhys and Simon, before his brutality towards those beneath him had put a halt to their friendship, and Rhys had felt forced to chastise him for it in public. In his anger, Vincent had threatened to kill Rhys, and had nearly made good on his promise at Cilmeri, in the devastating ambush where Rhys's lord, Llywelyn ap Gruffydd, the last Prince of Wales, had been assassinated. Rhys was glad the king's children weren't being cared for at the Tower of London, where they sometimes resided. To enter the castle there, he would have had to pass Llywelyn's head, which to this day was being displayed there on a pike. He shuddered every time he thought of it.

And then, a month ago, in the midst of Nefyn's tournament melée, Vincent had comprehensively apologized, told Rhys he was glad he hadn't died at Cilmeri, and thanked him for changing the course of his life that day in the Holy Land. In the weeks since, Rhys had thought long and hard about Vincent's apology and had come to the inescapable conclusion that he could not hate a man who no longer hated him, no matter how comfortable the emotion.

Still, the sight of him had stopped Rhys in his tracks and that familiar feeling of anger had risen up within him. Vincent's side had won Edward's war. Because of it, Rhys was here, in service to those who had shattered his world. He was so flustered, in fact, that he almost stumbled over one of the bailey's paving stones that kept the everpresent mud, with which every castle had to contend, at bay.

Seeing his dismay, as she would, Catrin put a hand on his arm and said in Welsh, "Remember what we've talked about. The past is the past. He wants to move on, and so do we. What's more, we have a job to do, and we have been ordered to do it with him."

Rhys took in a breath and let it out slowly—along with the anger that had colored his vision red for a moment. It was that same anger, following an old pathway and old pattern, that had told him to attack Vincent in Nefyn. Even if he still had been at odds with Vincent, Rhys wouldn't have wanted his anger to show. He was better than that. Since Cilmeri, he had learned how to be.

Oblivious to the turmoil inside Rhys, or at least pretending to be, Edmund said, "It may be that Pembroke is here too. That would be a pleasant surprise."

Pleasant would not have been the word Rhys would have used. *Aggravating* maybe. That would be because the Earl of Pembroke wasn't just any retainer to the King of England. He was William de Valence, Edward's uncle and—more to the point—one of the worst of the Norman oppressors in Wales. Rhys might be on the edge of forgiving Vincent, but he still felt fully free to despise Vincent's lord.

Vincent, on the other hand, appeared entirely composed, making Rhys feel petty and small. It was only the widening of Vincent's eyes that indicated he himself was at all discomfited. He also had a half-smile on his lips, as if he was actually *happy* to see them.

Then Vincent's overall expression became much more somber as he bowed before Prince Edmund. "My lord, please accept my condolences and those of your uncle, Lord Valence, on the loss of Alfonso. I am so sorry to be greeting you in this way at this hour. Lord Valence would have come himself if matters hadn't needed his direct attention on his estates."

"Thank you, Vincent. I will convey these sentiments to the king and queen when next I see them." Then Edmund turned slightly to gesture to Rhys and Catrin. "I believe you are acquainted with Sir Reese and his wife, Lady Catrin?"

Vincent bent his head. "I was honored to have witnessed your union in Nefyn." He straightened and put out his hand to Rhys. "Good to see you."

Somewhat numbly, because he was still struggling to come to terms with this strange version of his old enemy, Rhys grasped his forearm. "And you, Vincent."

As it turned out, being polite was not only the least he could do, but it was easy to do—at least in this moment with the sun shining down on them and the prince looking on. He could almost believe that Cilmeri could one day be no more than a bad memory.

Prince Edmund then spied Sir Geoffrey, the constable, coming out of the royal quarters. He glanced at Rhys for a moment, with what Rhys would have sworn was speculation, and then gave him a brief nod. "I will speak to the constable to ensure that you are given full range of the castle. Nobody will stop you from going where you wish and asking any question that arises. We will talk later."

"Yes, my lord." Catrin spoke for both of them, since Rhys's tongue remained stuck on the roof of his mouth.

Rhys knew what Edmund was saying to him under the surface: from this moment onward, he was the king's representative. They were here to investigate Alfonso's death, and the sooner they got started the better. Edmund had been a party to the plan they'd outlined on the journey, even if he thought they should be putting him to better use than merely being the person who paved the way for them. He insisted that, at the very least, he would keep his eyes and ears open.

In truth, that was all any of them would be doing.

At least Rhys couldn't suspect Vincent of having anything to do with Alfonso's death, for all that he was without a doubt the last man with whom Rhys would have wanted to join forces in this time and place. Truly, if someone had told him six months ago that he would be in the king's service, married to Catrin, and investigating the possible murder of the king's son at Windsor Castle—with Vincent—the last item would have been the most surprising thing.

Regardless, with a mental shrug, he reoriented himself to his new reality and said, "You made good time."

"As did you with a great deal farther to go. I arrived last night." He gave a little cough. "I was, I confess, somewhat surprised to receive the king's summons. They came from him, as they would, but since you are in charge of the investigation, they must have come from you." He paused. "Thank you for sending for me. Thank you for trusting me."

Rhys had thought he couldn't be surprised again by Vincent, but here he was gaping again. He felt like his brain was as mushy as the mud that had spattered his shins to the knees.

Catrin stepped in, being far quicker of mind than he. "We have much to talk about. Suffice to say, it is lovely to see a friendly face, Vincent. Do you know where we are staying? I would like to get out of my traveling clothes."

Vincent immediately looked contrite, giving Rhys time to put his thoughts in better order. "My apologies, Catrin. I didn't think. I was just so relieved to see you." He cleared his throat. "I hope you realize that all of England and Wales knows by now that you have ridden to Windsor. Rumors abound as to why."

Catrin looked from Vincent to Rhys. "We didn't know."

"Are you certain?" Rhys was proud of himself for speaking without emphasis, as if the answer to his question was merely of casual interest instead of urgent.

Vincent let out a laugh. "Quite certain. To know that the great Rhys ap Iorwerth is riding once again with Prince Edmund? How can you be surprised that everyone who is anyone would be interested in that? You saved his life. As rumor has it, you have recently saved the king's life as well. Twice."

Calling Rhys *great* was surely hyperbole. But perhaps the most telling part of what Vincent had said was that he'd pronounced Rhys's name correctly, down to the trilled *r*'s, instead of the usual Saxonization of it to *Reese ap Yourworth*.

Catrin moved a little closer to Rhys. "So they know he is a member of the king's guard?"

"Yes, they know this and more. They also know that he's been in the king's company since April, uncovering two terrible mysteries in the process. I heard all about it this morning from the boy who brought firewood for my hearth. Believe me, it is a tale worthy of the Knights of the Round Table we were all pretending to be at Nefyn. *A Welshman saving the life of the king.* It's what everyone wants to hear. Even more, it's what they want to *believe*."

"I didn't save his life," Rhys said.

"Haven't you learned by now how little the truth matters in these situations?" Vincent sounded entirely serious. "And I wouldn't go that far anyway. His life *has* been in danger. You can't deny it, not with what we saw at Nefyn."

No, I cannot deny it, and we are not only going to also be working with you, but with Miles de Bohun, who was right in the thick of it.

Rhys didn't say that, however. They hadn't told anyone about Miles's possible role in the sabotage of the viewing stand, nor about the ledger in which they'd found the information. He was also biting his tongue over the supposed accolades directed at him. He had known that joining the king's guard would make some of his own people see him as a traitor, and that the English might uphold him as an example of a *good* Welshman. That it had happened so quickly might make the job they had to do here easier, but he hoped he wasn't going to despise himself at the end of it.

"I am concerned about the attempts on the king's life. Of course, I am. There have been at least four in the last six months that I know of, never mind that I may or may not have saved him from any of them. But it is unwise to talk about this in public." While they'd been conversing, Rhys had been looking around the bailey. There was nobody else within twenty yards, but a cursory glance at the surrounding buildings found at least five separate faces poking out of doors and windows and then pulling back to remain hidden. "At Caernarfon, the king told me *the walls have ears*. But if a castle under construction wasn't a safe place to talk, Windsor is going to be far less so. Everyone here spies on everyone else out of self-preservation—especially now with Alfonso's death. You have to assume at all times that you are not only being watched but overheard."

"Then where and when?" Vincent asked, without objecting to being lectured about what he likely already knew.

"You know Windsor better than I do," Rhys said.

Vincent thought a moment. "The keep. Once you've settled and have dined, I would be grateful if you would meet me there as the bell tolls for Compline." He nodded his regards at Rhys's assent and walked away.

Watching him leave, Rhys focused on Vincent's use of the word *grateful*. It was a word he had never heard come out of a Norman's mouth before. In his past investigations, Rhys had prided himself on his ability to put himself in another man's shoes, but somehow, he was finding those worn by Vincent, of all people, to be a most awkward fit.

3

Day One

Catrin

"He is *so* sincere, Rhys." Catrin shook her head. "He pulls at my heartstrings, but how can we trust him? He's a Norman. What's more, he almost killed you!"

"For which he has apologized."

"Still—"

"I agree that we would be fools to," Rhys said flatly. "He knows it too. Which makes it harder yet again to distrust him."

"Regardless, Rhys, you need to make him feel wanted." Catrin could hear the warning tone in her voice. She didn't often tell her husband what to do, but this was important enough to talk about openly, ears or no ears.

Rhys let out a sharp breath. "I know that, Catrin. Vincent has extended the olive branch. Whatever is in my heart, or in his, I cannot be so churlish as not to take it."

Somewhat to Catrin's dismay, despite what she'd said to Vincent, they didn't even stop in their own rooms to change, never mind bathe, before beginning their investigation in Alfonso's suite of rooms in one of the towers. Possibly, if the king and queen eventually decided to raise baby Edward at Windsor Castle too, these would belong to him, since he was now the heir to the throne. For now, they were a memorial to the lost prince.

As Catrin stood in the center of Alfonso's receiving room, turning slowly on one heel to take in the whole of the room, she had to acknowledge that she and Rhys, two people who'd experienced great loss of friends and family (ironically, many at the king's hands), were the perfect investigators for this death. They completely understood the desire to know how and why Alfonso had died. Unlike the defeated Welsh, however, the king had the power to send them to unearth what he himself couldn't.

With a wry look at Catrin, Rhys entered the adjacent chamber where Alfonso's bed was located. Catrin stayed in the receiving room to go through Alfonso's collection of possessions.

The sight of them made her want to weep, and it was hard to focus on what she was supposed to be doing when all she could think about was what a sweet boy Alfonso had been and what an enormous loss to his parents his death was. She also couldn't help wondering if his death was also a loss to Wales. It was hard to know when a boy was ten what he would be like at thirty or at the death of his father.

That said, according to Edward's mother, King Edward had been focused and driven from birth, walking and talking long before it was normal for any child, determined always to *win*, to *conquer*.

That hadn't been Alfonso, for all that he'd enjoyed games and his training for war. She picked up a wooden ball that was sitting on the table. It matched a stick leaned up against the wall in the corner, very similar to the toys her own son, Justin, had played with as a boy. She could only be grateful that Justin had lived when so many did not. The stick and ball also indicated that Alfonso must have had at least one playmate, even if only his nine-year-old sister. Given their relative closeness in age, if Margaret had been a boy instead of a girl, she would have shared rooms with Alfonso instead of with her younger sister Mary.

Alfonso also seemed to have a fondness for carved men and horses, as he had a collection on a shelf above a table set against a side wall. Judging by the smoothness of the wood, discolored by years of a child's dirty hands, he'd played with them often. Well-used also was his wooden sword, fitted with its own sheath and small enough for Alfonso's ten-year-old body. To all appearances, Alfonso had been a bright boy with a sunny disposition. As she held his little wooden horse, she hoped very much that nobody had, in fact, wished him ill.

What was entirely absent were ledgers or documents, which Catrin would have gone through if he'd been an adult. But being only ten, Alfonso's household accounts would have been kept by his steward or possibly the castle constable. He did have books, however, which was something of a surprise, since by all accounts, Alfonso had been one to play outdoors and not for scholarly pursuits. She took down the first book and had to smile to see that it was one she herself often read aloud to Queen Eleanor: *The Song of Roland.* A second was a history of Charlemagne, translated from the original Latin into French. Both books were stirring tales of the twelve paladins of Charlemagne, recounting their battles against the Saracens. Further examination revealed that Alfonso had the Latin versions of both books too, though these were less worn.

King Edward favored stories of Arthur, and Alfonso had several of those as well, though the Norman Arthur could hardly be recognized as the one the Welsh knew. But once she saw the titles of the books at the top of the pile, Catrin could no longer be surprised Alfonso had kept them—and had read them, judging by the well-worn pages. He bore the same name as the king who'd commissioned them, the great Spanish king Alfonso VI.

Then a knock came at the door behind Catrin. At her *Come in!* it opened to reveal a beardless man with black hair, wearing a long black robe. At the sound of his arrival, Rhys stepped back into the main room.

"Señor. Señora." The man greeted them in Spanish and then switched to heavily accented French, putting his heels together and bowing to each of them in turn. "I am sorry to disturb." He put a hand to his chest. "I am Fernando de Galicia, Alfonso's steward, retained by the king to ensure that Prince Alfonso's every need was met and also that he learned Castilian, in homage to his uncle and namesake, King Alfonso of Castilla, God rest his soul."

Catrin glided forward. "Of course, we are pleased to meet you."

"Prince Edmund told me you would be here, and I took it upon myself to greet you. I understand you are sent by the king to inquire into the death of his son. I can assure you, without a doubt or hesitation, that Prince Alfonso died of a sudden illness and nothing I or anyone at Windsor did or did not do could have prevented it."

This came all in a rush, answers to questions they hadn't yet asked, but answers they also would have expected to hear from the man who oversaw the prince's care.

Rhys bent his head congenially. "I appreciate that you came immediately to speak to us. I can see that you cared deeply for Alfonso and are horrified by his loss."

Fernando took in a breath. "Gracias. Thank you. It is a terrible tragedy to lose him. We are all devastated." He gestured to the space around him. "As you can see, we left everything as it was the day he died, except for changing the linens, of course."

"Please tell me of Alfonso. It seems that you, of everyone here, might have known him best." It was shameless pandering on Catrin's part, but it worked.

"He was a sweet boy, obedient and clever—far cleverer than one might expect, given that he wanted all the time to be running and playing, wrestling with the stable boys, pranking the kitchen staff, or practicing with his sword and bow."

"He does have these books—"

Fernando spoke over her before she finished her sentence, seemingly eager to please. "He *loved* those stories. In his own mind, he was a paladin, just like Charlemagne's knights. And while he was proud to be named after his great-uncle, he insisted of late that we all should call him *Astolfo*." Here Fernando shook his head indulgently. "We humored him. Of course we did. Nobody could object to his enthusiasm. Well—" he paused again, "—except perhaps for his tutor."

"Alfonso was not the best student?"

"He hated formal lessons." Again, Fernando's smile was indulgent.

"Some of his books are in Latin, and one can see that they've been read."

Fernando laughed. "The books Alfonso loved had been originally written in Latin, so he was determined to read and understand them in the original."

He paused, his hand going to his mouth. "Excuse me. I must retire." His voice cracked as he turned away, and his cheeks were suddenly wet with tears.

Catrin felt like weeping to see it.

With Fernando gone, Rhys was less moved. "When he first arrived, he was very nervous."

"He, of all who work here, will likely be losing his position. What need will there be for a caregiver from Castile when none here have ties to Castile?"

"It certainly made him forthcoming." But then Rhys gave a low laugh. "He talked plenty. He just didn't say anything."

"He won't be the only one," Catrin said.

On the road, they'd discussed how to investigate Alfonso's death without offending his memory. They'd known there would be speculation about why they'd come. Gossip moved around a castle—and a country, as Vincent testified—rapidly. With their arrival today, rumor had to be proceeding like an autumn storm. By not eating in the hall, they'd added to it. It appeared that Edmund had known that and had put the bow to the crwth, as Prince Llywelyn used to say, and revealed the truth to everyone: *the king sent us to investigate Alfonso's death.*

"While true, it's their livelihoods—and lives—at stake."

That was a fact of life as well. With Prince Alfonso dead, five daughters remained alive and needed tending. If Catrin and Rhys uncovered something amiss in their treatment by any caregiver, all caregivers might be dismissed. And that was at best. At worst, the king's rage could see them hanged. They would know that too. They would fear it, and that fear would either keep anyone from speaking out at all—or cause them to turn on one another.

Either way, Catrin and Rhys would find themselves showered with a mix of truth and lies and not know which was which. She supposed that had been true in both of their previous investigations together as well.

"Answers in the negative are still answers," Catrin reminded her husband. "What I'm concerned about now is that, up until his tears, what Fernando said to us was well-rehearsed."

"If I were in his shoes, I would have prepared a statement," Rhys said. "It isn't as if everyone here hasn't had days to think about what to say. From the moment Alfonso fell ill, every one of the people in Windsor Castle feared they would be blamed for not doing enough for him. When Fernando reports that he spoke to us and that we are indeed investigating Alfonso's death, the line between what people want to be true and what they tell us is true will start to blur even more."

4

Day One

Rhys

While Catrin at long last *attained a bath*, to use her words, Rhys braced himself for his first real conversation with Vincent. If nothing else, Rhys was glad he'd managed to get a look around Alfonso's rooms before conferring with anyone else about the investigation. He was unsurprised not to have found much of interest, at least in terms of why Alfonso had died. If someone was responsible for Alfonso's death, he would have cleaned up after himself days ago.

That Alfonso was already buried could not be undone, not without the king himself ordering it. Short of finding a vial of poison left under the bed, which he already knew by looking wasn't there, any physical proof of cause of death was long gone.

Rhys had gone just a few steps from the guesthouse door, when a man left the kitchen carrying a tray of food. He took one look at Rhys and immediately turned right around and headed back inside. Vincent had implied that Rhys's exploits were well-known and respected. But there had been fear in that man's face. Rhys supposed the sooner he accepted his role as one to be feared, if not loathed, the easier all this was going to be.

Rhys exited the upper bailey, retracing his steps from earlier that day in the other direction, but instead of continuing on the gravel pathway to the gatehouse that led to the lower bailey, he took the stairway that led up the motte to Windsor Castle's old keep. The Conqueror, King William I, had built the original wooden keep as part of a motte and bailey castle, one of a dozen small fortresses thrown up in a ring around London to consolidate his conquest of England. In the process, he'd demoted the old castle of Windsor, once a favorite of the Saxon kings and located three miles down the Thames, to a royal hunting lodge.

Although in the subsequent centuries, Windsor had been turned into a palace, and thus expanded to three or four times the size of the original, these later upgrades had all been built around William's first castle. This keep, instead of being torn down entirely, had been rebuilt in stone. Rhys was quite sure it had been retained as a monument to King William and his, at times, desperate struggle to conquer England. Certainly it was a reminder of what had been required of the Normans to wrest the country from the Saxons and keep it. He himself could testify that, although the Saxons had long since been subdued, war was still a way of life to these English kings. Rhys swore his people would never become as cowed as the Saxons. Still, at this point, it was hard to see how they could avoid being wholly subsumed into England.

"You chose well," Rhys said to Vincent, having entered through the great doorway and found himself in a large receiving room. At one time this space had been the heart of Windsor, where the king had received the homage of his new subjects. "Is the place actually empty?"

"Entirely. I made sure of it. We cannot be overheard."

How completely Vincent had taken Rhys's caution to heart was simultaneously gratifying and disconcerting. Passing through the central hall, they reached the old guardroom, located at the end of a curving passage.

"What did Sir Geoffrey think of your request to clear the keep?" Rhys sat in the padded chair Vincent indicated and accepted the cup of wine he offered him.

Vincent's expression could have been withering, but instead it was amused. "You have been away from court too long, my friend."

My friend. Rhys mentally shook himself, struggling to accept what Vincent was telling him: he really did want bygones to be bygones, even as Rhys almost swallowed his tongue in his effort to avoid mentioning the fact that he'd spent six months recuperating from the wound Vincent had given him at Cilmeri.

"Nobody is going to gainsay any request coming from me, Rhys. William de Valence is the second-most powerful man in England, behind only the king."

"Don't let Prince Edmund hear you say that!" Rhys managed a laugh, and then realized he was genuinely amused. Rhys had missed Simon, his best friend in life, during their years apart.

It seemed he'd missed Vincent too, and it was strange how the hole left inside Rhys by Vincent's absence from Rhys's life had been easier to fill with hatred than forgiveness.

"He would be the first to admit it." Vincent made a motion with his head. "Regardless, nobody had the temerity to question me. You would do well to emulate my approach, Rhys. *You* represent the king."

"It's still an adjustment," Rhys managed to say.

"I can imagine." Vincent could have spoken dryly. If he'd been Miles he would have. Instead, his words conveyed understanding and compassion.

They were being absurdly nice to each other. Rhys felt compelled to consider how far he really was willing to go to clear the air. "Do you want to talk about—" He waggled his hand back and forth in the air as if to say, *you and me.*

"I want to talk about it if you want to talk about it. I said what I needed to say at Nefyn."

Rhys sat back in his chair, studying the other man. The entire situation was unlooked-for and also unaccountable. But still, it was before him. In that moment, Rhys decided the truth could no longer hurt him. "I don't need to talk about it. I am well."

Vincent laughed. "Are you? I all but killed you. You can't brush that away like a crumb from your sleeve. I know that. This will take time. But I'm also not going anywhere."

Normans never admitted they were wrong. They certainly didn't apologize. Only a very great need could have driven Vincent to do so. The niggling fear rose again in Rhys's mind that it was the only way Vincent knew to insert himself in Rhys's investigations.

And yet, it had been Simon, via the king, who'd asked for him to come, and Catrin was right that Vincent seemed entirely sincere about the way Rhys had changed his life.

"Have you become a saint?"

"Hardly." Vincent laughed, roundly and fully. "I know what your people in Pembroke think of me, and *saint* would not be the word they would use." He paused. "However, after Cilmeri, I went to a very dark place. My king had won. My lord was in high favor for his role in the victory, and I'd killed the friend who'd made me the man I'd become. I drank—"

This time the pause was longer. Rhys didn't want to prompt him, since this confession was his and his alone to make.

After another few breaths, Vincent continued, "I drank more than a man should who wants to retain his position." He gestured with the cup in his hand. "I still do, perhaps. Less now since Nefyn." He bent his gaze on Rhys. "You changed my life again."

Rhys stared at him. "You drink less since you learned I was alive?"

"That and—" the confession went to an even less looked-for place, "—then your Catrin moved the heart of my beloved, Joan, and she accepted my hand. We will be married in a fortnight, once her brother's affairs are fully settled."

"You credit Catrin for that?"

"She extended to Joan the hand of friendship, based on no knowledge of who she was, other than someone in need. Through her, Joan saw that her hatred for her brother was harming herself more than it had ever hurt him—and made no difference whatsoever to him now that he was dead. Catrin made Joan realize that it was her own decision whether to continue to allow his choices to rule hers."

Rhys would have to be cold indeed to deny Vincent's offer of friendship now. Sitting there, in a guardroom so much like the one in which they'd first served, he couldn't do so and be the man he wanted to be—for Catrin's sake, if for no one else's. Maybe Vincent missed Rhys as a friend. Maybe the two of them really could move forward together. Rhys hadn't made so many friends in this life that he could ever be casual about discarding even this one.

So be it. The honesty Vincent had meted out deserved some in return.

"In which case, you deserve the same truth you've given me, Vincent. I would have done the same as you at Cilmeri, if our roles had been reversed. For that, you do not need to apologize. You could have stabbed me in the heart. You didn't. You did exactly enough, in fact, to ensure that your companions left me alone."

"To bleed to death."

"To live," Rhys said, gently. "I lived."

5

Day One

Catrin

Catrin was being treated like a lady. While it wasn't a new experience, since she'd run her own household since she was sixteen years old, it was new again to her, because she hadn't been treated this respectfully since she'd joined Queen Eleanor's retinue. On one hand, a woman couldn't be afforded a higher honor than serving the queen directly. On the other, being a lady-in-waiting to the queen often amounted to being hardly more than a servant herself. It had been two years since she'd joined the queen's household, and she'd done it for long enough now that she'd almost forgotten what it was like to order others about.

Servants were much the same the world over, however, no matter in what castle one found oneself. Catrin had been here before too, not long ago, in fact, before the king and queen had set out on their long journey through Wales. Earlier, Eliza, one of the older servants, had brought Catrin wine as she'd been sitting in the guesthouse common room, a well-appointed area on the main floor, with a few cushioned chairs, two window seats, and a banked fire that had provided a pleasant amount of warmth at the ending of the day.

Now, as Catrin soaked in a warm bath, Eliza bustled about the bathing room. "It must have been so difficult to live so long in the wilds. I hope the queen is being treated well. They don't have bathrooms like this out in Wales, I suspect."

"Not many places. Not yet at Caernarfon, leastwise."

"I can't even imagine having a baby there! It doesn't bear thinking about!" Eliza laid out a cloth by which to dry Catrin when she'd finished her bath. "I said just the other day to my good friend Beth *I can't see what the king was thinking, taking his poor pregnant wife so far from home!*"

Honestly, Catrin could only agree. It *was* dangerous to take a woman who was eight months pregnant on a long journey in a carriage. That said, Catrin herself had been born in Wales, as were hundreds of babies every day. Rather than mention that fact, Catrin stood up in the bath and began to dry herself off. "How goes it with you, Eliza? Are you still seeing that fellow you like—Roger I think you said his name was?"

"He brought me flowers the other day." She snorted a bit, though Catrin could tell that she was pleased that Catrin had remembered and that Roger had been so thoughtful. "I'm just an old woman. I don't know what he was thinking."

"He's thinking that he's sweet on you."

Eliza blushed, indicating she was sweet on him too. "It is kind of you to remember."

It wasn't particularly kind, since speaking to Eliza so familiarly was the preamble to pumping her for information, but Catrin continued anyway. "Is marriage not far away?"

"Between you and me, I think he would have spoken about it by now, but with the prince's death—" She swallowed hard. "Nobody here at Windsor can marry between now and Christmas, not with the grieving."

"I'm so sorry." Catrin's skin was dry by now, and Eliza began to help her into her nightdress and robe. "I didn't know Alfonso well, but he seemed to me a lovely boy."

"Oh he was! But these things happen. What can one do? He was so full of life." Eliza, who herself was endearingly full of life, wiped at the corners of her eyes with her fingers. Then she smiled and added, "I almost forgot that was his name. He insisted everyone call him Astolfo instead of Alfonso."

Catrin tipped her head, having heard the same thing already that evening from Fernando. She feigned ignorance, however, sensing that Eliza had a story to tell and wanted to tell it in her own way. "That name sounds familiar, but I can't remember how I know it. Wasn't he named for his uncle? I saw the books in his rooms. It looked to me like he was very proud to be named for Alfonso of Castile."

"He was, my lady. Of course he was! He read those stories many times to his sisters—and to those of us who were fortunate enough to be tidying the room or changing the linens at the time."

"They are wonderful, aren't they?"

"Can you read yourself, my lady?"

"I can."

Eliza shook her head, as if the mystery of reading was be-yond her comprehension, and perhaps it was. "Then you may re-call that in those stories Astolfo was the twelfth paladin, the son of the King of England. Alfonso wanted to be just like him." She sighed regretfully, looking past Catrin to the middle distance, where Catrin imagined she was seeing her own paladin, the lovely Roger—or maybe remembering again the sweetness of Alfonso.

"I do recall." It was in Catrin's mind that she would be wise not to pursue any further conversation about Alfonso for now. She didn't want to barrage every servant she came across with ques-tions about his death, not right at the start. Servants, like lovers, needed to be wooed.

But Eliza herself, now that the topic had come up, wasn't ready to let it go. With a sideways look and a stubborn set to her chin, she said, "I know why you're here."

The words came out hard—perhaps harder than she'd in-tended because her face reddened. Still, she didn't back down and didn't waver in whatever determination had caused her to speak out.

"Do you? Why am I here?"

"You think one of us murdered him. I can tell you right now that none of us would have harmed Alfonso."

Catrin kept her expression as serene as possible. This was a delicate moment, and she had a sinking feeling that if she said the wrong thing here, she would never get another piece of infor-mation out of anyone, no matter how often she asked or how serious the questioning. So she spoke as gently as she could manage. "Is that what they're saying in the kitchen?"

"And the tavern." Eliza still didn't waver, not even in the face of Catrin's calm demeanor. "The king needs someone to blame, and it's to be one of us."

"It would be unfair to pretend that we aren't here to learn more about Alfonso's death. But we are *not* here to blame anyone who is not guilty. We are here for the truth, not a scapegoat."

Eliza's expression told Catrin she didn't believe her and, what's more, that Catrin was losing her.

"Can you tell me who first mentioned any of this?"

Eliza's obstinate look finally wavered. "What do you mean?"

"Who was the first to say that we had come to find a scape-goat?"

"I-I-I don't know. I heard it from Roger." Then she frowned, for the first time thinking for herself. "No, that isn't right. We'd both heard the rumor separately. I think Roger was at the tavern with his friends."

"What friends?"

Eliza made a dismissive gesture. "Peter, George, Jehan, Ralph. The prince had sent word ahead that he was coming, you see, and the messenger mentioned that Sir Reese was in the party. Everyone is saying it. How can it matter who said it first?"

Catrin smiled. "You're right, of course. It doesn't matter. Thank you for speaking to me, Eliza."

Eliza curtseyed, and when she came up, her expression looked slightly mollified, though still not happy. Seeing it, Catrin tried one more time. "Please let me assure you again that neither my husband nor I wish any of you ill. I cannot make promises about what the king will or will not do in the future, but we are not here to blame the innocent."

"The king could make you." Eliza's earlier defiance returned enough to throw the words at Catrin.

"No, he couldn't." Catrin's flat tone put a look of surprise on Eliza's face. "The king knows that Rhys always tells the truth. I can see you don't believe me, but you can ask anyone you like, and they will tell you it's true. Honesty is the quality the king values in my husband more than any other."

6

Vincent stood. "If we leave now, we should be just in time."

"In time for what?"

Vincent grinned. "It's a surprise—not my idea, I might add. I told him you didn't like surprises."

"Told who?" Rhys didn't get up, his suspicions returning full bore. "That's it? You cleared the entire keep and now you want to leave?"

Vincent paused with the door half open. "You didn't want to talk earlier, and I assumed that was because you didn't want to say what you had to say in front of Catrin. Or do what you had to do."

Rhys was nonplussed. "Did you fear I would attack you?"

"It was a possibility."

A bit thunderstruck, Rhys rose to his feet. "I would have thought you'd want witnesses if I was going to murder you in cold blood."

"I didn't think you'd kill me. You didn't kill me in Nefyn." He shrugged. "I decided I owed you a few good punches."

"I already got in a fair number in the melée."

"I had some bruises, I admit, and I could barely lift my arms afterwards." Vincent let out a low laugh. "That was my last tournament."

Almost against his will, Rhys agreed, "Mine too, God willing."

And on that rather positive note, they left the keep, descended the hill to the middle gatehouse, walked through the outer bailey, and then through the outer gatehouse into the town. Rhys didn't even bother to try to discover where they were going. By this point, he was so amused—and perhaps even bemused—by the entire evening that he found he didn't much care.

Once in the town, Vincent made for an inn, naturally called *The King's Arms*, which had a fairly respectable representation of Windsor Castle's keep painted on a sign hanging above the door.

Putting his hand on the latch, Vincent hesitated. From within, they could hear roars and cheers. "Follow my lead?"

"Whatever you say."

"*Whatever you say.*" Vincent snorted. "When have you ever been so amenable? We'll see how long that attitude lasts." It was a way of speaking to each other that would have been customary in the Holy Land when they were friends. It was certainly the way that Simon and Rhys spoke to each other now. A funny feeling formed in Rhys's belly at the thought that he really might be getting his friend back. Maybe even a *better* friend, because this version of Vincent was far less prickly than the old one.

With a last twitch of his mouth, Vincent opened the door, bringing them into a warm, raucous room that was bigger than Rhys had expected, judging from the outside, even as the crowd was large enough to make the room feel small and crowded. Towards the center of the room, two men were seated at a table with cups arrayed in front of them. The one facing them was in his middle fifties, wearing clothing of a merchant in subdued colors. By contrast, the man seated with his back to them was dressed in bright blue and yellow, with a flamboyant matching hat pulled low on his forehead.

As they pressed closer in order to see better, just two more onlookers in a sea of them, the second man put out both arms to silence the crowd and spoke in Gasconese French, with an accent Rhys hadn't heard in many years. "Quiet everyone. Let me think!"

Rhys frowned, feeling as if he knew the voice. Then, as the man lifted his cup, preparing to drink its contents, he gave his outstretched wrist a little twirl.

Rhys laughed under his breath. "Miles."

Vincent glanced at him. "Is that laughter pleased or displeased?"

"Heaven help me, *pleased*. I think." He made something of a noncommittal motion with his head. "I admit that sometimes I can be sardonic."

"Sometimes?"

Rhys laughed outright at Vincent's deadpan comment. They really were getting into the swing of bygone days. "I am not surprised to see him in Windsor. The king sent for him as well as for you. It's the circumstances that are surprising. Someone is going to recognize him if he keeps on this way."

"Are they? Would you have if you didn't know him so well?"

Miles's accent and the twirl had brought Rhys back to the Holy Land, as did so many of his memories these days. There, Miles, Vincent, Simon, and Rhys had sat together many nights, gleefully mocking the mannerisms of their French allies. As with many things he did, Miles's impressions were the best, dead-on at times, and just over-the-top enough to leave them all holding their bellies with much needed laughter.

Then, in the present, Miles turned his head, responding to a comment one of the patrons made, and Rhys saw his profile. He had trimmed his beard to almost nothing and sported a flamboyant mustache that curled at the ends.

Vincent was right. Miles looked nothing like himself. Without those memories, and the prior knowledge that he was coming to Windsor, Rhys wouldn't have known him.

"He can't help himself, can he?"

"It seems not."

"What exactly is he doing—or don't I dare ask?"

"He is investigating, like we are."

It looked to Rhys as if he was drinking, but he was willing to hold his skepticism in abeyance until he learned more. "Miles can drink any man on any continent under the table and then walk a straight line afterwards. Wouldn't it have been better to save the secret of his hollow leg for later if we really need it?"

"Not so loud. Only you and I know about that." Vincent put a finger to his lips, shushing Rhys, though the crowd was rowdy enough that nobody could have overheard. "Besides, that isn't what he's doing. I admit his current behavior looks somewhat unconventional, but this is an interview for a position at the castle."

"He is applying for an actual job?" Rhys blinked. "How is drinking a man under the table going to get him that?"

The last time Rhys had witnessed one of these contests, Miles had lasted one more cup—eleven to his opponent's ten—as he always did, before that man slumped off his stool onto the floor. That time, the patrons had roared their approval and left the drunken loser to sleep off his ale where he'd fallen. Miles had sauntered away with clear eyes and an insouciant grin. He hadn't even experienced a sore head the next morning. He'd been in his early twenties then. Rhys would have thought he'd learned a bit more moderation by now.

But, as Vincent had indicated, drinking to excess wasn't exactly what Miles was doing. For starters, Miles and his competitor were drinking wine, not ale. As Rhys and Vincent—and the patrons of the tavern—looked on, the proprietor poured a small amount of wine into each man's cup. With astonishment, Rhys realized he knew him too, also from the crusades.

"That's Tom!"

Tom was tall, thick, balding, and had been a leader among a band of men from east London. Unlike Miles, and probably Rhys as well, the difference in appearance between forty-five and sixty, as Tom had to be now, was much less than from twenty to thirty-five.

Vincent shushed him. "You can speak to him later."

"He must remember Miles."

"Miles did introduce himself earlier. Now hush!"

Rhys found himself holding his breath along with everyone else as he watched Miles sip the wine and roll it around on his tongue.

"See?" Vincent said in a whisper.

"I still don't know what he's doing, but it's definitely better than downing an entire flagon in a single breath."

Miles's opponent was already less alert than Miles, as was generally the case with the men Miles went up against, no matter what they were drinking. He wasn't staggering yet, however, and at the prompting of Tom-the-soldier-turned-innkeeper, he was the first to speak. "St. Emilion."

"No," Miles said immediately. "It's Castelsagrat."

With Miles's answer, Rhys finally understood the game they were playing and the job Miles wanted: this was a wine tasting contest. Each man was guessing in turn the name of the region or vineyard in Gascony from which a particular wine had come. Miles's opponent was Windsor Castle's butler, in charge of all drink at the castle: wine, ale, and mead. Tom had just referred to him as Butler James.

Now Tom nodded at Miles. "Yes. It's Castelsagrat."

As Miles's arms went up in the air in triumph, the crowd cheered, and the butler sat back in his seat, laughing and shaking his finger at Miles. Beneath the general chatter, Rhys heard him say, "Present yourself at the castle gate at Terce tomorrow and tell them I sent for you. They'll point you in the right direction to find me."

"Thank you, Butler James. I won't let you down." Miles rose to his feet, steady as a rock, like always.

"See that you don't."

Miles sketched a bow and then set off towards the back of the inn, presumably to the latrines, which were always much needed at such an establishment.

"That's our signal." Vincent weaved his way through clusters of laughing men, who by now had congealed around a new pair of contestants. These were back to the old game of drinking ale as quickly as possible. Likely one or both of them would end up in the yard as well, upending the contents of their stomach into the straw that had been piled in a trough behind the inn expressly for that purpose. A man who couldn't hold his ale long enough to get out the door was universally mocked—and banned from the tavern for a time. He would also be responsible for cleaning up his own mess once he was sober.

As Rhys stepped out the back door of the inn, to his utter and total surprise, Miles himself was upchucking into the straw.

Miles flung out a hand. "Don't say anything. I know what this looks like, but I have a good excuse: that was the most awful wine I have ever tasted."

"Poor Castelsagrat," Vincent said.

Miles straightened, holding his belly but relatively sober and somewhat recovered. "I don't know how the butler could have said *St. Emilion* with a straight face."

"Maybe he wanted you to have the job and so let you win," Vincent said mildly.

Miles narrowed his eyes. "You besmirch my honor, sir."

Rhys looked from one man to the other, at first fearing they might come to blows over the matter, but then Miles's lips twitched, and Vincent took a step forward, laughing. "I would never."

"Lies do not become you, Vincent." Miles clapped Vincent on the shoulder and shook him. "Thanks for coming."

Realizing that all truly was well, Rhys felt able to say to Miles, "That was an impressive display; I forgot you could do that."

"What can I say?" He shrugged. "Ever since I was a boy, I've been able to taste and remember."

"It's a gift," Vincent said to Rhys, back to sardonic.

Just then, a man came out the back of the inn, heading for the latrines, and the three of them edged away from the doorway and the light that shone through it onto the graveled yard. It was good to be farther from the trough of straw as well.

They found better darkness near a corner of the inn's stables. At this late hour, given the fullness of the common room, there was plenty of activity about. For once, that made them less likely to be disturbed rather than more, since the two stable boys were kept hopping by the demands of the patrons coming and going, and nobody was looking at them twice. If the yard had been empty, they would have been far more noticeable.

Rhys rubbed his forehead. It wasn't so much that a headache was coming on, but that these two *friends*—oddly, that's what he felt he could call them—were an inch or two from giving him one. In between conversations with Miles, he kept forgetting the man's ability to talk the bark off a tree and say nothing while doing it. Vincent didn't appear to be much better.

"What exactly is your plan, Miles?" Rhys asked him.

"The name is Gilbert le Gascon, my lord."

Rhys endeavored not to snort. "Gilbert, then."

"I have just been hired by Butler James to work in Windsor's cellars. I thought that would be obvious."

Rhys really wanted to roll his eyes but said instead, "I gathered that, but *why?*"

"We are looking into Alfonso's death, are we not? How better to learn the truth of it than from the inside? It came to me that you might need someone who wasn't overtly among your company."

As Miles had been talking, Rhys found himself focused on his huge mustache. It was a risk, growing it, because it made him memorable. Rhys would have chosen to be as nondescript as possible, as a better way to disguise himself, but that wasn't Miles's way. In truth, becoming unmemorable was exactly what Rhys had chosen to do during his sojourn in Caernarfon all last year. The Welsh villagers had known who he was, but none of the Normans had connected him with the Rhys who'd served in the Holy Land all those years ago.

Now Rhys eyed Vincent. "You're telling me that you agreed to this?"

"He outranks me, Rhys. But he's right too. No matter your reputation, we need all the help we can get."

"Alfonso's dead, Reese. We—" here Miles gestured between him and Vincent, "—decided that whoever killed him must either be so highly placed he is untouchable, or so entrenched nobody would ever suspect he is a villain."

Vincent nodded. "Just like whoever has been trying to kill the king."

7

Day One

Catrin

"First of all, we cannot assume that Alfonso was murdered. We are not here to assume or speculate." Catrin was wrapped up in Rhys's arms, having coerced him into a bath too before he'd come to bed. It had been pouring rain on his walk back from the inn, so he'd been soaked anyway. The rain continued to come down hard, thudding on the slate roof above their heads. "If I've learned anything from you, it's that."

It was very late now, and she was tired, but Rhys needed to talk after his encounter with Miles and Vincent, and she needed to listen.

"I can't control them, Catrin, which should be obvious from the fact that Miles seems to have taken matters into his own hands."

"We talked earlier about not trusting Vincent. What about Miles?"

"I confess I want to trust him, just like with Vincent." He rolled over onto his side so they were facing each other. "Both of them make me want to."

"What about the ledger?"

"I am holding the contents of the ledger in abeyance for now, *cariad*. If nothing else, the king isn't here for his life to be threatened."

Back in Nefyn, at the end of their investigation there, Catrin had discovered a ledger written by the primary culprit, a man named Bernard, who was steward to the Earl of Richmond. In an ink which was only revealed when Catrin held the paper up to a candle, he'd written that a group of Marcher lords and their representatives had been conspiring to increase their wealth and power at the expense of the king.

Bernard had fallen short of accusing them of plotting to assassinate the king and, in fact, seemed to deliberately *not* do so. That the barons would want to undermine the king without killing him made sense to Catrin. Many didn't care for him personally or approve of his rule in general, but without him, England would descend into chaos. What's more, the loss of the king's iron hand might enable another one of their number to rise to the top, whether as regent or ultimately as king himself.

None of them wanted that.

It was comforting, in a way, that these Normans could be so predictable in their machinations. They might despise the king.

Catrin was quite sure that Humphrey de Bohun swallowed down his hatred every time he was in the king's presence. But they hated each other more.

The ledger had also identified Miles as the man responsible for the sabotage of the tournament's viewing stand. The night before the main events began, it had collapsed directly onto the spot where the king would have been sitting the next morning. She and Rhys had kept this information to themselves. It was too dangerous to share with anyone until they could determine if it was even true. Which left them working with men who were, at one and the same time, friends and possible enemies.

"We both have spent far too much time hating these last few years, my love."

"I've been *so* angry, Catrin. I'm discovering, in large part thanks to you, that I have been so angry because it's easier than being anything else."

"And what else might that be?" Catrin was breathing easily, glad beyond measure that Rhys was finally able to articulate some of this to her. She had thoughts about what he needed, but the more he came to his own conclusions, the better. In general, he'd always had a level head on his shoulders. Somehow, despite all he'd been through and survived, he maintained a hopeful view of the world. Or maybe it was more accurate to say that he'd renewed one.

"Sad and afraid." He swept a strand of her hair out of her face. "I'm tired of being angry. I'm tired of hating. I don't want to live in fear of *feeling* or of loss anymore."

"I'm not Father Medwyn, but I know he would tell you that you need to find a way to encompass everything you feel." Father Medwyn was the priest at St. Peblig's Church in Caernarfon, a man Rhys had known since he was a youth and whom he trusted. "We can't control what happens to us, only how we respond to it. We *will* feel fear and loss again. We will grieve again. The only alternative would be never loving again. That's no way to live. In fact, I suspect Father Medwyn would say that it isn't living."

"I wasn't living when I was alone in Caernarfon." He'd closed his eyes, and she suspected that this conversation had been easier from the start because it was taking place in the dark, and she couldn't see his face clearly. "Trusting remains hard, however."

"Especially trusting these Normans!"

"Heaven forbid!" At first he laughed, but then as Catrin snuggled down again in his arms, he sobered. "This is what you've been talking about, isn't it?"

"Is it?"

His eyes were open now, literally and figuratively. "We can't wait for things to get better, or our lives to be different, to be whole. The world may always be desolate and full of despair. Always. Wales is never going to be free from Edward, not this year, not next year, maybe not until long after we're dead. Maybe not ever. We need to be happy—and find happiness—where we stand—"

Whump! A muffled concussive sound came from below them, like ten people simultaneously beating a tapestry to clean it. Rhys broke off in the same instant Catrin sat up.

"What was that?" She was on her feet, and Rhys was already moving towards the door, his boots in his hand, before she finished her sentence.

He pulled open the door. The corridor was clear, but he was frowning. "I hear crackling. And smell more smoke than I should. I—" He glanced back to look at her, fear in his face. Fear for her, she knew, far more than for himself.

They'd left the shutters open because they both liked sleeping with fresh air around them. But the air had suddenly become less fresh.

"Get the blanket from the bed." He'd already pulled on his boots, and now he plucked his cloak from the wall.

Catrin knew what to do without further instruction: she pulled the wool blanket off the bed, dumped all the water from the pitcher on the sideboard on it, and bundled it up so the liquid would soak in a bit. The smell of smoke was stronger as they descended the stairs, and they arrived in the common room to find it full of black smoke.

Being relatively new, the guesthouse had a stone fireplace set in the far wall, directly under their bed chamber, as it turned out. Sparks were flying everywhere, and smoke filled the room, stinging her eyes. It was so thick she could see little else. She started to cough.

That was all the impression Catrin got before Rhys whipped the blanket out of her arms and shoved her towards the back of the guesthouse. "Get us more blankets, anything to smother this fire. Water will only help if it spreads."

She didn't wait to be told twice, nor ask what he was going to do. It was raining outside, so they didn't have to worry so much about the fire leaping from the guesthouse, which was freestanding, to the nearby kitchen or other buildings. And the roof was covered in slate in the first place because stone didn't catch fire.

But the entire interior of the building was wood and could be consumed if they didn't get the fire under control. The guesthouse had a bath room and laundry on the ground level, so first she grabbed every blanket, cloak, and cloth from the supply cupboard and ran back to Rhys as fast as she could.

"Rhys!" Upon her return to the common room, her voice went high in panic when she couldn't see him through the smoke.

But then he was there, taking the bundles of fabric from her. "Now water!"

It had been very late when Rhys had returned, so they'd left the bath to be emptied in the morning. She plunged into the bath room, grabbed the two buckets the servants had used to fill the tub, and scooped up the now cold and dirty water.

Carrying two full buckets at once almost wrenched her arms from her sockets, but she was in too much of a hurry to carry only one, although the effect was that she sloshed a portion of the water onto the floor in her haste.

By the time she arrived, Rhys had opened the shutters and the front door, and the smoke was dissipating. They ran back and forth with four more buckets of water, throwing it on the walls and the floor, just to make sure they had extinguished every spark.

With the fire out, Catrin stood weaving on her feet. "What happened, Rhys?"

"Someone added an entire log of pitch wood to the fire. As you know, it is wonderful for starting a fire, but not so wonderful if you put too much in." As he was wearing his boots, Rhys kicked aside what once had been the blanket on their bed to reveal a partially-burned log that had rolled out of the fireplace onto the floor.

Because they'd acted so quickly, all it had burned were a few floorboards in front of the hearth, though the explosion of pitch wood had also left scorch marks on the walls and furniture.

"I remember my father cursing one of Prince Llywelyn's tenants for putting a log of pitch wood on his fire at a time when he was too drunk to hear the sputtering hiss as it lit," Catrin said. "By the time he realized what he'd done, it was too late to stop. He burned down his own house and three of his neighbors'."

Rhys canted his head. "I remember that. That may be, in fact, why I realized so quickly what this was."

"We could have died." Catrin limped over to a chair and sat. There were burn marks on the back rail, but it was otherwise sturdy. "We really might have if we hadn't been awake already. We were lucky."

"You always see the good in everything, Catrin. I'm afraid I can't, in this instance. We *were* lucky not to have been asleep. And maybe we were unlucky that someone made a mistake with the pitch wood. But I'm thinking what happened here doesn't have much to do with *luck* at all."

8

Day Two

Miles

It had been a long time since Miles had been so far out of his depth. In truth, he had no idea what he was doing. He'd never worked for anyone in his life, other than his nephew—or the king—and the *work* he'd done consisted entirely of going where they pointed, even if what he did once he got there was often up to him. Having admitted this fact to himself, however, he decided that working for the butler might in the end be hardly different. Whether it was Humphrey, King Edward, or Butler James, when they said *jump*, it was his job to ask *how high*.

With that conclusion drawn, he became much more cheerful, to the point that he was able to whistle a somewhat out-of-tune ditty as he approached the guardhouse.

The guard stopped him, as he would, since Miles was a total stranger and for once not riding a horse or well-dressed.

"I am Gilbert le Gascon. I am expected by Butler James."

It had been a toss-up in Miles's mind whether he should call himself *Gilbert* or *William*. Or maybe *Roger*. These were common names among Normans, and they also happened to be the first names of three rivals to his nephew's power in the March, the border regions between England and Wales: Gilbert de Clare, William de Valence, and Roger Mortimer. Any name would have been appropriate for the man Miles was pretending to be, and he wanted people thinking of him, if they thought of him at all, as belonging to a different lord than the one he did belong to. The Bohun family was the only one of which he was aware that used the name *Humphrey* (repeatedly, for some reason). It was an old Norman name but one that had never been in as much use as many others.

In the end, Miles had settled upon *Gilbert*. He was currently in league with Vincent, William de Valence's lieutenant. In Humphrey's opinion, Gilbert de Clare was the most objectionable of the three magnates. Upon the death of his father, Gilbert had been made the ward of Miles's father (also named Humphrey but whom they routinely called *the Second Earl*) until he came of age. Then, in a not so ironic and definitely uncomfortable twist, upon the death of the Second Earl, Miles's nephew Humphrey had been made the ward of Gilbert, who was six years older.

By then, the Second Barons' war had come and gone, and with it any possibility of friendship between Humphrey and Gilbert. They'd started out on the same side during the rebellion against the king, both allies of Simon de Montfort, until Gilbert had betrayed them all, freeing Prince Edward from prison and then leaping into the fray on the royal side with the same fervor he'd exhibited for Montfort up until then. Miles's brother (nephew Humphrey's father) had died from wounds incurred at Evesham. The memory of that death—and Gilbert's betrayal—was seared into every Bohun's soul. At the time, Humphrey had been sixteen and Gilbert twenty-two. It didn't help that they'd continued to be rivals not only for the king's favor but for land—and thus power—in the March.

That said, with Reese forgiving Vincent for all but murdering him at Cilmeri, a possibility so remote Miles had never even considered it, anything could happen.

Regardless of their animosity towards one another, neither Humphrey nor Gilbert, at the moment anyway, wanted the king dead. Miles could admit that might be a temporary state for both of them, if only because neither was currently in a strong enough position to take the regency outright from the other one. To attempt to magnify their personal war might throw the entire contest to Prince Edmund, or even Roger Mortimer. All these great earls were jostling for power in the March and the king's favor. Each man's desire to one-up the other was so great it was a wonder that Gilbert hadn't also sent someone to inquire into Alfonso's death.

The thought pulled Miles up short. He considered himself disguised reasonably well in his Gascon clothes and utterly out of context for anyone who might recognize him—or he would be as soon as he established himself with the butler. Miles hadn't been to Windsor itself in over ten years, shortly after his return from the

Holy Land. This fact had made him fairly confident he could successfully get himself a job at the castle—that and the support of Tom the innkeeper, who would have made sure Miles won the contest with Butler James if Miles had not managed to do so on his own.

Even Tom hadn't immediately recognized Miles for who he really was, though he'd thrown himself into the deception with enthusiasm. At the moment, Tom was in his inn, and Miles was feeling very exposed in the enormous lower bailey, encompassing a distance of some five hundred feet from the inner gatehouse on the eastern end to the stables on the far western end.

He picked up his pace, ready to get out of the no man's land in which he found himself. Arriving at the kitchen door, which was open to let out some of the heat from the ovens, he was immediately struck by the chaos before him—and the order within that chaos. Breakfast had finished, but the cooks were well into preparation for the next meal. There was some talking, but little chatter. Everyone appeared to have a set task, and nobody except him was loitering.

And then, even before he had to interrupt someone to inquire for Butler James, the man himself appeared out of the back, wiping his hands on a cloth. "Good. You're here. Today's shipment is just arriving on the Thames. You can help."

"Of course, Butler James."

Windsor Castle guarded an important crossing of the Thames but wasn't situated exactly on the river as were some Norman castles. The chalk cliff upon which Windsor stood was many yards back from the bank and a hundred feet above the river. Supplies for the castle were carted from the docks along a narrow and fortified lane into a rear entrance that gave access to the cellars beneath the great hall in the lower bailey. From there, food, drink, and goods were sent throughout the castle to where they were needed.

The supply entrance reminded Miles a bit of the situation at Chepstow Castle, the seat of Roger Bigod, with its precarious balcony overlooking the River Wye. In an emergency, the castle could be resupplied from the river, using ropes and pulleys. Perhaps at one time the Thames had run right up against the bottom of Windsor's cliff, but no longer. From the start, then, the digging of wells inside the castle had been necessary, and they'd been used to great effect during the several sieges to which Windsor had been subjected, the most recent during the reign of King John and the first Barons' War.

"Your name tells me your family's origins are on the Continent," Butler James said as they left the castle and descended the path to the dock. "How is it you have traveled here?"

"I am a by-blow." Miles lied in what he hoped was a convincing manner. "My father arranged for my apprenticeship in a vineyard, since I displayed a facility for wines, but there was the matter of the master's daughter..." He allowed his voice to trail off and made his expression appropriately contrite.

The butler snorted. "It was wise of you not to tell me about this last night. There will be none of that here, or you will find yourself out of a position right quick!"

"I never did touch her." Miles pulled on his forelock. "She used me to hide her attachment to another. I chose to leave rather than accuse her of lying."

"So you're an honorable man, are you?" The butler laughed mockingly. "We'll see." Then he raised a hand to the men ahead of them on the dock. "Allen! Jehan! God be with you!" The first was a large strapping fellow, who seemed to heave about the crates and boxes with ease, but the second man was somewhat aged, slender and pale, though with a big beard. He hadn't been working and was the first to greet Butler James.

Miles followed a pace behind, understanding that his words had engendered the intended response, which was to make Butler James wary. He had succeeded to the point that the other man seemed to have moved away with alacrity. The goal was to walk the perfect line between showing himself to be capable, even indispensable, while at the same time slightly down-on-his luck and untrustworthy.

Reese had asked Miles last night why he'd chosen to apply for this particular position. At first, Miles had replied with the most obvious answer: that it was open, a fact he'd learned during earlier conversations with castle workers. It was also a job for which he was uniquely suited. He genuinely could judge the location and quality of wine, and it had been a trick with which he'd amused his friends from Hereford to Acre and back. He'd just never put it to work before beyond the earning of a few coins for his amusement in a tavern.

It was only later, as if it wasn't important, that he'd admitted he had no other option if he was to work inside the castle. Any position that involved his more usual skills—those associated with his status as a knight or the son of an earl—would put him too far above the people upon whom he was supposed to be spying. It might also attract the attention of the higher echelon of workers and visitors to the castle, some of whom might actually know him and see through his disguise.

So once he'd discovered, after snuffling about the edges of the castle for a day, that the wine cellar had an unfilled position, it had seemed like a gift from God. He'd learned, over the years, that his gut could tell him quite a lot about the world. Miles thought Reese's did too, even if he claimed to be all about steady inquiry and facts. Reese couldn't have appeared as omniscient as he did, as often as he did, if he hadn't learned to take a chance on a guess.

All three of them—Reese, Miles, and Vincent—had renewed their alliance not just because of the king's orders. They all had a sick feeling in their guts telling them that something was awry at Windsor Castle. Miles didn't know whether that feeling was because of Alfonso's death or something else.

But he was determined, if at all possible—with the help of these old and unlikely friends—to tease out the truth if he could. He'd known before Reese had said so that it wouldn't be easy. The instant Alfonso had died, these people had put up a barrier as high and thick as Windsor's curtain wall. Miles had chosen to disguise himself because the best way to take a castle wasn't by breaching the walls directly, but by subterfuge.

And he'd just been let in the postern gate.

9

Day Two

Rhys

From the shadows of the inner gatehouse, Rhys had watched Miles enter the kitchen before he himself, still shaking his head at Miles's magnificent disguise, crossed the lower bailey and approached the door of Windsor's physician. His rooms were part of a large wooden building, two-stories high, located to the north of the castle's beautiful chapel.

Nobody had known about (or rather, nobody had *reported*) the fire in the guesthouse before Rhys had sought out Constable Pickford at dawn. He could only think that the rain had kept the guards inside, and the hour had been so late—or early in the morning, rather—that nobody else had been about.

Rather than roust the constable immediately, Rhys and Catrin had slept for a few hours, rolled together in a blanket they'd salvaged, on a pallet they'd dragged into the bathing room. Although Constable Pickford had been horrified at how close the guesthouse had come to burning to the ground—and them with it—his assumption was that the fire was an accident. Rhys, on the other hand, thought that being almost killed in his sleep the very night he arrived was far too coincidental to actually *be* a coincidence.

But, for now, Rhys had decided not to air his opinion any more forcefully. The constable was right that it could have been a mistake on the part of the servant who'd last stoked the fire. And yet, when Rhys inquired as to which woodman had been responsible for the guesthouse most recently, none claimed to have gone anywhere near it since two helped Eliza warm water for Catrin's bath. Nobody could say who had put the log on the fire after that. It certainly hadn't been Rhys! It wasn't part of their protocol to stoke fires overnight this early in the autumn. But someone had to have done so and then tiptoed out.

The physician did not respond to Rhys's initial knocks. Rather than wait on the doorstep, Rhys pushed at the door, which opened easily, and poked his nose inside. He didn't want to get off on the wrong foot by entering where he was not welcome, but given the fire in the night, he felt an urgency in his belly that told him not to wait any longer. As it was, the fire had delayed this investigation by several hours. He couldn't help thinking that had been, at a minimum, the point.

"Doctor?" His voice echoed into the darkness of the room, a contrast to the bright sunlight of the morning outside. September was often the most beautiful month of the year in Britain.

"Who's there?" The voice came from an adjoining room.

Widening his eyes in order to adjust them more quickly to the lack of light, Rhys entered fully and passed through the main room to reach the far doorway from which the response had come. By the time he stepped into this second room, the physician was fumbling with the shutter over the window.

Light flooded the room, and Rhys now found himself blinking away the glare. "I am Rhys ap Iorwerth."

"The king's quaestor?" The physician was blinking repeatedly as Rhys had done, though Rhys's eyes were much happier with the new level of light in the room. "*You're* the one they were talking about in the hall last night?" The physician shook his head, laughing a little under his breath. Even though it was mid-morning, he was still in his dressing gown. "I never caught the name."

"Do I know you?" Rhys peered at him, searching his face. The man reeked of ale, and his drunken state was why he was avoiding standing directly in the light.

"If I am as changed as you are, I suppose it's no surprise you don't recognize me." The physician made a sweeping gesture with one hand. "I know you to look at only because you gave me your name, and there has only ever been one *Reese ap Your-worth.*"

"Peter de Beauchamp." Rhys blurted out the name, brought up from the recesses of his memories of those long-ago days.

Just saying the physician's name out loud recalled sun-dried bricks and an endless, suffocating heat, even at night. In the summer, many days in the Holy Land felt like walking into an oven while underneath a wet blanket. Really, Rhys shouldn't have been taken aback that he knew the man, and it was absurd to be surprised whenever he encountered men from his past, especially since he had been the one to separate himself from them, rather than the other way around. Perhaps instead he should assume that he knew everyone and be pleasantly surprised when he didn't.

"At your service, Sir Reese." Peter bowed with an exaggerated flourish and almost fell over. He steadied himself by putting a hand on the edge of a nearby table. "I thought you'd left."

"I'm back." Rhys stated this fact without emphasis.

"And in the king's service now." Peter grunted. "You may have served Prince Edmund all those years ago, but you were always King Edward's favorite."

Rhys surely would never have said so himself. "I go where I am bid these days."

"As do we all." Peter was still standing in the shadows to one side of the window. The breeze coming through it helped dissipate the smell of ale coming off his body, worse now with every word he spoke.

"I had been thinking that by now everyone at Windsor knew I was in the king's service again and why I have come."

"I don't listen to gossip." Peter snorted. "Perhaps I should join the layabouts in the tavern or hall more often instead of eating in my rooms." He pointed to a tray on the side table containing the remains of his dinner. "But the fact that you're standing here tells me all I need to know: the king is angry that his son is dead, and he sent you to find someone to blame."

"Have I found him? Were you this drunk when you attended the prince—"

"Of course I wasn't drunk! What do you take me for?"

"I take you for a drunkard," Rhys said flatly, pushing back at the notion that it was unreasonable to wonder at the motives or actions of the people who'd tended Prince Alfonso when he died. "Why should I believe differently, given what I see before me?"

"I wasn't drinking to excess then. In fact, I have all but abstained from drink for over ten years, ever since—" He broke off, his face paling.

"Ever since what?"

Peter was still drunk enough to be having trouble containing his thoughts and spoke what had to be the truth: "Ever since the death of Prince Henry."

The two men gazed at each other, Peter in horror that he'd spoken out loud and Rhys less by what he'd said than at the pain behind it. The physician was referring to King Edward's second son, who died in 1274, just after Edward returned from the Holy Land.

"You had something to do with Henry's death?"

"No!" The response was immediate and emphatic. "Other men were his main attendants."

"Then why the guilt I hear in your voice—and by your own admission, your manner?"

"Because the fact that I was drunk meant I couldn't save him. Maybe he couldn't have been saved by anyone, but I've learned more since then about the disease he had, and maybe—"

He had tears in his voice as he became a weeping drunk instead of an obstinate one.

That also wasn't a sufficient defense, but for now Rhys let it go. They'd arrived at the heart of the matter a bit quicker than Rhys had intended, but it also showed him how easily an intelligent man could add one to two and come up with three. This particular physician had always been intelligent, when he allowed himself to be so.

Rhys reached for the flagon beside the bed and sniffed the contents. Miraculously, it contained water, not wine, and smelled relatively fresh from the well. Rhys poured out a measure into a cup and handed it to Peter, along with the end of a stale piece of bread from what was left of his dinner. Together, the water and bread could counteract the effects of last night's ale in Peter's stomach.

"Speak to me of Alfonso. What illness did he have?"

Peter's voice was steadier now, on firmer ground. "You can call it whatever you like: the flux, ague, grippe. It began with vomiting. As it progressed, he had stomach cramps and diarrhea. It became clear that there was nothing I or anyone else could do for him."

This was the first time Rhys had heard Alfonso's illness described in detail. "Those symptoms are common when someone is poisoned."

"Of course they're common!" Peter threw the words at Rhys. "Don't you think I've thought of that? Of course I've thought of that. Unfortunately, if he was poisoned, the possibilities for what poison was used are wide and varied. Many, if not most, result in symptoms similar not only to many illnesses but to the specific symptoms Alfonso exhibited."

This was the most coherent Peter had been, indicating to Rhys that, even in his inebriated state, he'd thought long and hard about this. "Name one."

"I am loath even to speculate as to what could have been used, if one was used."

"Hyacinth," Rhys said, throwing out the first flower that came to mind.

"There you go. That's one." Peter threw up his hands. "I know of a dozen common plants that can kill a man. *If* Alfonso was murdered, don't you think we all know that the chances of the culprit being a long-time family retainer, who either turned traitor, was being blackmailed, or has secretly been working against King Edward all this time, are high? Don't you see *we know that!*"

All of a sudden, Peter found a chair and slumped into it, his head in his hands. From the looks, he'd been torturing himself with the possibilities since Alfonso had died.

"Such a person could have had a hand in the deaths of the other royal sons too." Fresh from his night dealing with pitch wood, Rhys had an image of himself throwing a log on a fire. "Henry and John died of illness."

"At the time of John's death, the king and queen were on crusade. John was the ward of his great-uncle, Richard of Cornwall. You and I were in the Holy Land with them then, so you know that I could not have played any role there. Earl Richard himself died the next year, before Edward returned to England. It is unlikely he was ever questioned as to the whys and wherefores of John's illness."

"But Henry died three years later, after we'd all returned, when you were there."

"Are you really accusing me of murdering him?" Peter looked blearily up at Rhys. "I am a fool for ever mentioning him." Peter's face returned to his hands. "I was not the children's primary physician at that time, you do accept that, right? And it can't be news to you that Henry was often ill. He'd had scares before."

"I did know that. What symptoms did he have?"

"What symptoms *didn't* he have? Most notable were stomach aches; skin rashes; his throat was often sore; his digestion was poor; he excreted too much urine. Like Alfonso at the end, his eyes were often sunken."

"How did he actually die?"

"He grew weaker and weaker. He ate and drank, sometimes in great quantity, but it did him no good. One day he simply did not wake."

"What kind of skin rashes?"

"Bumps and blisters, mostly on his elbows and knees. He had poor skin tone, and it was discolored in places."

Rhys stared at Peter's downturned head, his heart starting to race. The bumps and blisters were not familiar to him, but the other ... they'd just encountered those very symptoms in Nefyn. "As in arsenic poisoning?"

"Of course not." Peter reared back. "Arsenic kills quickly, and that death looks different from Henry's."

"Arsenic can kill in small doses over a long period of time." Rhys himself had known little of this before a few weeks ago. It was the changes to the skin that allowed a physician or healer to distinguish arsenic poisoning as a cause of death from the dozens, if not hundreds, of other poisons that instigated nausea, vomiting, and/or diarrhea. And that wasn't even to mention the suite of diseases that displayed similar symptoms. Thus, the conundrum with Alfonso.

"Yes, nausea and vomiting are common, but Henry had no muscle cramps or tingling in his fingers and toes. Besides, nobody could have harmed the child over such a long period of time, not to produce those kinds of results. It would have taken months and years of—" He stopped, stuttering. "No. Nobody would do such a thing. The attending physician at the time diagnosed him with a condition known to the ancients as *diabetes mellitus,* based upon the fruity smell to his breath before he died."

Rhys had heard of the disease. Known as *honey urine* in the common tongue, it was a condition for which there was no cure, as was the case with so many illnesses. In its worst forms, when it attacked young people, it could kill within weeks.

"You didn't see any relationship between what Henry suffered and how Alfonso died?"

"No. Alfonso was not a sickly child and showed no sign of illness before he was suddenly very ill." Peter shook his head vehemently. "His death wasn't at all like Henry's."

"Have you ever seen anything like what Alfonso experienced?"

"Of course I have. Didn't I just say? *You* have. In the main, it looked like dysentery. How many hundreds of men have we seen die exactly the way Alfonso did?"

"Except—" Rhys waited for Peter to continue the thought the best he could.

The old physician obliged. "Except nobody else fell ill. With dysentery, someone else *always* falls ill. Entire armies have been laid low by it. Kings have died of it." He pursed his lips for a moment.

"What thought just made you pause?"

"There *was* something about the progression that wasn't right." It was the first time Peter had acknowledged that anything was truly amiss. "He had too few symptoms until he had them all, and he died too quickly." He went back to staring at the floor. "There is a second possibility, you know, even though you're going to think it's more remote."

"And what is that?"

"That *if* Alfonso was murdered, a fact I refuse to concede, it was at the hand of someone newly attached to Windsor Castle."

"Do you have someone in mind?"

"Do you know how many people we employ here? Hundreds! No, I have nobody in mind. You might ask the constable his thoughts."

"I intend to." In fact, conferring with the constable of the castle as to when each servant or retainer had been hired, in reverse order, was near the top of Rhys's list of tasks. That an outsider had murdered Alfonso, *if* he had been murdered, would certainly the preference of everyone at Windsor.

It also remained perfectly possible that all three boys had died from natural causes. Or only one of them. Or none of them.

"Had Alfonso shown any signs of illness before?"

"Of course not, or I would have said. Alfonso was sick for a few days, and then he was gone." Fresh tears tracked down Peter's cheeks.

"Clean yourself up, Peter." Rhys gazed down at him, unmoved. "You may not lose your position if I determine what you say is true, but if you continue down this path, you'll lose it by your own actions anyway."

"Arrest me or don't, Reese. Do your duty, and I will do mine. I have nothing more to say."

10

Day One

Catrin

For some reason, Geoffrey Pickford, Windsor's constable, had not been easy to find. Over the course of a quarter of an hour, Catrin had been sent from his rooms to the hall, to the garrison captain, to the kitchen. She was ready to give up and was starting to wonder if the entire point was for her to give up, when she finally spied him coming out of the keep in the middle bailey, the place Rhys had met Vincent the night before.

"Sir Geoffrey!" Catrin raised a hand to gain his attention.

He hesitated on the step down from the main door. For a moment, she wondered if he was going to pretend he hadn't seen her and disappear back inside.

But then he seemed to think better of retreat and came all the way down the steps to meet her where she was standing in the gravel pathway that surrounded the base of the motte.

"May I aid you in some way?" Geoffrey's expression was that of someone who had a hundred other things he ought to be doing. "You have not experienced any more trouble in your lodgings, I hope! I have sent men to restore the floor and others are going through the kindling and logs piece by piece to ensure that we don't repeat the error of last night."

"They are doing good work. That is not why I'm here." She was endeavoring to continue to give him the benefit of the doubt, but it was hard. "I don't mean to keep you. I am here at the behest of my husband, to—"

He cut her off. "To ask about Alfonso's death. I know."

Geoffrey's expression continued to be a cross between exasperation and superiority, to the point that Catrin was wondering if she was misunderstanding something. His nose was so far in the air she could see up his nostrils, compounded by the fact that he was a relatively tall man and had remained on the bottom step of the stairway to the keep, so Catrin had been having to look up at him even more than usual.

"Prince Edmund explained everything to me yesterday. I'm sure the king knows what he is doing, but I am disturbed not to have been consulted as to these inquiries. At a minimum, Captain Thaddeus and I together should have been the ones to conduct them."

"We serve at the pleasure of the king." Catrin could think of nothing else to say. The man was discontented. She could attempt to soothe him, but his attitude was his own responsibility, not hers. "So you believe there was nothing untoward in the death of Alfonso?"

"Of course there wasn't! The very notion is absurd."

Geoffrey seemed to realize after he'd spoken that he was effectively calling the king absurd. He waved a hand in front of his face as if swatting a fly. "I would have explained as much to the king himself had he come—or had Sir Reese asked."

The king was seeing to his newly conquered domains, a matter about which Catrin had her own objections. Their mutual discontent with the king's actions could have united her and Geoffrey, but Geoffrey was now looking away, implying yet again that he had a list of duties as long as his arm from which she was keeping him.

Catrin was well past irritated herself. "My husband would be with me, but we had trouble finding you after our initial conversation this morning." This was an outright lie. Rhys had gone to talk to the physician and had never looked for Geoffrey. She pledged to confess the sin to a priest at the earliest opportunity, though she found it hard to ask forgiveness for lying to a man she found so odious. Probably that just made the lying worse. "I'm aware that you have many duties, and he sends his apologies. We were hoping to see the list of names of everyone you employ at the castle and when they were hired."

That at least was true.

"Of course. If your husband comes to my quarters, my clerk will assist him." Geoffrey blew out another breath.

Catrin was genuinely starting to wonder if he didn't keep records of the information she was asking for. Or maybe they were embarrassingly incomplete?

"I really would prefer these details don't become common knowledge among the staff, who are unsettled enough. And now with the fire in the guesthouse!" He glared at her as if somehow *she* were responsible for a log of pitch wood being thrown on the fire. "Children sicken, and sometimes they die. These things happen. It is the way of the world." He gave her a sharp nod and turned to head back up the stairway, effectively ending the interview.

Catrin watched him disappear back into the keep. Though it looked as if he'd left the door open a crack. He had been leaving the keep when she'd hailed him, so he might have gone back up the stairs as the only way he could think to get rid of her. Now, he was watching her, waiting for her to leave before he departed again himself.

Rhys wasn't going to be happy when she relayed the gist of the interview. Her husband presented a calm demeanor to the outside world, but one of the best ways to rile him up was to disrespect his wife.

Geoffrey, meanwhile, had to know that his behavior would appear strange. If his intent was to put her off the investigation and convince her that all was well at Windsor, without a doubt, he had failed utterly.

11

Day Two

Rhys

"I had nothing to do with the prince's death. Nothing!" Rhys had made it hardly more than two steps from the physician's doorway when a young man accosted him, getting down on his knees and raising his hands in supplication. He couldn't have been more than thirty, with a mop of black hair and a trace of a beard, as if he normally shaved in the morning but hadn't yet today. His clothes were rumpled too, implying he'd slept in them.

Rhys grasped the man's arms and pulled him to his feet, embarrassed for him, but also ready to question him since he'd presented himself so openly. "Who are you?"

The anguish in the man's face indicated he'd pushed himself to the edge mustering his courage to come to Rhys and been waiting for him to appear, else he wouldn't have been in front of Rhys so immediately. "Charles Fortin."

Rhys tried to keep the impatience out of his voice. "Yes, but what is your relationship to Prince Alfonso?"

"I was Prince Alfonso's tutor." The moment he said Alfonso's name, Charles burst into tears and appeared entirely unaware this display was taking place in the lower bailey.

To save Charles from himself, Rhys got him walking towards what he thought might be a likely spot to hide, just inside a stairwell up to the battlements. If Charles was going to offer himself up, Rhys was willing to accept his sacrifice.

And then, to add to the oddness of the scene, on their way towards the curtain wall, a young woman hurried out of the kitchen carrying a large cup of ale, which she thrust into Charles's hand. "You need this, I'm sure."

Charles initially refused the cup, trying to push her hand away and in the process almost spilling it.

Rhys smiled his thanks at the woman and forcibly wrapped Charles's hand around the cup. "Drink."

The young man had been Alfonso's tutor, and for that reason might be considered of above average intelligence, but he was not a heavy thinker in this moment and obeyed like one used to doing so.

While Charles drank, Rhys looked at the maidservant, who had gorgeous, thick auburn hair and bright blue eyes. "That was thoughtful of you."

She bobbed a curtsey. "I'm Darla. Cook Hal asked us to keep an eye on you and let him know if you were heading his way. But then I saw poor Charles. You aren't going to blame him for anything, are you? He is harmless." She said all this in a light, friendly voice, implying she had no idea the scene was in any way out-of-the-ordinary.

"I'm not going to hurt him."

Darla gave him a beatific smile. "That's what Eliza said after she helped your wife with her bath last night. Hal didn't believe her. I do."

By now, Charles had drunk the full contents of the cup, almost in one go. He was no longer crying, but his shoulders hung dejectedly. It would be hard to conceive of a more pathetic sight.

"Thank you, Darla." Rhys himself was a little befuddled by her manner.

"You're welcome." Darla headed back to the kitchen with a spring in her step, pleased with a job well-done.

Amused and bemused again, Rhys went the other way in order to settle Charles on the bottom step of the stairway to the battlements. Nobody else was about, which couldn't be normal. Rhys found it likely that Darla had not been the only one watching him. The entire castle would know by now that Charles had melted down in front of him like a spent candle.

Charles was clenching and unclenching his hands. "I would never, ever do anything to hurt Alfonso or jeopardize his health in any way. You have to believe me."

Rhys didn't have to believe him, in point of fact, but it made no sense in this moment to say so, and he sensed he'd get more from Charles with gentleness than by taking a hard line.

"Take a breath, Charles, and then tell me everything you remember about how Alfonso died."

"The illness began with vomiting. One moment he was well, and the next he wasn't. He couldn't keep anything down, even for an hour." Charles had come to Rhys because he thought his life hinged on this conversation, and he showed no reluctance to be as forthcoming as possible. Rhys could understand the impulse to preempt any accusation by facing it head on, and he was willing to listen. "He had diarrhea, and after a few more hours, the diarrhea became bloody. I could tell that he wasn't getting the sustenance he needed. We tried everything to get him to keep liquid down. Those sunken eyes—" He broke off, practically shaking at the memory. "His pulse became thready. Then came seizures and blood in the urine. It took two days for him to die."

"You seem to know a great deal about the progress of his condition."

"I stayed with him the whole time. Fernando and I. I heard everything the physicians said as they came and went."

"Physicians?"

"Peter, of course, but others too, called in from London to consult, as well as the herbalist and hospitaller from the monastery. Even the midwife. Don't mistake this Peter with the one we had then. He was not a drunkard. Nor was he proud! Anyone whom he thought might be able to contribute was called. None could help."

"What did they try?"

"Everything! Don't you understand that yet? This was *Alfonso*! That beautiful boy." Charles's voice held nothing but pain and anguish, and he collapsed forward onto his knees. "Nothing worked."

"What was Alfonso doing in the days and hours leading up to him falling ill?"

"That I cannot tell you for certain, beyond his usual sessions with me. Fernando would know better."

Fernando was on Catrin's list to interview this morning, after she'd tracked down Constable Geoffrey.

"Did anyone else in the castle become ill?" It was what he'd discussed with the physician earlier, but he would be asking this question, and all these others, again and again.

"No." Charles's head came up, and he spoke slowly, really thinking for the first time. "Not that I know."

Rhys had been crouching in front of him, and now he straightened to lean back against the wall. His knees couldn't hold that position for very long anymore. "Nobody?"

"Not that anyone said."

"What about the food taster?" Since Alfonso would have had one.

A hitch was back in Charles's throat, as if he was going to cry again. "He remained well throughout Alfonso's illness, though he died afterwards, of course."

Rhys stared at him. "What did you say?"

Charles frowned. "Didn't anyone mention it? He was found dead one morning a few days after Alfonso died. He loved Alfonso, as we all did. He was old, and his heart couldn't take the loss."

Rhys continued to stare at Charles, who then made something of a despairing gesture with one hand. "You are thinking Alfonso was poisoned, I know. That's why you spoke with the physician just now."

"There are many poisons that disguise themselves as common illnesses. That's why Alfonso *had* a food taster."

"George wasn't ill before he died. We would have seen it. He would have said. His heart gave out." Charles was certain, but also a little obstinate.

"How long had George been part of the royal household?"

"Since before Alfonso was born." Charles's own fears that Rhys would blame him had dissipated as Rhys's attention had turned to George. "You can't be thinking *he* had anything to do with it? Surely if he were responsible, he would have acted sooner. Why wait a decade? I would say the same about any one of the retainers here. Alfonso was ten years old. If anyone at Windsor wanted him dead, surely there were better opportunities sooner."

Charles was right, perhaps, but by voicing his concerns, he'd also given Rhys a new question to ask—though not of Charles, who had acted as if Rhys was being unfair in questioning the circumstances of Alfonso's death. Didn't he understand that Rhys *had* to ask? He obeyed the king, as they all did. And this was what the king had ordered.

But as Rhys studied the top of Charles's head, downturned again in grief, he had to admit that Charles had a point. If Alfonso was, in fact, murdered, *why now?* Had something changed recently to encourage the killer to act? And if so, what was it?

Baby Edward's birth was an obvious change, but equally plausible were events far beyond Windsor Castle, such as the conquest of Wales. For a Welshman to have taken it upon himself to murder the heir to the English throne was so plausible as to be the first thing to consider. Unlike an attack on one of King Edward's castles in Wales, which would require a considerable force of men, the assassination of his son might require only one.

Rhys and Catrin, however, as far as he knew, were the only Welsh people in the castle.

Of course, the fall of Wales to England was hardly the only event that could engender animosity amongst Edward's subjects. Some Saxons hated him still, and there were plenty of those about. The Scots had no love for him either. And that wasn't even taking into account the possibility of a foreign power—France, Aragon, the Holy Roman Empire—from objecting to Edward's interests on the Continent. Any one of them could see a pathway to ridding themselves of a powerful English king by murdering his heir to the throne.

Charles's tears had lessened again, so Rhys held out a hand to help him to his feet. "Can you think of anything at all that might help me learn more about Alfonso's last days? Who was with him when he first took sick? Had anyone visited him who didn't usually?"

"We have had no visitors. And I think it was Princess Margaret who was with him." Charles's expression was one of despair. "We did everything we could to care for Alfonso. All of us." He choked up for a moment. "We loved that boy."

12

Day Two

Catrin

Catrin and Rhys had decided that Catrin should be the one to speak to Fernando alone first. She didn't have anything close to as much experience with investigating as Rhys did, but she had done her share of interviewing since she'd met him, and it seemed reasonable to both of them that Alfonso's steward would find Catrin less threatening than he would Rhys. Last night, Fernando had poured out a large volume of talk, even before they had asked him any questions. There seemed little doubt that on the walk he'd been rehearsing what he wanted to say.

What hadn't been particularly helpful had been the litany of denial of wrongdoing. It really might be that he had done nothing wrong. But sometimes the best way to defend oneself was to attack first—something Catrin had learned in the years of playing with her older brothers and Rhys.

That appeared to be Fernando's new strategy from the moment he opened his door at her knock. "I was hoping to speak more with you—"

He cut her off with a sniff and put his nose in the air, the second man this morning to do so to her. "This is really too much. I told you everything I knew last night. And I'm offended, quite frankly, that your husband would send you instead of coming himself." The Castilian in his French accent grew thicker the further he got into his sentence.

Catrin herself was suddenly offended on her own behalf. Just because Rhys served the king in an official capacity didn't mean that her role as the queen's lady-in-waiting—and Rhys's wife—was of no importance. "We just have a few—"

Fernando closed the door in her face.

She stared at the oak through a count of ten. Then she shrugged, lifted the latch, and entered the room.

Fernando wasn't immediately in sight. Confused, because he'd been *right* there a moment ago, she strode across the room, to another doorway on the far side. When she reached it, she found her quarry leaving through yet another door, which led to a different corridor. He hauled a trunk behind him. Judging by the bits of paper and discarded clothing on the floor, he'd just finished hastily packing.

At the sight of Catrin, a look of pure and utter astonishment crossed Fernando's face, and when she bounded towards him, his expression turned to genuine horror.

"Señora!" He backed into the corridor.

In entering the room uninvited, she had violated every tenet of courtesy. In truth, she had expected Fernando's reaction, was pleased to see it, and felt better about her impulsive choice, especially since he genuinely appeared to be running away. "Are you going somewhere?"

"I have arranged for a carriage to take me to London. I serve no purpose here now."

"The carriage will have to wait. You cannot have forgotten that my husband and I have been sent by King Edward to determine how his son died. I do not care if you find my presence offensive or if you would rather speak to my husband. We are equal partners in this endeavor, and I expect you to remember that fact from now on!"

Fernando's mouth opened and closed like landed fish.

Catrin kept talking. "I need to know specifically the exact order of events leading up to Alfonso's death: when he was last well, what signs of sickness he exhibited first, and what you did about it. If we are to clear you of any wrongdoing, we require an intimate understanding of his daily routine, his lessons, who he saw, and how often and when. I expect you to provide all this information to me now."

In a whirl of skirts, she settled herself in a chair by the window, crossing her legs at the ankles and folding her hands expectantly in her lap.

Fernando's response was to continue to stare at her. "But—" He wanted to run. She could see it in his face.

"I was just speaking with Windsor's constable. Should I fetch him?"

Fernando's shoulders sagged. "No." He dropped the end of the trunk. "That won't be necessary."

"Thank you, Señor Fernando. Please come back inside the room so we don't have to shout." Catrin smiled sweetly. She could have called him by only his given name, but her intent was not to demean him so much as to overawe him.

When she'd entered the room, she had deliberately swathed herself in the persona of Queen Eleanor, emulating her affectation of high dudgeon. Catrin had always thought it was something of an act when the queen did it, though that didn't really make it any less intimidating in the moment. When the anger had the desired effect, and the response from her underlings began to follow the course she wanted, the queen would moderate her tone.

So Catrin did too. "Please sit—" she pointed to a stool near the end of his bed, "—and speak to me now." And then, as if she had just noticed the disarray of his room, she said, "You really intend to leave Windsor forever?"

It was a question to which Fernando could give a clear answer. "I desire to return to Castilla immediately. There is nothing for me here." He sniffed dismissively, indicating his courage was returning. "The weather in England is appalling."

It was a perfectly acceptable day today, even if the sun of earlier was covered by clouds threatening rain. Catrin loved the way the clouds moved across the sky, every moment different.

Still, she couldn't deny the truth of Fernando's words. The weather in Britain could be foul at any time of year.

Instead, she simply continued to smile gently. Catrin had learned from a master, and in this moment she could be thankful for the queen's unintentional tutelage. "If you can answer my questions, I can then speak to my husband about allowing your departure."

She had the power to keep him here, and Fernando knew it. She'd been sent by the king and queen, at whose pleasure he also served. In addition, given that Catrin had run her own household for twenty years, she'd had experience with retainers such as Fernando long before she'd come to serve Queen Eleanor. Many believed themselves of a higher station and more indispensable than they actually were and thought they had the right to set the terms of their own employment. In a few cases, they'd been correct in their estimation of their worth, but it was sometimes unwise for the lady of the manor—especially one only sixteen years old—to acknowledge that she knew it.

Though still hesitant and keeping a wary eye on Catrin, Fernando at last sat on the stool she'd indicated. It put his head lower than hers, with his knees raised somewhat awkwardly, just as she'd intended.

"My apologies, Madam. Please ask your questions, and I will endeavor to be of service, as always."

"Thank you. We will begin with a discussion of his last days."

Fernando took her words for the order they were. "He was well, and then he wasn't. He could not keep anything in his stomach, and then he experienced diarrhea. The doctor could give you the full list of symptoms." He put his hands to his eyes, and Catrin realized with a pang of guilt that he had started to weep again, as he had last night.

"I'm sorry to be here." She put out a hand to him, though with his own hands before his face he couldn't see it. "Surely you can understand why the king sent us?" She wasn't asking for forgiveness so much as understanding.

To Fernando's credit, he gave it to her, though still speaking from behind his hands. "I know why. We all know why. The king would have been neglecting his duty if he hadn't sent someone. Please know that I would have given anything for Alfonso to still be alive. If we could go back in time to a month ago, every single person in this castle would be determined to do whatever needed to be done differently to ensure that he never fell ill. When he was dying, I begged God to spare him and take me instead."

Now Fernando leaned forward, overcome, and sobbed into his forearms. The quick speaking, confident steward was gone, replaced by a grieving man. Possibly, he had held his grief in check up until Catrin had released it.

"I'm so sorry for your loss."

In the end, there was nothing she, or anyone else, could say.

13

Day Two

Miles

"Was Alfonso one to come often into the kitchen?" Miles asked.

Up until this point, Miles had allowed the general conversation at the meal to go on around him with very little contribution on his part. This wasn't because everyone had been speaking in English, which he wasn't supposed to know. The official language of the court was French, and thus, the staff were to speak it even amongst themselves.

In his regular life, Miles understood English well but spoke it poorly. Gilbert le Gascon could be forgiven for not having even a rudimentary grasp of the language. In his guise as Gilbert, Miles had answered all their questions about who he was, as honestly as he could under the circumstances, still trying to walk that line between being open and slightly roguish. Truthfully, he wanted to be all things to all people: for his overseers to trust him enough to do his work unsupervised; for the innocent to talk to him without guile; and for the dishonest to see a fellow conspirator in his shaded answers.

Regardless, it would take time for anyone to trust him—time he might not really have. Reese and Catrin were charged with uncovering truths, and he and Vincent with helping them, but he knew without the king telling him directly that there was a sunset on their window of time for this investigation. They had a few days, perhaps a week, to come up with some answers, if answers were to be found.

He had to put those thoughts aside, however, since they would do him no good in the immediate moment. One couldn't rush confidences. That said, once the conversation moved on to talk about Reese and Catrin, he thought his first opportunity had come.

"Not often, Gilbert." Butler James answered first, calling Miles by his pseudonym, which Miles was perpetually attempting to remember referred to himself.

"Rarely down here." This reply came from the man who oversaw the preparation of vegetables. "The royal children have the full run of the upper bailey, where there's another kitchen, but they are here less often unless they are on their way out of the castle."

If nothing else, his new position had Miles eating well above the common, hardly different from what he would have been fed had he been dining in the upper bailey with Prince Edmund. In point of fact, it was the exact same meal that had been served a moment ago to the diners in the great hall. Those workers were, in general, of no greater station than those around this table. They just worked elsewhere in the castle. The only kitchen workers not present currently were the servers, who were still hustling back and forth to the hall replenishing dishes. They would eat in a second shift and get the leftovers. Such was the lot the world over of someone who provided food to others. Until today, Miles had given no thought at all to when those who served him ate or what they ate when they dined. Needless to say, today had been an education.

Butler James ripped at a piece of bread with his teeth. "After we eat, you'll be delivering wine there."

That was something to look forward to, and Miles ceased his questions. It wouldn't do at all for anyone to wonder why the new wine dispenser was curious about the dead prince.

Fortunately, the conversation continued without him. "What about that quaestor, Sir Reese?" one of the bakers said.

"We don't have to think about him," Butler James said reprovingly. "Don't mind him, and he won't mind us."

That seemed to be the general agreement around the table until one of the younger cheese girls said, "But what about the fire? They say—"

Cook Hal cut her off. "Never you mind what *they* say. It was an accident. Someone up there didn't do his job. You do yours and keep your head down while you're doing it."

The girl subsided, her eyes on her food. Miles very much wanted to pursue this line of inquiry, but he reminded himself that he was trying not to stand out, and he'd prefer not to be censured until he meant to be.

Fortunately, the woman in charge of basting meat made a sad sound. "Alfonso was very sweet."

Clearly, in her mind, to go from speaking of Reese to Alfonso was an entirely logical progression. To that end, the primary bread maker, a woman, lifted her cup. "To Astolfo, as he liked to be called." There were nods all around the table, and everyone raised their cups and repeated, *to Astolfo, Prince of the English.*

Miles was deciding whether it would be appropriate to ask who Astolfo was, even though he already knew from his own foray into heroic tales as a youth and from his conversation last night with Reese, when the baker added, "The king must be out of his mind with grief."

"He's got another one, though, doesn't he?" This came from one of the vegetable choppers sitting next to Miles. As in the great hall, everyone at the table had their proper place. At one end sat Butler James. At the other was Cook Hal, the man in overall charge of the kitchen. The middle seats of each long row going down the sides of the table were given over to the head baker and the man in charge of the meat. The lowest in status—or in Miles's case, the newest employees—sat near the ends, because they were responsible for getting up to fetch more food or run errands for their betters.

That put the vegetable chopper on the end, next to Hal, who slapped him upside the head. "We don't talk that way at table."

The chopper didn't look so much cowed as resentful. As the youth was sitting next to Miles, he was able to overhear the mumble in English that followed: "I'm just saying. It would be different if the baby had been a girl."

Speaking English got him another slap.

Whether or not he should have shared his thoughts, the man was right. He also had the most cavalier attitude Miles had encountered so far about the loss of the prince. In a low voice, Miles returned to French, which not only had to be the sole language he could know, but the only language he could speak at the table without getting whacked on the back of the head. "It sounds to me like there's some in the castle with their own opinions."

"And some outside as well. My friends see things a bit differently."

"I'd like to meet these friends of yours."

He shrugged. "All right."

"What is your name, friend?"

"Cedric."

It was a Saxon name, one which was becoming more unusual over time, especially in a Norman castle. Still, the citizenry of England remained almost entirely Saxon, even if the most common name in London was Roger or William or, in fact, Gilbert. By now, two hundred years after Miles's ancestors had crossed the English Channel with King William, untold lesser Norman men, who had made up the bulk of the invading army, had intermarried with those they'd conquered.

It was through that ancient, adventuring Humphrey that Miles's family had been saddled with the moniker *Bohun*, which meant *beard*. Back then, beards were unusual. Even Duke William had been clean shaven. That long-ago Humphrey had followed the duke because he'd been a younger son, like Miles, with little wealth of his own. By risking his life, he'd established his family, which had grown to be one of the wealthiest and most powerful in England. Since then, the Bohuns had prided themselves on their huge beards, their prowess in battle—and their willingness to take risks.

That trait had come out as strongly in Miles as it had in his nephew, both of whom had been pressed hard by the Second Earl. Miles's older brother had been the Second Earl's heir, but even coming so long after all the other sons, Miles had always known that he'd had his father's respect. It wasn't even fair to say that all his father had left him was his name and his family pride, since he'd even given Miles Waresley, a small estate near Huntingdon, from which he earned enough not to be wholly dependent on his nephew.

Miles was still trying to make his father proud, even these many years after his death. He thought the Second Earl would be pleased by the way he had renewed his friendship with Reese and amused by Miles's current position at the castle. Even now, his father's last words echoed in his head, ten years after his death: "Bohuns are more capable than other men, Miles. We are out of the ordinary and always have been. Whatever you do and whatever you become, don't be ordinary."

14

Day Two

Rhys

Rhys was moving across the bailey, thinking of where to go next and if that might include food, since he'd heard the bell calling the workers to eat, when he was hailed from the entrance to the chapel. "Reese!"

It was Prince Edmund waving at him from the porch of the chapel, flanked by two of his guardsmen. Rhys instantly changed direction. The wind had picked up, bringing with it the first few drops of rain, so Rhys was happy to find shelter before it started up more.

Within a few heartbeats, the weather had changed from a relatively sunny day to an overcast one, and then the rain began coming down in earnest, drumming on the roof, with other drops careening off the stones of the bailey. It was easily loud enough to drown out their conversation, were anyone close enough to listen, though that didn't seem to be Edmund's primary concern.

"I see you are on a quest, so I won't keep you, but I wanted to let you know that you and Lady Catrin are invited to dine today with the family in the hall in the upper ward." Edmund spoke as if an invitation to eat with the royal family was a daily event. It would be for him. "I know I don't need to tell you to be circumspect in your questions about Alfonso in front of the children."

"Of course, my lord. I have said it many times, but I wanted to say again, now that we are here, that I am sorry for this loss. I wish we were not at Windsor, doing this job. It grieves me, and I hate that I am opening a wound in everyone every time I ask about Alfonso's death."

"Is that a roundabout way of telling me that you haven't had much luck in your inquiries?"

"I wouldn't necessarily say that, my lord. We are still in the first hours. Certainly those who might be responsible for Alfonso's death have not stepped forward to lay bare their souls. I do not expect it. Thus, it might be a few more days before we can reach any real conclusions." He paused. "If we do ever reach a firm conclusion. I hate to say this, but we are coming into this investigation late, my lord. Alfonso died on the 19th of August. There may be only so much we can learn so many days after the fact."

Edmund let out a forceful sigh. "It is to be expected. I assure you the king knows it too."

That was nice of Edmund to say, and Rhys believed that King Edward did realize that sending them to Windsor was like firing an arrow into the dark. One never knew if it would hit the target, bring down something unexpected, or land harmlessly in the grass. That didn't mean he couldn't be wrathful if the target that it hit wasn't the one he wanted.

Now Edmund rested a hand on Rhys's shoulder. "I also heard about the fire in the guesthouse last night. Constable Geoffrey insists that the pitch wood was included in error."

"Sir Geoffrey can believe what he likes. I am more inclined to suppose that someone very much doesn't want us to be here."

"For that reason, you and Catrin will move into different quarters tonight. I want you to take the queen's rooms."

Rhys drew in a breath. "My lord, are you sure—"

"You will not argue, and if anyone objects, they can take it up with me, including my sister-in-law."

Rhys swallowed down any further objections. "Yes, my lord." And then he gave Edmund a quick rundown of the investigation so far, including the fact that he wasn't to be surprised if he saw Miles wandering about in the guise of a servant.

Even that news didn't dismay the prince. But then, he had rubbed shoulders with the Bohuns far more than Rhys in the last decade.

"None of this is why I called you over, Reese. The priest is within. He mentioned to me that he would be happy to speak with you."

Rhys tilted his head, reading significance into this comment, though at the same time not entirely sure what he was meant to understand. "I will go to him immediately, my lord. Thank you."

Edmund departed with his guards, leaving Rhys to enter the chapel alone. He was wary, but endeavored to project a confidence he didn't necessarily feel. The chapel within Windsor Castle was twenty feet wide and some seventy feet long, meant to rival Sainte-Chapelle on the Île de la Cité in Paris. It was built over an understory which contained the crypt, as well as storage and the vestry.

To reach the chapel itself required climbing a set of stairs, which exited the stairwell into a narthex. This portion of the chapel was separated from the nave by walls that extended from both sides, though they did not meet in the middle, and ended at a height of eight feet. Rhys went through the open doorway, walking at a steady pace towards the lectern where the priest was standing, frowning down at whatever was laid before him.

Rhys halted a few paces away. "Father—"

The priest, who had not looked up, put up a hand, cutting him off. His eyes moved back and forth, indicating to Rhys he was reading. Then he raised his head. While he wasn't exactly smiling, the severe look was gone. Rhys's first impression had been that the priest was tall, but that was only because he'd been standing on the lectern. Once he descended the steps and was on the same level as Rhys, he proved to be slightly shorter and significantly more rotund, with thinning hair and white in his beard.

"I am Father Giles. You must be Sir Reese, the king's quaestor."

"Yes, Father."

"Come. There is wine to share." The priest swept a hand across his forehead and sighed. He was behaving as if they'd reached a disturbing point in the conversation, though so far fewer than a dozen words had been exchanged. Perhaps the very idea of talking to Rhys was disturbing.

With faint hope, honestly, that he was about to learn anything revelatory, Rhys followed Father Giles to a narrow door in the very back of the church. He wouldn't even have known it was there if they hadn't gone through it, since it blended in so well with the wooden paneling that made up the lower eight feet of the chapel. Above were spectacular stained-glass windows, some of which depicted the life of St. Edward the Confessor, the last Saxon king of England these Normans acknowledged. William the Conqueror had claimed that Edward had made him his heir, which then became his excuse for invading England in 1066. It wouldn't surprise Rhys at all if, in similar fashion, later generations canonized a Welshman who betrayed his people to the Normans.

Or perhaps his country's defeat was so complete, no Welshman would ever achieve sainthood again. The Welsh church had once been independent. Now that it had been forced into conformity with the Norman church and Rome, only two Welsh saints were honored in the entire calendar, one male and one female: Dewi and Gwenffrewi, whom the Normans called David and Winifred. They'd even stolen Gwenffrewi's bones from her grave in Wales and moved them to an abbey in Shrewsbury.

So perhaps, as Rhys followed the priest down the stairs and into the church's receiving room, his attitude wasn't as accommodating as it could have been. The priest, on the other hand, went straight to the sideboard and poured a cup of wine for each of them. Rhys accepted it with thanks, since he was thirsty. As he swallowed the wine, he also swallowed down his resentment and reminded himself why he was there.

Father Giles gestured him to a chair, while he himself moved around the main table in the room to his seat on the other side. Books and papers were stacked in piles, but there was a cleared space where the priest could put his cup.

Rhys took the chair that was offered, took another sip of wine, and waited.

Initially, the priest seemed content merely to drink in silence. Rhys was just deciding that he had let him consider what he was going to say long enough when Giles sighed again. "I gather you spoke to the Earl of Lancaster?"

"I did."

Silence.

It was growing more obvious by the moment that the priest thought that what he had to say was momentous. His extreme reluctance had Rhys wondering if he'd underestimated him, and this issue was so fraught because Giles would have to violate the sanctity of the confessional to speak of it.

Finally, the priest overcame his reservations. "I must tell you of my concerns as to the situation regarding Alfonso's death."

Rhys straightened in his seat. "I would very much like to hear whatever you have to say."

"Mind you, this is for your ears alone. I didn't speak of it to Earl Edmund." Father Giles too shifted in his seat. "I merely said I had a matter to discuss with you. I didn't want to upset him, and I am loath to gossip. It is a great sin."

Rhys happened to agree that gossip was a far worse sin than many, though not perhaps murder itself. Both eroded trust and tore families and communities apart. Each in its own way was also a mainstay of any murder investigation. So he nodded encouragingly, trying to look interested but not too intent, since he didn't want to scare the priest back to silence. Of the people Rhys had spoken to so far, none had offered him more than grief and denials.

At long last, the priest stopped hesitating and came right out with his concern: "I feel I must draw your attention to the chief nanny, Mildrith. She is a troublemaker, I fear she will tell you things that are untrue."

"Do you suspect Mildrith of anything untoward?"

"Not—" Father Giles motioned with one hand. "I don't mean to imply that she had anything to do with Alfonso's death, even if many of the king's children died while in her care. She is far too outspoken for a woman of her station."

Rhys blinked at the way Father Giles had tacked the last comment at the end of an even more provocative statement. As the husband of another woman whom this priest might call *far too outspoken,* Rhys found himself instantly giving this Mildrith the benefit of the doubt—as clearly others had done if she had continued to be employed by the royal family throughout the deaths of the children in her charge. Rhys could see now why the priest had been circumspect in the presence of Prince Edmund, whose wife had lost a son during her first marriage (to the King of Navarre), when the nanny had dropped him over a battlement. By mistake, of course. One would hope. *Dear God, one can only hope.*

Father Giles cleared his throat. "She and Physician Peter had an argument about the proper course of treatment for Alfonso." He paused, prompting Rhys to think to himself *ah, here's the real truth.* "I suppose it is fair to say that the three of us had an argument about it. And then, in the immediate aftermath of his death, she insisted that Alfonso's illness might not have had a natural cause. The castle's constable, Sir Geoffrey, ordered her to cease speaking of it on pain of dismissal."

Since Rhys and Catrin were here at Windsor with the very same thought, it seemed hypocritical to censure someone else for sharing it. Rhys had learned long ago, however, not to discuss his opinions with his informants. "What did she think had happened?"

"She insisted that we consider the possibility that a human hand could be involved. You see, none of the other children with whom he'd played in the previous days, nor anyone else in the castle for that matter, was ill." Father Giles made the sign of the cross. "It is a mistake to think that way. God strikes down whom He wills, and calls home to Himself whom He wills. *If we live, we live for the Lord; and if we die, we die for the Lord. So, whether we live or die, we belong to the Lord.*"

The quote was from Romans, one Rhys had heard a hundred, if not a thousand times, at funerals and elsewhere. What the good father did not know, however, was how the king was haunted by this idea that Alfonso was dead because God had willed it. Of course, everything that happened was God's will in the end, but King Edward feared his own deeds had brought retribution down upon his house.

"So you, yourself, believe Alfonso died of a natural illness?"

"Yes."

"You have no doubts?"

"None at all."

"You mentioned that Mildrith had been at the bedsides of the other children when they died. Is that because you *don't* feel the same about their deaths?"

Father Giles blinked. "I never meant to imply any such thing! I merely wanted to point out that just because she has been intimate with the children does not mean she should be trusted."

That wasn't at all the impression he'd given Rhys. Really it looked to him as if Father Giles wanted to have it both ways: for Alfonso's death to have had a natural cause *and* for Mildrith to somehow be responsible for not only his death but that of the other children.

"How many of the children's deaths have you attended?"

Rhys had known before he spoke that the question would appear critical, even accusing, to the priest, and it rendered Father Giles momentarily speechless. He recovered enough to say, "Of course, many have lived at Windsor at one time or another. But I saw nothing untoward in their deaths. Children die, I am sad to say, in staggering numbers."

"The king has had, some would say, more than his fair share of grief."

"Such is the lot of the mighty." The priest shook his head. "God raises them up, and he brings them low. It is not for us to question by what means."

All of that was true too, but no real help to the king.

The priest eyed him. "You don't remember me, do you?"

Rhys just managed not to roll his eyes at another member of the king's retinue he didn't recognize. "I'm sorry. I do not."

Father Giles nodded. "Over a decade ago, I was visiting Southwark Cathedral, at a conference called by the Bishop of Winchester, when you were brought in to investigate the death of the boy in that bathhouse. You would not have been introduced to me, so it is no slight to you that you don't remember my face. It was a long time ago, and you were busy. Honestly, I wouldn't remember your face if I didn't already know it was you."

Rhys hadn't thought about that investigation in many years, even with renewing his service to the king. It had taken place after Rhys's return from the crusade, when he'd still been in the service of Prince Edmund, before he'd left to join Prince Llywelyn's personal guard. Even though Father Giles would have been within his rights to see this defection as a betrayal, Rhys heard no censure in his voice, just acknowledgment of what was and what had been.

Rhys's reception in this royal castle was turning out to be entirely different from what he had expected. Instead of rejection, he'd encountered acceptance. Instead of anger, he was hearing concern. It was almost making him reexamine his prejudices. It turned out, just like in Wales, that people were people, and everyone would be far better off taking everyone as they came.

15

Day Two

Miles

Miles was opening his mouth to say something encouraging to the worker beside him—because Miles had a feeling that now might be the time for risk, at least with him—when the kitchen door flew open. A serving girl stood on the threshold, her hand to her mouth.

At the sight of her, the head cook looked up, a half-eaten chunk of cheese in his hand. "What is it, Darla?"

"I went to see Bobby. I know I'm not supposed to seek him out while we're on duty, but—" Her face crumpled, and she threw her apron over her head so it covered her face. From behind it, despite her sobs and the cloth over her mouth, her next words came clearly enough. "He's dead! Someone stabbed him in the belly!"

Darla was to all appearances devastated, but Miles's spirits instantly lifted, and he found himself on his feet. *That was more like it!* It was one thing to try to investigate a death, particularly an emotionally painful one, that happened weeks ago. It was quite another to have one plop into his lap on the very day of his arrival. Of course, it wasn't *his* arrival that might have prompted the murder, and if anyone was having trouble with the idea that Alfonso was murdered too, they would find it less difficult to believe now.

"Did you tell anyone else? Raise an alarm?" The butler proved himself to have a cool head in an emergency.

"Nobody was about, so I came here. I didn't know what else to do. He was just *there*, in the corner of the storage room where we usually meet. I know we weren't supposed to be there. Nobody was supposed to know—" Her explanation said plenty about her relationship with him, how often they might have met, and what they might have done together. "I *loved* him!"

"Quiet everyone!" Butler James put out a hand to those around the table, many of whom had been thrown into turmoil by Darla's news. Some were gazing at the girl in horror, a few of the women were openly weeping, and several men cursed. "We are all upset, but we don't know what the situation is yet, and until we do, you have jobs to do." Then, to Miles's utter delight, he pointed directly at him. As it turned out, by standing, Miles had made himself noticeable. "Take Darla and find the captain of the garrison and that—" the butler snapped his fingers twice, "—Welsh quaestor who arrived last night. This will be a better use of his time."

Better than what? could have been the obvious question, but Miles had realized within the first hour of his employment that not only was everyone still talking about Alfonso's death—and grieving his loss—but there was no uncertainty as to why Reese had come to Windsor. They knew his history on crusade; they knew he'd joined the king's guard; and they knew enough to both fear speaking to him and fear not speaking to him. In other words, his reputation had preceded him. Miles could have told Reese after Nefyn that it was only a matter of time before the whole of England knew that he was back in the king's service and was someone of whom villains should beware.

Miles didn't know exactly why the butler was sending him on this particular errand. He didn't care either. It would allow him to be involved in the investigation without inserting himself into it on his own initiative, which was something he very much wanted to avoid. Again, it was all about standing out in exactly the right way.

Rather than give Butler James time to change his mind, Miles collected the somewhat bewildered Darla and left the kitchen with alacrity. He had no actual idea where he might find the captain of the garrison at this hour, other than, perhaps, eating in the hall or in the main guardroom, but he figured that enough castle guardsmen would be about for him to learn that answer easily enough. In fact, just as he and Darla left the kitchen, he spied one coming from the main gatehouse.

Miles raised a hand to hail him. "You there!"

Only after he'd spoken did he realize that he was behaving like Miles de Bohun might, not as Gilbert le Gascon would. It was too late to take his action back, however, so he hustled up to the guardsman and made his apologies. "I'm sorry to call to you that way, but I have urgent news for your captain. Can you point me to where he might be?"

Thankfully, the man accepted Miles's apology with a flick of his fingers. "I'm sorry to tell you that he isn't in the castle at the moment. He was called into town about a fracas at an inn."

"At this hour of the day?"

"Fracases can befall inns at any hour." The guard made a motion with his head as if to ask, *how could you not know that?* Then he said, "What of it?"

Miles's momentary deliberation was long enough for Darla to blurt out, "Bobby's dead! I found him stabbed to death in the stables! There was blood *everywhere!*"

It was more than Miles would have said, but no less than the truth.

"I'll fetch the captain. This is more important than a tavern brawl." The guard did an immediate about-face and headed back towards the gatehouse, but then he stopped and looked at Miles over his shoulder. "You probably should find that Welsh quaestor. Helping with something like this is the least he could do."

Clearly Butler James was not the only one who thought Reese, and thus all of them, were wasting their time looking into Alfonso's death.

"Do you know where he might be?"

Though the guard had set off again, he pointed towards the inner gatehouse and said, without breaking stride, "He's right there. I'm off."

Really, Miles's involvement was looking more and more reasonable as each person to whom he spoke sent him in the same direction: towards Reese. Everyone in the kitchen had heard Butler James give Miles the order to find him, and the guard would tell Captain Thaddeus the same.

Consequently, Miles hustled Darla over to Reese, who was just coming through the gatehouse from the middle bailey. When he reached him, he ducked his head in a manner appropriate to a wine dispenser meeting a knight and said in a voice that carried, "Sir. I'm sorry to intrude, sir. But have you heard the news? A boy's been found dead in the stables. Bobby is his name. Darla here found him. I was sent by the butler to fetch you. My name is Gilbert le Gascon." He spoke in a rush, trying to throw out all the necessary information in as efficient a manner as possible, and also in a way appropriate for the dispenser he was pretending to be.

Reese glanced from Miles to Darla to the guard disappearing through the gatehouse, and then to the stables, where at the moment there was no activity. "Do you mean the stables here in the lower bailey?"

Miles nodded, and Darla again poured out what she knew: "I know I'm not supposed to see him during the day, but yesterday he asked, so of course I went. And then he was just *there.* Stabbed!"

"In the stables? It doesn't look like anything is amiss there."

Darla had collapsed into a shower of tears, so Miles was able to speak. "She didn't raise the alarm but ran back to the kitchen to tell us."

Reese put a gentle hand on the girl's arm. "When was the last time you saw him before now?"

She didn't stop sobbing, but she managed to say between hiccups, "Yesterday afternoon, like I said."

Reese was being very gentle. "Run back to the kitchen, now, my dear. No need to see him again. I'll come find you after you've settled, all right?"

Darla's sobs quieted. "Yes, my lord. Charles said you were nice." The girl departed.

Reese took in a breath. "Let's see what this is about, shall we?" He set off towards the stables with Miles hustling to keep up. Then, under his breath, he added, "How on earth did you arrange to be the one to fetch me?"

"I was at the table when Darla came in, and Butler James ordered me to find you."

Reese was almost laughing now. "I see you have properly installed yourself in your new post."

Miles plucked at his forelock, prompting another suppressed laugh from Reese. "Of course, my lord. Anything to serve."

Windsor's stables, in keeping with the overall style of the castle, were extensive, with long rows of stalls around a central aisle. The horses here had better accommodations than most people. Like the castle itself, these lodgings were fit for a king. The main door in the side of the stables was some ten feet wide as well and equally high, sufficient for a mounted man to ride through. Upon initial entry, Miles and Reese halted, so their eyes could adjust to the lower light. Before them was a wide space for attending to horses, and then, farther on, a dozen stalls took up each side of the aisle.

The first person they encountered was a gray-haired man mucking out a nearby stall while the horse who lived in it munched contentedly from his feed bag. He was very thin (the man, not the horse), but Miles could see his muscled arms through his shirt. Miles and Reese had momentarily cast shadows on the floor to partially block the light coming through the doorway, which prompted the man to look over.

He squinted, continuing to work at first. And then, as Reese and Miles came all the way inside, he ducked his head, his eyes skittering first over Miles (and then dismissing him as of no importance) before addressing Reese. It wasn't often in his life that Miles was pleased to be dismissed. "May I be of assistance, my lord?" He spoke in French but with an English accent.

"Did you see a girl, a maid named Darla, come in and out of the storage room within the hour?"

"No, sir. Should I have?"

Reese didn't answer in the affirmative, but simply said, "The storage area would be found where?"

The stable man ducked his head again. "I don't mean to be rude, sir, but may I ask to whom I am speaking?"

Miles jumped in on Reese's behalf. "This is Sir Reese, the king's quaestor and a member of his guard."

"Oh!" The man blinked several times. "Pardon me, my lord." He bobbed a third quick bow. "My eyes aren't what they used to be. Nor's my hearing, truth be told."

That had been obvious by the fact that he hadn't known about Darla, who was not exactly a quiet girl. Now that Miles was closer, he could see the rheum in the man's eyes. "What is your name?"

"Edgar." For the first time the man really looked at Miles—or attempted to. "And who might you be?"

"Gilbert, the new wine dispenser."

Edgar nodded, as if that was to be expected, and gestured to Miles's right. "It's there, my lord."

"I'll need a lantern," Reese said.

"Of course, my lord." He hurried away while Miles and Reese entered the storage room. Within stables, lanterns needed to remain unlit most of the time, since the danger of fire was so great. While the stables were very clean, hay and straw dust were everywhere and even a single stray spark could bring the whole place down around them.

But the lantern was required because, though the storage room was built on something of the same grand scale as the rest of the stables, with a high ceiling and sturdy rafters supporting the roof, it had no windows. Stables were always designed to allow plenty of air flow for the sake of the horses, but there was no need for that here.

Even so, they had enough light filtering through the doorway to see the shape of the room and what it contained, mostly gear for riding, such as spare saddles, bridles, and the like, but also a small, slumped form in the far corner. Given the dimness of the room, it was little wonder nobody had noticed him earlier, especially Edgar, who probably couldn't even see that far.

Reese hastened across the room to crouch next to the boy and put his hand to his neck. After a pause, he said, "He's dead."

"What was that?" The gray-haired stableman had returned at the same moment Reese had spoken. "What did you say?" His shock was such that he let go of the lantern.

Miles, fortunately, hadn't moved more than a pace into the room and was able to grab the handle of the lantern in time to stop it from overturning onto the floor. The last thing they needed was another fire.

"Do you know who this is?" Reese asked in English, the stableman's native tongue.

Edgar approached warily, Miles beside him, now with the lantern, with which he illuminated the body. The stableman had to bend to see the boy's face, but once he saw it clearly, he reared back. "That's Bobby."

Thus had been the serving girl's identification.

Bobby was lying on his back with a disconcerting dark stain underneath him. When Reese had crouched beside the body, he'd avoided putting his boots in it. As Miles held the lantern lower, he was able to see the obvious gash in the young man's belly beneath the rib cage and knew the stain was blood.

"How old was he?" Reese asked.

"Just nineteen last week. He was walking out with my granddaughter, Bess."

Miles wondered if that would be news to Darla.

"I'm sorry, Edgar, for your loss," Reese said.

"I didn't like him." Edgar's chin jutted out. "He had a roving eye."

Miles wasn't going to disagree, given Darla's story about why she'd come to the stables in the first place.

Reese's expression didn't change. "I'll need to speak to anyone who has been working in the stables today. Gather them in the central space by the door and don't tell them what this is about."

"Yes, my lord!" Edgar was through the door in a flash to do Reese's bidding.

Miles, meanwhile, had discovered a second entrance to the storage room, located in a side wall. "Well, we know how someone could enter and leave without being seen." He looked out, noting the blank wall of the next building some ten feet away, and then closed the door again. Reese might have liked the light, but not the observers who might be attracted by the open door.

Reese took this news of a second door in stride. Instead, he pointed to the wound in the boy's belly. "You'll note the angle of the blade was upwards, indicating it went into the flesh below the ribs and thrust towards the heart. The killer knew what he was doing."

"That means he was a soldier? A member of the garrison, perhaps."

"Or merely someone who was a soldier at one time. There are plenty of those about. Or he could simply be versed in the human body."

Miles's eyes widened. "You suspect the doctor?"

"I suspect no one and everyone. At this stage, I'm simply making observations."

"Maybe this was a lover's quarrel and has nothing to do with Alfonso."

"Maybe." But then Reese gave a vehement shake of his head. "I can come up with a thousand possible scenarios to explain how Bobby died. We have to reduce it to one, and it has to be the right one."

"I would have thought that speculation would be helpful." Miles *always* pushed back. He couldn't help himself.

"There's a real danger in drawing conclusions and sending myself in pursuit of a line of inquiry too soon that later proves to be fruitless. Better to keep my options open until we know more. I haven't even examined the body properly yet." He looked Miles up and down. "It does concern me slightly how easily you infiltrated the castle. Not to denigrate your skills, but if you can do it, someone else could too."

"I could take offense at that but I think I won't. You're speaking truth."

Reese gave a little grunt. "Just now, I was discussing this very subject with the constable's clerk, and he tells me that Windsor employs almost two hundred people. One more or less is of little note. He knew the butler needed an underling but hadn't known you were hired until after you were already at work. He seemed unconcerned by that fact."

"I would hope that those employed in the upper bailey are vetted more closely," Miles said. "Though, the last thing Butler James said to me before Darla arrived with the news of the body's discovery was that he was sending me there after our meal."

"We will have to make sure you keep that appointment. That investigation is why we're here."

"Surely the deaths are connected!"

"Are they?"

"Aren't they?"

Reese merely raised his eyebrows, prompting Miles to guffaw. "You really do try not to assume anything, don't you?" He shook his head, not sure he could be so disciplined and patient. "Can you tell how long he's been dead?"

"Some hours by the feel of him, perhaps as many as half a day. The body is warm and stiff. As it's past noon now, that puts the time of death late last night or in the early hours of the morning."

"Is that about the time I was drinking wine with the steward?"

"I'm thinking that's a bit too early. It would be after that." Reese shot Miles an amused glance. "You are not off the hook."

Miles chose to take him at his word. "I tell you truly that I was not inside the castle last night."

Reese sat back on his haunches, genuine surprise in his face. "Do you think I suspect you?"

"You said *everyone*."

"You're right. I did. But to be honest, I don't suspect Catrin either."

"You seem remarkably calm for being faced with a dead body."

"Dead bodies I understand."

"You are a strange man, Reese."

"Some might say you have to be a little bit—" Reese paused as he fought for the right word, "—*off* to do what I do."

"Like milk left out too long in the sun?" Miles shook his head, somewhat disbelieving. "You said earlier not to assume anything, but you are assuming Bobby was murdered. Couldn't he have killed himself?" Maybe just asking the question indicated that Miles was a bit *off* too, but he thought, under the circumstances, the question should be asked.

"If he'd stabbed himself, the knife would still be here, close to his hand. It isn't. That means someone took it. Was there blood on the serving girl when she came into the kitchen?"

Miles thought a moment. "No. Not even on her hands."

"She said she was meeting Bobby in secret."

"Which would make sense if he was walking out with Bess."

Reese indicated that Miles should set the lantern near the boy's head. Bits of straw littered the floor around the body, and he swept some away with one hand. Others were stuck to the floor in the pool of blood that had formed underneath the corpse.

"You are adapting to investigating with somewhat distressing ease," Reese said, somewhat absently.

Miles didn't know about that. He was quite certain he had a long way to go before he could approach a murdered boy with anything like the confidence or equanimity Reese was exhibiting. "I would have expected more blood."

"With this quick a death, it could be the right amount. When a man is bleeding out, the blood pulses with every heartbeat, but when the heart stops—"

"—the blood stops as well."

Reese frowned. "Have I said that to you before?"

"In those early days in the Holy Land, you had the enthusiasm of a new convert, my friend. You told anyone who would listen of your discoveries, and Simon and I listened at length."

Reese was the one to duck his head now. "My apologies." He motioned for Miles to help him roll the body over, which they did, prompting an immediate recoil on Miles's part.

"Ouch!"

Bobby had been lying on an upturned rake and had two puncture wounds to show for it. "That must have hurt."

Reese shook his head. "He was dead by the time he hit the tines."

"How could you possibly know that?" Miles asked.

"Do you see how the flesh punctured by the tines is yellowish-pink?"

Miles gave a hesitant nod. "I suppose?"

"That indicates the wounds didn't bleed."

"So we know how he died." Miles's expression turned thoughtful. "How are we going to discover who killed him?"

Reese glanced up at Miles. "Do you really want to know?"

"Of course. Why wouldn't I?"

"You have been going your own way a bit. I don't want to interfere with what seems to be a fairly well thought-out plan."

Miles put a hand to his heart. "As I said, I am always willing to learn."

Reese snorted his disbelief but explained anyway: "I approach every investigation from the standpoint that all men want the same three things: wealth, love, and power. With one thrust, someone deprived this boy of all three."

"I know you don't want me to ask questions—"

"I didn't say that. Questions can be helpful. I am a quaestor, and what is that but *one who asks questions?* So ask away. If I don't know the answer, I'll tell you."

"Why kill a lad like him? Even more, why kill *this* lad?" Miles had straightened to look down at the corpse, and he answered his own question before Reese could, "Because Bobby knew something, or the killer thought he knew something, and it cost him his life."

Reese waggled his head noncommittally. "I always want to know *why*. It's important to me to understand why a man does what he does, but we don't need to answer that question to find the killer."

"I don't understand."

"We have the how—by stabbing; we have a good estimation as to the when—sometime last night. Someone will have seen something, somewhere, that will get us the *who*. And then the *why* will take care of itself." Reese rose to his feet. "Before this moment, we had suspicions only. Now we know there's a murderer in the castle. He exists. We have only to move forward from here."

16

Day Two

Catrin

Having spoken to the physician, the tutor, and the priest, Rhys had come to find Catrin in order to relate to her what he'd learned. He'd also repeated Father Giles's slight to Mildrith, particularly that he'd called her a *troublemaker*.

Catrin had laughed, remembering the few times she'd encountered Mildrith. Although they'd never exchanged more than a handful of words, those had been enough to make her fully believe that Mildrith could have rubbed the priest the wrong way, especially if he really thought that women should be seen and not heard (had he *met* Queen Eleanor?). Afterwards, she went immediately to question this paragon of womanhood for herself.

Mildrith was similar in age to Catrin, a few years short of forty. She was also a widow, albeit with no children of her own—at least none that lived. If not for Catrin's son, Justin, Mildrith's story could have been Catrin's story, which served to create an immediate bond between them. This sharing of information occurred within moments of Catrin's knock on her door. Mildrith was a good listener. Her attention had Catrin talking about herself—perhaps far more than she usually did, and maybe more, in retrospect, than she should have.

Mildrith also was one of those people who had no trouble talking, and unlike Fernando, what she had to say did not appear rehearsed. Her life story poured out in a steady stream. A less confident person than Catrin might find Mildrith's personality to be overwhelming on first acquaintance.

Somewhere in the midst of Mildrith's flow of words, Catrin managed to ask, "Wasn't Alfonso too old for a nanny anymore?"

"Oh, he was, being ten years old. But I've been with the royal family from the beginning, since the first daughters were born. I care for Elizabeth now."

The royal daughters had been living with Alfonso at Windsor since the end of the Welsh war. The eldest, Eleanor, was fifteen. She could have been married by now, since royal children often married young, and she was currently engaged to the son of the King of Aragon. But that kingdom was under interdict from the pope and, until the decree was lifted, King Edward refused to give away his daughter.

Next oldest was Joan, who had been born in Acre on crusade, lived until she was five with her grandmother in France, and was now twelve and also awaiting a royal marriage. Her first contract had been with a son of the King of Germany, but the young man had died three years earlier. Rumor had it, in fact, that she would soon be affianced to none other than Gilbert de Clare, the

Earl of Gloucester and Catrin's former husband's lord. This could only happen if the pope granted Clare an annulment to dissolve his marriage to Alice de Lusignan, niece of William de Valence, Vincent's lord.

Margaret and Mary were next at nine and six. Since the age of three, Margaret had been betrothed to the son of the Duke of Brabant, but it would be a few more years before their wedding. There was talk that Mary might be destined for the church, but for now, the girl remained at Windsor. That left the youngest daughter, Elizabeth, born two years earlier in 1282. So far, she wasn't affianced to anyone.

Mildrith handed Catrin a cup of wine, poured from a carafe. In the hall, ale was served almost exclusively, but amongst this level of retainer, the drink was wine. It was no wonder that Miles had latched upon the empty position of assistant to the butler as the best way to gain entry into the castle community. Catrin was honestly surprised she hadn't seen him about his work as yet, refilling carafe after carafe, given how much was being consumed.

Catrin took a sip, noting the wine's robust flavor. She reminded herself that, after months in Wales in which mead was the drink of choice, she wasn't used to this quality of wine, nor the quantity in which it was being dispensed. She should be careful not to drink too much.

The wine appeared unnecessary for loosening Mildrith's tongue, but Catrin waited until the nanny had swallowed a few sips before asking, "Please tell me of Alfonso."

Mildrith began talking immediately, as if she had been waiting for weeks to be asked that question. Given that the castle steward had muzzled her, maybe she had. "From the moment I laid eyes on that boy, I loved him. His disposition was almost always sunny, and he wasn't sickly like Henry had been. That made life with him so much more pleasant. He enjoyed everything and was eager to please, which encouraged all of us to please him."

During the brief moment Mildrith took a breath, Catrin asked, "Did you look after him from the very beginning?"

"Oh no. Alfonso was born in Gascony during the king's return journey to England from the crusade. I was still with Henry then, who lived another year. When the family arrived in England in 1274, Alfonso was already almost a year old. Joan had been left with her grandmother in France. Henry died a few months later, in October of that year. The queen was pregnant with Margaret, and I was brought back to help care for Alfonso while we waited for the birth."

Here she met Catrin's eyes. "Your noble husband departed for Wales around that time. I remember. Some were quite upset." She paused, looking inward as she remembered. "We remain grateful he had been on crusade to save Prince Edmund's life. The honor he holds now is, of course, well deserved. And how nice to see him married to you! If you don't mind my saying so, my lady, you were never very happy with Sir Robert, God rest his soul, and it is a blessing to see you so full of life. Marrying Sir Reese has taken ten years off your face!" Here she put out a hand. "Not that you looked old before, don't get me wrong. Fresh as a spring day I always used to say you looked. But now you look like a girl only a few years out of pigtails."

As she paused to take another breath, Catrin, who knew for sure that she did *not* look like she had when she was sixteen, managed to insert another question. "Were you present when Alfonso died?"

"I was. We called him Astolfo, at his own insistence. Did someone say?" Without waiting even for Catrin's head to nod, Mildrith plowed on. "It was such a horrible day. Horrible." She shuddered. "One of the worst days of my life. He had all the usual childhood illnesses and survived them, you see. We all thought he was out of the woods. And he was hardy! Nobody else was ill either. I don't know everything about these matters, as that useless doctor has told me more than once, but even someone who has never had children knows that when one child falls ill, others do too, and very often one can trace the chain back to the person who went out into the streets of London and brought the illness back to sicken everyone else! That priest claims that all illness is God's doing, and I don't doubt that for a moment, but I couldn't have cared for children for as long as I have and not have seen that when the first one comes down with measles, a few days later the next one does, and if you don't keep the rest away, sooner or later, you have an entire castle full of sick children!"

In her umbrage, she took another breath, allowing Catrin to speak again, "But that didn't happen with Alfonso—excuse me, Astolfo?"

"It did not! He'd been playing with his sisters—he was always rescuing them from one danger or another: dragons, Saracens, or what have you. He was happy and well one hour and then he was sick the next and kept getting sicker until he died. There was nothing anyone could do." She flung out a hand. "I don't blame that doctor. Even if Alfonso was poisoned, there would be very little anyone could do." She stopped again, as if realizing for the first time how outspoken she'd been. It looked to Catrin as if the effort of holding back an elaboration of her opinions all this time had been making her almost swallow her tongue.

Catrin, of course, very much wanted to hear those opinions. "You were told to keep that notion to yourself, I hear."

Mildrith tossed her head. "As if I would ever say anything about the matter to the princesses, poor dears. Distraught, they are! But I did speak to the doctor when the priest was present, as well as the constable. Have you met him yet?"

Catrin managed a nod before Mildrith was off again. "Sir Geoffrey came on right after the old one died. I have liked him well enough up until now. He'd been training for stewardship all his life, you see. One of the Pickfords. Saxon by heritage, but then, so am I. His family managed to keep their lands after old William came in. One of the few who did."

There were, in fact, more Saxons at Windsor Castle than Catrin had expected. Everyone called themselves English these days, though the Welsh name for them, *Saesneg,* made no distinction between whatever they were now and the Saxons they had once been. Rhys had lamented the lack of Saxon spine in standing up to the Norman conquerors, but the reality was that they had stood up for years. While it wasn't the two hundred the Welsh had managed, they didn't have mountains to hide in like Catrin's people did. Consequently, when they'd fallen, the fall had been long, and they'd landed very hard indeed—as hard as the Welsh, truth be told. As Mildrith had rightfully pointed out, the Saxon nobility who'd lived through their rebellions (in the same way that noblemen who'd survived Llywelyn's war, as Catrin's brothers had), were few and far between.

What King Edward was doing in Wales was no more or less than a way of life for these Normans.

"If you've been with the royal family all this time, were you present at the deaths of any of the other children?"

"Of course I was with them when they died! I was their nanny, their one constant in a sea of changing retainers and servants. If I wasn't there when they were ill, who would be?" Mildrith made no attempt to qualify this fact, or apologize, or hide the truth.

Catrin felt she had to put in, "Neither of the other boys died at Windsor." John, the eldest of the dead sons, had died as a ward of his uncle while at Wallingford; and Henry had been at Guilford, where he was being cared for by the Queen Dowager, Eleanor.

"I went where the children went."

In truth, everything she was telling Catrin made perfect sense. It was common for noble families to retain the same nanny throughout the years, to oversee the care of each child in succession. As the children grew, she was replaced by tutors or other guardians more suited to the child's specific needs. Alfonso's primary caretaker had been Fernando, although he'd also maintained a stable of tutors and instructors, as befitted his station as the future King of England.

"At the time did you think something was amiss at any of these other deaths?"

"No." Mildrith deflated. "Did someone say so? I don't think much of that doctor, since he has a little too much faith in wine as a cure. But that priest!" Now she gave a violent shake of her head. "Prayer is all very well and good, but prayers don't cool a little boy's forehead when the fever takes him, do they? Prayers don't hold his head over the bowl when he's vomiting up his insides!"

The grief in her voice was heartbreaking, and Catrin had no doubts anymore, if she'd ever really had any, that Mildrith had nothing to do with Alfonso's death. Her love for her charges shone from her face. "Do you have any evidence of wrongdoing by anyone?"

Mildrith shook her head. "The reason I stopped talking about how Alfonso might have died, as Sir Geoffrey asked, was because I couldn't point a finger at anyone. Everyone loved him. None of us would ever want to harm him." Her voice caught in her throat, and she bent her head to hide sudden tears.

Then a wail came from the room behind Mildrith. She and Catrin had been seated in a well-lit solar, around which various toys were scattered as would suit a small child. Instantly Mildrith leapt to her feet, wiping at her cheeks with the backs of her hands, and disappeared through the open doorway, returning a moment later with Elizabeth. The little girl was very blonde, plump, and sweet. She'd been sucking on the tip of one finger, which she pointed at Catrin.

Obligingly, Catrin came forward and let Elizabeth wrap her small fist around Catrin's finger. The child seemed more composed than usual for two, with an intent look that seemed to see right through Catrin. Admittedly, at the child's age, the typical range of abilities, whether physical or mental, was very wide. Then she wriggled to get down and ran to a toy horse, sized perfectly for her to ride, and sat on it, bouncing up and down while talking like a running brook, just like Mildrith.

For once, Mildrith was silent, not overriding the child. Catrin was able to crouch before her. "I like your horse very much. What's his name?"

"Tencendor." The word came out clearly enough, being relatively simple for a young child to say, without *r*'s to trill or the difficult *ll* sound which could flummox Welsh children at that age.

"That was the name of Charlemagne's horse." Catrin turned to look over at Mildrith.

The nanny nodded. "Alfonso named him, of course. She would sleep on that horse if I let her."

"There are worse things, and it's a nice way to remember her brother, which perhaps she'll appreciate when she's older." Catrin straightened. "If you can think of anything else that might help us determine if something untoward happened to Alfonso, please find me, day or night."

Mildrith looked down at her hands, which were clasped to-gether. Now her speech did not come quickly. As when they'd first begun talking, during the time Catrin had been sharing her own story, Mildrith showed herself capable of stemming the flow. "I will do so. Of course I will, though I have thought and thought al-ready. Everybody loved him."

It was what everyone had said. By now, Catrin was really hoping Mildrith was right.

17

Day Two

Rhys

Rhys headed for the main storage room door. "Let's talk with the stable workers."

But Miles didn't move. "Are you sure about leaving the body lying here? Shouldn't we take it to the laying out room?"

Rhys turned back. Not even Catrin had been such an enthusiastic student. She'd asked good questions, but even she hadn't been as outspoken as Miles. "He isn't going anywhere."

"Yes, but—"

"The issue, Gilbert," Rhys said the name with something of a wry tone, "is that I have competing concerns at the moment. Better to see the faces of everyone who works here when they learn of Bobby's death, rather than waiting for the arrival of the garrison captain and a host of officials. It might even be that speaking to me, a Welshman, will be easier for them. Honestly, that's the first time I've ever had that thought!" He shooed Miles out the door and closed it behind them.

If it was Rhys's honesty and competence that had drawn Miles to Rhys all those years ago, it was Miles's curiosity and insight that had drawn Rhys to Miles. Most noblemen spent no time at all putting themselves in the shoes of anyone other than those above them, and that was in the service of conspiring to take their place. As should have been clear from the start, and certainly was becoming more obvious by the moment, Miles wasn't a usual nobleman. This younger son had long since accepted that he was never going to rise higher in the world than he was right now except by his own merits. It was his nephew who was the earl, not him. Only through Humphrey's favor, or the king's, might Miles achieve real wealth of his own.

That perspective had made him ambitious, clever, and at the same time thoughtful. It was also likely the reason he and Rhys had been able to become friends despite their differing backgrounds and stations.

As Rhys had asked, Edgar had gathered the stablemen in the central area by the entrance. By now, it was well past midday. Guessing by the crumbs being brushed from one man's sleeve, until very recently he'd been eating in the hall in the lower bailey, as likely had most of the workers here. That was why Darla had gone to meet Bobby in the storage room, knowing that few would be about at that hour. And if the only worker remaining was Edgar, who could neither see nor hear well, the loving couple would have had a good chance of not being disturbed.

Rhys faced eight stablemen, ranging in age from twelve to seventy, Edgar's approximate age. That was just barely enough men to cover all thirty horseboxes. They needed so few workers because only a fraction of the stalls were currently occupied. Most of the horses had been taken to Windsor's pastures and stables on the Eton side of the Thames where, in good weather, they would stay until their masters needed them. Those stables were also where Prince Edmund's two horse boys had gone.

Adjacent to the storage room were two somewhat cavernous rooms, one for straw, necessary for the horses' beds and to provide additional roughage in their diets, and a second for hay, piled nearly to the ceiling, since the harvest had just happened. Even with diminished numbers, collectively the horses consumed an enormous amount of food, and their beds needed to be mucked out every day.

"We have some bad news." Rhys didn't wait to assuage their curious looks. "We have just discovered the body of Bobby, a young man who worked here. He was found in the storage room."

To a man, Rhys's audience rocked back on their heels. Several let out exclamations along the lines of "No!"

Rhys had been trying to watch every man's face at once, and none of them struck him as anything but shocked at this news.

"How did he die?" This was asked by a young man with hair the color of the straw he worked with. "The kitchen girls will be so upset."

"I can't imagine why," Miles said under his breath to Rhys.

Rhys made no sign that he'd heard Miles. Nor did he remind him that he wasn't supposed to know English. Thankfully, Miles subsided.

"He was stabbed," Edgar said. "I saw it with my own eyes just now."

Rhys endeavored not to roll his own eyes. He would have held that piece of information in reserve, since it was usually unwise to blurt out the details of a murder in the first moments of questioning suspects. Darla already knew, however, and was telling everyone that Bobby was dead and how he'd died. Keeping the information from the stablemen was futile, and even petty, given that Bobby appeared to have been a friend to some.

"So it's murder. And you suspect one of us." This came from an older, bearded fellow, speaking in a resigned tone, as if life had treated him badly for a very long time, and he would have been a fool to be surprised about it now.

Rhys tipped his head. "As Edgar just made clear, it *is* murder. Someone is responsible."

"I-I-I didn't mean—" He broke off, his initial cynicism giving way to fear, which hadn't been Rhys's intent, since he'd spoken mildly. "It wasn't me. It wasn't any of us." He made a sweeping gesture with one hand. "We've been at our meal."

"Bobby died long before the meal. When was the last time any of you saw him?"

"Yesterday afternoon." The straw-haired man's face was screwed up as he thought. "He was whistling."

"What's going on here?"

Rhys turned to see a tall man with red hair tied in a thong at the base of his neck, just arriving.

At the sight of Rhys's face, the man immediately ducked his head. "My apologies, my lord. I didn't recognize you from the back." As Fernando had done, he put a hand to his chest. "My name is Donegal. These men are my responsibility, and I can answer for them."

Everyone around the circle relaxed a bit, glad their commander had arrived to save them.

"Are the stables occupied at night?" Rhys asked.

"They are," Donegal said. "We have lodging in the back of the loft, with one of us on duty during the night. That was Jon there."

Another man, this one more Rhys's own age, with short brown hair and a scar on his cheek, lifted a hand. "Me. But I didn't hear anything." His eyes went wide. "Or see anything! Could Bobby have been murdered right under my nose? How could I not have noticed?" He seemed genuinely upset.

Donegal put out a hand. "It isn't your fault, Jon. Nobody is blaming you."

"Didn't you miss him when he didn't show up to work this morning?" Rhys asked.

"Bobby worked in the upper kitchens. You'll have to talk to them." This was contributed by Edgar.

Rhys swung around, wondering why Edgar hadn't mentioned that earlier. "You're telling me he wasn't a stable boy?"

All around, the men and boys shook their heads.

"Who among you knew him best and perhaps could tell me more about his movements yesterday and last night?"

As one, they looked to one of the lads, a boy who could have been anywhere from fifteen to twenty-one. Bobby hadn't had much in the way of facial hair either, and both young men were lean and on the small side. "Me. I'm Tim."

"Do *you* have any idea why Bobby was in the stables last night?"

"No." Tim's face crumpled, though he didn't actually cry. "If I did, I would have said already. I have no idea what he was doing here. Me, I was in the tavern, talking to my mates." He gestured to Miles. "You were there."

Rhys was unsurprised by Tim's denial. It was all he'd heard so far, and he was growing used to it. But as he'd told Miles, this death was different from Alfonso's. By whatever means Alfonso had died, Bobby had been murdered—and only last night. "I'll need to talk to each of you in the coming hours. For now, you may go about your business." They dispersed with an alacrity that might have been amusing under different circumstances. Then Rhys turned to Miles and said in French, more for Donegal's benefit than Miles's, "You should go too. It would be helpful if you could keep your ears open."

Miles ducked his head, repeating his words from earlier, for the benefit of any men who might still be close enough to overhear. "Of course, my lord. Anything to serve."

18

Day Two

Miles

Miles found himself fascinated by the way the castle's workers were continuing to go about their daily business as if nothing had changed. It was one thing when Alfonso had died a fortnight ago. But this boy had died that very day. And unlike the prince, who'd been sick, Bobby's death was sudden. He'd been *murdered*.

And yet, Miles could see that everyone still needed to do their jobs. People had to eat. Rooms required cleaning and horses' stalls mucking out. The staff did it all without complaint. In truth, they took pride in the work they did. Miles could be astonished, but he was a bit humbled too.

More than that, he was ashamed of how much he'd learned about the functioning of a castle just in the first hours of his employment. He thought he'd been good to the common folk who served him. He tried not to lord over them in the manner of so many of his fellow noblemen who didn't even view them as people.

But he did it anyway without realizing, and now he knew it. He was never going to look the same way again at the boy who cleaned and laid the fire in the hall.

And because the work of the castle had to continue, Butler James sent Miles to the cellar in the upper bailey to replenish their wine stocks, as he'd said he would.

At first James had appeared somewhat miffed that Miles had taken so long with Reese, but once Miles explained what he'd learned (in the guise of Gilbert le Gascon, of course), he'd immediately been forgiven. And as Butler James questioned him as to the details, it became clear that one of the reasons he'd sent Miles to find Reese in the first place was to learn the details about Bobby's death.

This made Miles instantly suspicious, but since Reese hadn't told him not to talk about what he knew, and Miles was subject to James's authority, he laid out all the details. The Gilbert le Gascon he was pretending to be would have had no reason to withhold even the smallest tidbits of information. Miles had been *right there*, standing over the body. It wasn't long before James knew everything he did. Or rather, *almost* everything. Miles wasn't about to tell him any of his conversation with Reese or what he couldn't possibly have learned with a poor to nonexistent grasp of English.

Butler James was excited enough as it was. "This Reese seemed to like you, to appreciate your presence?"

As the answer was *yes,* Miles saw no reason to deny it. "He suggested that he might need an extra hand or pair of eyes in the coming days, and I might present myself to him when I was off duty." Miles cleared his throat, suddenly worried that James would take that as an indication that Miles wanted to be relieved of his duties—or that Reese wanted him to be. "I told him that I had just started in the job today so of course I needed to fulfill all my new tasks as I learned them. But that I would speak to you about helping him when I wasn't needed."

"Hmmm." Butler James harrumphed, but Miles could tell he was pleased. "It is important to stay on the good side of the king's quaestor, but I also agree that we cannot shirk your new tasks. It wouldn't look good to the rest of the staff and might make them feel like I was favoring you above your station. You *did* just start today." He gave a sharp nod as if confirming a thought. "I will send you now to Hugh, who manages the cellar in the upper bailey. He isn't quite my counterpart, as he doesn't deal with the intake of supplies and the overall dispensation of drink, so is beneath me in authority, but you will obey him as you obey me."

By *cellar*, James meant that Hugh managed the alcohol stores—not only wine but also ale and mead, when they had it—in that part of the castle. Having grown up in the March, Miles was fonder of mead, a wine made from honey rather than grapes, than many Normans. Reese and Catrin would be missing it about now. It occurred to Miles that he should see what he could do about procuring some for them. It was his job now, after all.

Really, it was the least he could do for inserting himself into their investigation, never mind that it was at the king's request. Reese had accepted not only Miles's presence, but his help too,

without any demur. Not that perhaps he felt he could object. Another result of living in the March his entire life was a well-tuned
sense of everyone's proper place. As the son of an earl, even with
little wealth of his own, Miles outranked Reese. Reese had been
appointed by the king, but otherwise he was the son of a minor
Welsh nobleman. Mostly Miles rubbed along pretty well with everyone, but neither he nor Reese could ever forget that, at any time,
Miles could assert his superiority.

Miles hadn't yet been to the upper bailey of the castle, and
he was curious to see what improvements Edward had made since
he'd been crowned king, which was the last time Miles had been
here (Edward had been crowned at Westminster Abbey. During
the course of the proceedings, Miles had accompanied his father to
Windsor).

The castle was built on a rocky bluff above the River
Thames. The original builders had managed to dig deep enough to
hit groundwater, so the castle had a well inside the walls, but they
hadn't bothered to excavate an understory in most of the buildings, building up instead of digging into the earth.

Thus, if his intent had been to enter the upper bailey's
kitchen, which was a long, free-standing building on the Thames
side of the castle, Miles would have had to mount stairs. But since
he was transporting a large quantity of wine at the order of Butler
James, he wheeled his little cart to the lower doorway, which allowed direct access to the cellar.

Compared to the warmth of the late summer day, the cellar
was cool and dark, as it needed to be given what it contained. He

knew enough to close the door immediately behind him to keep the coolness inside. A tall man with short, copper-colored hair and a beard to match stood at the far end of the room, speaking to another, smaller man. They were both bent over a worktable lit by a lantern, flipping through a ledger.

Miles trundled his cart down an aisle between open shelves on one side and stacked casks of ale on the other. Windsor Castle brewed its own ale every week to provide fresh drink for its occupants. That job belonged to an entire army of workers, overseen by a man with the Flemish name of Wizo. The residents of the castle drank upwards of five hundred gallons of ale a week.

Butler James had made clear to Miles that Wizo too was subordinate to him. Even if James had been merely the wine steward (rather than the butler, and thus in charge of all the cellars at Windsor), his status would have been higher, because wine was of a higher status. It was a more costly drink, imported from France, and reserved therefore for the high tables and nobility.

Wizo had been at the noon meal and appeared to be a jovial fellow, perhaps in part because of the large quantity of ale he consumed. He also seemed to view every order Butler James gave him as optional. And, in truth, he wasn't wrong about his own importance. What he produced served more people and could not be foregone under any circumstances. The king wanted wine at his table, but he could make do with ale if he had to. If Wizo and his people ceased to produce ale for the castle residents, they would get water instead.

But because wine was also integral to the happiness of the royal family, Miles had gainful employment and a real excuse to move about at will.

The red-bearded man turned to look as Miles approached, dismissing the clerk in the same motion that bid Miles come forward. "I don't recognize you." Despite the gesture of welcome, the statement came out somewhat combative.

"I'm Gilbert le Gascon. I'm—"

"—the new dispenser that Butler James hired." Hugh cut him off.

Miles halted a few paces away, still holding the handle of the wine wagon. He had very little experience with anyone cutting him off in mid-sentence, barring his own father. As the Second Earl had died shortly after Miles had returned from crusade, it hadn't happened in a very long time. Even Humphrey didn't make a habit of it. "Yes. This wine came in today. He sent me to ask how much more you needed."

In addition to rarely facing someone who outranked him, Miles had also never spent much time in the cellar of any castle in which he'd ever lived. He might have used such places for hide-and-seek as a child, but his father had been *very* particular about his wine and entering for rough play had been forbidden.

As in the case of his lack of real knowledge of the way servants lived, Miles chided himself now for not paying closer attention long ago to the acquisition of supplies. Managing the drink stores in a castle, not to mention the food, was a massive undertaking—and one he had never before appreciated. Throughout his life, food and drink appeared at the table, or in the kitchen when he wanted something outside of regular mealtimes, and he never thought much more about it than that. Knights and sons of earls didn't have to.

Even when he'd been in the Holy Land, he'd had a servant to take care of his needs. He ate with the other noblemen most days, and could buy what he wanted from the market if he was hungry in between meals—or send a servant to do it for him.

"Tell Butler James I will let him know what is necessary. Now that Prince Edmund is in residence, not to mention Sir Vincent and that Welsh quaestor and his wife, I will need to refigure." Hugh paused, frowning. "Do you think Sir Reese and Lady Catrin drink wine? Or would they prefer ale?" Hugh looked hopeful—and sounded less abrupt than upon first meeting. Perhaps the details of the ledger he'd been discussing with the other man had put him out of temper for a time, and it wasn't his usual manner to be abrupt with underlings.

"They will both definitely want wine."

Hugh deflated.

Then Miles added, thinking of his friends and genuinely trying to be helpful, "Though I might suggest that if you have mead, they'd prefer it. They are Welsh, after all."

"True, true." Hugh's brow furrowed, and then he put up one finger, telling Miles to wait. "I believe we have some. I received a small cask yesterday. I told Butler James nobody would drink it, but he said it came on the barge." He gave a sigh. "Like always."

The comment was said so sadly that it caught Miles's attention. "May I ask what you mean by *like always*?"

"These past months, mead was Prince Alfonso's favorite drink—heavily watered down, of course," he hastened to add. "Most days, he refused to drink anything else. Everybody else despised it, but he would not be dissuaded."

Miles wanted to keep asking questions, since once again Alfonso's name had come up without him needing to mention him, but he felt he needed to phrase whatever he said very carefully so as not to put Hugh off. "The prince was the only one in the castle who drank mead?"

"None other has a taste for it, not when the best wines from Gascony are available." Hugh had gone to the shelves, presumably searching for the mead.

"How did Prince Alfonso even know to drink it?"

Hugh was barely listening, counting on his fingers instead. Miles held his breath, not wanting to offend, but also hoping for an answer. Hugh got to the end of whatever he was adding up and then glanced over at Miles. "He read about it in one of his books and insisted we procure some."

"Did Prince Alfonso ever come down here?"

Hugh had moved on to making space for the drink Miles had brought, but it took less of his attention, and this time he answered immediately. "We saw him often. He was ever one for adventuring, as he used to say. Why do you ask?"

Miles made a little gesture that was half about appeasement and half dismissing the question as unimportant (even though it was very important to Miles). "I know he died. Everyone I've spoken to in the lower bailey is suffering. It must be much worse here for those who knew him better."

At last, Hugh entirely stopped what he was doing and turned to Miles. "Yes. It has been hard." His words were spoken matter-of-factly, with sentiment but with utter certainty, as if discussing the state of the harvest in a bad year. "The boy was nothing but a delight. I have worked at Windsor since the old king's time and have known all the children." He gestured with one hand. "Most of us have. When one dies, it isn't just the king who grieves. You should keep that in mind when you go upstairs." He paused and then said somewhat gruffly—to the point that Miles realized he might be holding back tears. "It was good of you to mention it."

"Certainly." Miles ducked his head, acknowledging that he'd made a good impression without meaning to. That hadn't been his intent, but he accepted it for what it was. He couldn't wholly suppress an innate desire to be liked and accepted by these people. Mostly, he managed to do just fine pretending that he didn't care. His current employment, along with his intent to deceive the residents of Windsor, had been entirely *his* idea.

Hugh didn't notice the way Miles was dithering. Perhaps he'd needed a moment to gather himself too. "You'll need to deliver wine to all the rooms where we have guests as well as to the royal apartments. I understand you can read?"

"Yes." It had been one of the principal qualifications for his hiring and the reason his post had been vacant for some months.

His ability to distinguish one wine from another was useful, but more of an amusing trick to entertain patrons in a tavern.

"Here's the list." Hugh handed Miles a piece of paper which associated particular rooms with particular vintages. The remaining children's rooms, for example, all required a sweet wine that was more water than wine.

On that note, he made his way up the stairs from the cellar and into the kitchen. No surprise that in a castle this large, a great deal of food and drink was served each day, and it would have been foolish to attempt to transport it after it was cooked from the lower bailey to the upper—thus, the need for two kitchens. There were two halls too. Because the upper bailey was reserved for the family of the king and their personal guests, retainers, and servants, Vincent's lodgings were in the guesthouse in the lower bailey. Thus, he had not been burned out of his room last night. His lord, William de Valence, was the king's uncle and, if they'd come together, likely Vincent still would have been housed in the lower bailey while Earl William would have had a place in the upper one next to Reese and Catrin.

Miles, in turn, were he to present himself in his usual form as Miles de Bohun instead of Gilbert le Gascon, would likely have been placed beside Vincent since, like Vincent, he was lower down in the hierarchy of noblemen. Humphrey, as the Constable of England, should have had a room in the upper bailey, but even that would depend upon who else was staying at the castle and how generous the king was feeling that day. Humphrey hadn't tested his welcome in many years and, were he to come to Windsor, might decide to avoid the issue entirely by finding his own lodgings at a nearby monastery. At Windsor Castle, the rank and station of visitors was judged to a hair's breadth.

Meanwhile, on a daily basis the hall in the lower bailey was used by the majority of the workers in the castle, though it could be turned into a meeting place when the king called a conference of his barons.

There was some irony there for Reese: in becoming kingsman, quaestor, and spymaster, he had achieved a privilege that had never been afforded Miles. Nor Vincent, in point of fact. Of course, Miles's lodging last night at the inn hadn't been nearly burned to the ground either.

Constable Pickford might be dismissing the fire as an accident, but Miles wasn't at all sure he was right. It was in Miles's mind to inquire about that too, if he had a chance, thinking that if Bobby had been murdered out of a fear that Reese had come to investigate, it might have happened in conjunction with trying to get rid of Reese entirely, or at least harm him enough that he would be unable to continue.

This kitchen was not in the uproar Miles might have expected when one of its own had just been found dead in the stables. Instead, those present were moving about in icy quiet. One young woman was beating on bread dough as if it were the murderer. Miles stood watching for a few moments before someone noticed him. And although the kitchen in the upper bailey served fewer people overall, it was much larger, even to say lavish, compared to the utilitarian facilities in the lower bailey.

"May I help you?" A tall man, thinner than Miles thought usual for a cook, approached and spoke in perfect French, implying to Miles that he was not English in origin. He confirmed that assumption a moment later after Miles gave his name and explained that he was the new wine dispenser.

"At long last! A Gascon! Too few here understand wine. I'm Cook Armand. Did you understand that it will be your task to ensure that the wine our steward chooses is properly conveyed to the great hall and all the rooms? Prince Edmund is particularly discerning. He might run you off your feet, sending you back and forth to the cellar to acquire him a different vintage."

Miles hadn't entirely understood that most of his time would be spent in the upper bailey, but this news was all to the good for his real purpose here. He was getting the sense that his new employment was something of a make-it-up-as-you-go situation. They'd needed another body to fetch and carry, and that body seemed to belong to Miles. A regular server was perfectly capable of distributing carafes chosen by Hugh, but wine was taken *very* seriously here at Windsor, as it should be. The royal family should never be inadequately cared for.

Meanwhile, Miles had questions he could ask in his position as Gilbert le Gascon. He dropped his chin and said in a low voice that didn't carry, "You heard about the boy found dead in the stables?"

Armand let out a very French puff of air. "We can think of nothing else!" He spoke louder than Miles had expected and appeared in no way concerned that everyone in the kitchen could hear his exclamation.

"Was he not missed when he didn't show up for work this morning?"

"Pah!" The cook could have taken offense at Miles's question, or wondered why he was asking at all, but Miles had endeavored to make sure his voice was conspiratorial rather than accusatory. "Bobby was always about the place, doing as he was bid. I didn't notice because I didn't need him."

Then he gestured to the woman kneading bread. "Jane is Bobby's cousin, and she told us she'd seen him earlier that morning." The cook glared at her. "She lied."

The young woman in question had glanced at Armand when he first spoke, and at the addendum to his sentence, burst into tears.

19

Day Two

Vincent

Vincent didn't have much experience—or, to be exact, *any* experience—with murder victims, but he'd entered his fair share of laying out rooms over the years. Before today, none had been for the purpose of investigating murder. Rather, these rooms were designed to facilitate the washing of a dead body in preparation for burial and were similar the world over. Even if a body lay for a time inside the church before the funeral, it was never washed in the church. Often, the washing took place in the dead person's home.

A castle was different, however. Castles existed because war existed, and conquering kings needed to defend themselves from the people they'd conquered and from the aspirations of their own barons. Occasionally, they also had to fend off foreign invaders. At a minimum, men killed one another regularly, and every castle needed a place to wash a body—and sometimes more than one at a time.

This laying-out room was on the large side, befitting the grand scale of Windsor. It was adjacent to the laundry, so water didn't have to be carried far. In lowland castles and monasteries, which were close to a water source that could be diverted through the castle itself, the laying-out room, like the laundry, could be placed right over a fresh water channel. Windsor, unfortunately, was built on a high plateau, so even though the Thames was close by, it had not been diverted through the castle itself.

"The killer made a mistake, leaving the body like that." Catrin spoke thoughtfully as she stood opposite Rhys, looking down at the remains of their new victim. Rhys had left the door to the laying-out room open, which allowed Vincent to overhear Catrin's words. Then he stepped through the doorway and made himself known.

"Once Bobby was dead," Rhys shot a ghost of a smile that might be in welcome in Vincent's direction and kept talking, "he may not have had a choice. Murdering a man in the back of the stables is one thing. Moving a body is quite another. You might be surprised how difficult it is to get rid of one."

"All the more reason not to kill him inside the castle."

"It might not have been planned," Rhys said.

Catrin didn't appear convinced. "It's because you're here, obviously."

"We don't know that," Rhys said mildly, in a tone Vincent recognized as meaning he was working hard not to be drawn into an argument.

"I suppose there was no way for him to know what you knew. He assumed the worst and acted." Catrin's eyes brightened. "Your very presence is terrifying, Rhys."

She pronounced Rhys's name the Welsh way, as Vincent himself had worked very hard to learn how to do. Fortunately, with his lord's lands located primarily in Wales, it hadn't been difficult to find tutors.

"I am late to the discussion, I realize," Vincent said, "but the news of the discovery of the lad's body is all over the castle. No surprise, I suppose."

"I didn't attempt to instruct anyone not to talk about it. By the time Miles found me, the entire staff of the lower kitchen knew." Rhys glanced over at Vincent. "Did you see anyone hovering outside on your way here?"

"No. In fact, the bailey appears uncharacteristically deserted."

Catrin looked rueful. "Nobody wants to get any closer to the body than they have to. As any self-respecting common man knows, it's easy for their betters to latch upon the closest person when things go wrong, regardless of whether or not that person is to blame." She shot Rhys a wry look. "They don't know that you would never do that."

Rhys's eyes remained focused on the body he was undressing. He'd never been very good at accepting compliments, even, it seemed, from his lovely wife.

Now, she looked over at Vincent. "I'm glad to see the two of you getting along, I was worried that I might have to mediate between you."

"All is well, Catrin," Rhys said in Welsh. "You may let it lie."

Vincent didn't speak Welsh himself, but he understood enough to make sense of Rhys's words. He didn't let on that he understood, however, not yet ready to give away all his secrets.

All *was* well. Mostly. As Vincent looked down at Bobby's body, he remembered why he'd been relieved—once the initial umbrage at being overlooked had receded—when Rhys had become *the* quaestor instead of him way back in the Holy Land. He certainly hadn't wanted to be the one in charge of investigating the death of Clare's captain in Nefyn in July. That had been his lord's idea, not his.

And while Vincent was quite clear on the fact that Rhys didn't entirely trust him yet, he felt he was getting close to a real accord. Thrusting one's sword through the belly of a friend, quite literally, had a way of engendering distrust. At least Vincent hadn't stabbed him in the back.

Besides, Vincent wasn't entirely transformed. To this day, it still irked him that all that time ago in Acre, Rhys had told him off in public for whipping that soldier instead of pulling him aside to speak in private. He could see why Rhys had done it, since Vincent hadn't been willing to be pulled aside at the time, but Rhys had been an arrogant, self-righteous bastard about it. And then he'd left the princes' service for Wales without, as far as Vincent could tell, a backwards glance. Vincent had apologized for what he'd done, but he'd never heard the same from Rhys, not even something half-hearted about how they'd made the mistake of being young.

Vincent was feeling younger these days than he had in years. Part of that was his upcoming marriage to Joan, whom he genuinely loved. And part had to do with the way the burden of his past was lifting. He'd despised himself for a long time. If Rhys wasn't man enough to take some responsibility for their decade-long animosity, so be it. Vincent could let that go too.

He shared none of this with Rhys or Catrin, who was still talking: "What they don't realize is that we will investigate with or without them. For now, they've closed ranks. Every person I've spoken to describes the workers at Windsor as one entity, working together in harmony: *none of us would have harmed Alfonso.* It might even be true. But this boy here was not Alfonso."

"And he was definitively murdered," Rhys said.

Vincent grunted, feeling he could contribute something to the conversation. "The castle has too many workers for every one of them to be content. I haven't investigated murder before, but when wrong has been done in a castle, eventually someone starts talking."

Catrin made a *maybe* motion with her head. "I suppose you may already be right, despite my pessimism. Alfonso's steward and his tutor sought Rhys out before he could come to them, to speak of all the ways they had nothing to do with the prince's death."

Rhys's mouth had a wry twist to it. "I am willing to be patient. For now."

"It isn't as if they don't know where to find you, *cariad*," Catrin said. "By now, even if they weren't acquainted with you from before, everyone in the castle knows who you are and why you're here."

As she was speaking, Vincent found he couldn't take his eyes off the body. It didn't smell particularly bad, though it might very soon, especially in this warm weather. While he might have little experience with murder, death, on the other hand, was an old friend.

"What did Captain Thaddeus say to you?" Catrin was looking at Vincent again. "Rhys told me you had gone to speak to him."

"I told him that if he didn't leave this investigation to Rhys, he was a fool." Vincent made a *puh* sound with his lips. "Fortunately, he wasn't difficult to convince. Captain Thaddeus is ambitious but fervently wishes to have nothing to do with an investigation into Alfonso's death—or this body, with the assumption the two are related."

"Which is still an assumption," Rhys said.

"I'm assuming it, whether you want me to or not." Vincent gave a bark of a laugh. "See, I listen to you no better now than when we were young." As soon as the words were out, Vincent wondered if he should take them back.

But Rhys laughed, and they had a moment of camaraderie, even standing over a dead body.

Vincent felt free to carry on: "It seems to me that it was foolish of this killer to assume he was about to be caught. It isn't as if we've learned anything substantial about Alfonso's death." It was the truth, but the instant he spoke, he kicked himself for the way he said it, since his words could be viewed as disparaging of Rhys's skills. Knowing it, he put out a hand. "I didn't mean—"

Rhys continued to chuckle. "You don't have to apologize, Vincent."

Rhys had intended the words to make Vincent feel better, but instead, given Vincent's earlier thoughts, they stung. He fought his umbrage, even as resentment curled in his belly. Deception was something with which Vincent—and every Norman, truth be told—had long experience, so he continued to smile and pretend that all was well between them, just like Rhys had told Catrin it was.

But in that moment, he was lying. He eyed the Welshman, wondering if he was too.

20

Day Two

Catrin

Earlier, Catrin had been worried that she would need to be a mediator between the two men. Now she felt like an interloper. If Catrin hadn't been certain it was her husband standing in front of her, she wouldn't have believed how well the two men were getting along. Their accord seemed real to her, but inside she shook her head. Even after twenty years living among Normans, and being married to one, she still struggled to read them.

Rhys continued, "I could argue that we do know some things by now, but before the discovery of Bobby's body, you are absolutely right that we were nowhere close to identifying a possible killer at the castle. We had interviewed a few people. That is all. Again, you are speaking *as if* Alfonso was murdered, which I will not concede. I don't want to assume it and head down the wrong path. We have two deaths: Alfonso's and Bobby's. We will take each separately for now."

"Three deaths, Rhys," Catrin hastened to remind him.

"Three?" Vincent looked from Catrin to Rhys, who hurriedly explained about the supposedly natural death of George, the food taster. That was yet another thread to pull, but not one anyone at the castle wanted to talk about either. George had been old. *These things happen.*

Catrin was really starting to distrust the phrase, even if, at times, *these things did.* "So where does that leave us—"

She broke off as a rider came through the main gatehouse and dismounted to look around the lower bailey with evident curiosity. He was wearing traveling clothes rather than the tunic and armor of a soldier. Nevertheless, she would have recognized him anywhere. A stable lad ran to take his horse's reins, and the newcomer relinquished them with a smile and a pat of gratitude.

"What is it?" Vincent came to the door to stand beside her. "Is something wrong?"

"Not wrong at all. My son has just ridden into Windsor."

"I'm very happy for you, my love," Rhys spoke from behind them, still at the table, "but I can't help thinking that Clare has sent Justin to join the festivities."

Rhys had to be right. That Justin had come to Windsor now couldn't be a coincidence, a fact which Justin made clear once Catrin ran across the bailey to fetch him. She was a mother before she was anything else, even Rhys's wife, and an opportunity to see her son twice within a few weeks, after a long drought, had her eyes alight. Even murder couldn't detract from her joy at seeing him.

Her emotion dimmed, somewhat, once she brought Justin to the laying-out room and remembered the boy on the table. It wasn't as if she'd forgotten about him in the excitement of greeting Justin, but it was a reminder of why they were here. Why they were *all* here.

For Justin's part, he came to a halt at the foot of the table. "This is not what I expected to find when my lord sent me to Windsor to aid in your investigation of Alfonso's death."

"I have found that it is best to have no expectations." In her brief absence, Rhys had thrown a sheet over the body and now approached to embrace his stepson. "Then one is never disappointed."

"Says a man who has risen in a few months from the underling of Gwynedd's coroner to a valued member of the king's guard. And married to my mother!" Justin clapped his stepfather on the back as they hugged.

"You should be careful, Rhys," Vincent said in a low tone. "You forget to whom you're speaking. This is Catrin's son. Her gifts are his, and he sees more than you expect."

Catrin wasn't sure that Justin understood the depth of the pain behind Rhys's supposedly offhand comment. Vincent clearly had. It was too late to take it back, however, and Rhys made no attempt to do so.

"Vincent. Always a pleasure." Justin formally greeted the other man. The two were both knights and retainers to great lords. Although they differed in age, there was no difference in rank between them.

Vincent bobbed his head. "Justin. I know that your lord and mine have had their differences—" At this, Justin let out a snort, prompting a smile from Vincent, who then continued, "—but I see no reason why we can't work together."

"If you and Sir Rhys can do it, I would hope that you and I could."

Catrin squeezed her son's elbow, impressed and proud that he had the temerity—or maybe just the innocence—to speak outright on a subject few others would dare broach.

Then Justin squared his shoulders. "I know I have just arrived, but I'm ready to assist. What can I do to help?"

Rhys then laid out for Justin the entire investigation so far—without hesitation—and concluded with, "How's your English?"

"Excellent." Justin had listened to Rhys with a quiet intensity, and the only emotion he'd shown was when Rhys had told him about the guesthouse fire, at which point he'd put his arm around Catrin's shoulders and pulled her to him.

"Since nobody knows you yet, I'd like you to take another run at the stablemen. I questioned them all, including the master of the stables, a man named Donegal, and Jon, the man on duty last night. They gave me next to nothing. His closest friend, Tim, wept—and then claimed that he couldn't imagine what had brought Bobby to the stables so late at night. But if anyone might know more than he's letting on, I'm thinking it would be him. See if you can discover it."

"I will do my best." For a moment, Justin's already upright posture became poker straight. Then he eased into a more relaxed position. "Do I tell them I'm working for you?"

"Tell them you're my son," Catrin said, impulsively. "Suggest that I am worried about spending another night in the castle where people are getting murdered. Feel free to imply that the burning of the guesthouse wasn't an accident. Constable Pickford won't like it, but he doesn't get to tell me what to say." She almost laughed at the way she was invoking her inner Mildrith.

"The workers are very proud of their place at Windsor and the work they do," Rhys added. "If you imply that something is amiss here, they might leap to its defense by explaining what Bobby could have been up to."

"Yes, sir. You can count on me."

Justin set off, determination in every line of his body.

As he watched him go, Vincent's tone, once again, was dry. "It is as Miles said: you draw able men to you. You can't help it." Then he looked at Rhys. "You haven't yet given me my task."

Rhys neither argued with Vincent nor put him off. "I know you speak English. Do you feel like taking on the garrison? The questions may be tedious, but we have to ask if anyone knows anything about what might have happened last night. And ask again."

"I can do that. What are you going to do?"

"Catrin and I have been invited to eat with the princesses this afternoon."

At his words, Catrin startled. "I forgot we'd been asked. Are we late?"

"Not yet."

Vincent suddenly smiled. Though he'd laughed often since they'd arrived at Windsor, this smile was different. It transformed him, taking ten years off his face, in the way Mildrith had said marrying Rhys had done for Catrin. "I see what you're doing. You and Catrin are the public face of this investigation. Everybody knows who you are and why you are here. You will, of course, be asking the sisters about their brother. Gently." He sobered, but his eyes didn't dim. "Meanwhile, the rest of us will see what we can discover in the nooks and crannies where nobody's watching. You truly are a spymaster at heart," he paused before adding, "my friend."

It sounded, as before, as if he meant it.

21

Day Two

Miles

Jane was plain of face, a fact that was more than made up for by her womanly figure and the thickness and richness of her hair, which was the color of walnut. She appeared to be approximately twenty years old. As he'd been made aware over the last hours, he was the privileged son of an earl. So while Miles had never been one to dally much in the kitchen, he'd had his moments. A few decades ago, she would have caught his eye. Now, not so much, and not aided by the fact that she was sobbing into her half-kneaded loaf.

Before the bread that resulted could be overly salted by her tears, Armand shooed her away from it towards a bench on one wall, which was hastily vacated by an older woman who'd been shelling peas. Miles followed, not because he had any official business with her, obviously, but because nobody else had made any move to comfort her. He thought Reese would be pleased that he was taking the opportunity presented to him. Besides, Miles was curious and wanted to see if he was capable of eliciting something useful from the woman.

Since Armand was already badgering another worker to finish Jane's kneading, Miles thought it might even be appropriate for him to play the friendly newcomer. He sat next to her and, after a moment's hesitation, put an arm around her shoulders. Jane leaned into him, weeping with great heaving sobs.

With that, Miles realized the slight flaw in his plan, in that Jane was in no condition to tell him anything. He needed to get her calmed down, and he didn't think he would successfully manage it while still in the kitchen. Lifting a hand to catch Armand's eye, he then motioned towards the door, asking without speaking, *Why don't I take her out of here?*

Armand was no happier than any man would be about having a weeping woman in his kitchen, and he nodded that Miles should do exactly that. He might even have looked relieved that Miles was there to take care of her instead of leaving it to him.

Once outside, the upper bailey didn't prove to be quite as full of places to hide as the lower bailey, but it did have a kitchen garden, and he guided her towards it. Once they reached fresh air, and as Miles had hoped, Jane stopped sobbing quite so fervently. He figured he might as well get the questions started before she realized he had no business asking her anything. For now, he wasn't much worried that Armand would be concerned about where he'd gone. While he had his orders to replenish the wine throughout the upper bailey, Armand was not his direct supervisor. Hugh was. And since his domain was the cellars, Miles thought he had a few moments' respite.

"Why did you lie?" Perhaps that wasn't the best question to begin with, since it prompted another round of tears.

Finally, he again got her calmed down enough to answer. "We ate our evening meal together, as we often do, chatting for a long while after as we often did." Jane had one hand covering her face and spoke around it. "Then he went off to meet a girl. When he didn't appear this morning, I figured he was still with her and had slept late. I've covered for him before, you see."

Miles managed to refrain from saying *ah ha!* But he was glad she wasn't looking directly at him. He didn't usually struggle not to be expressive. Putting on an emotionless mask was practically a requirement for every Bohun every day and as easy as swinging his cloak around his shoulders. But in becoming Gilbert le Gascon, he seemed to have lost the skill. "What girl would that be?"

He already knew it was Bess, or in a pinch, Darla. But it seemed important to ask.

Jane wrinkled her nose. "I don't actually know that he did go to see a girl. When he left, he was typically vague about where he was going and whom he was meeting, I just assumed it. Now ..." She shook her head.

Miles deliberated as to whether he should mention the two girls with whom they knew Bobby had had a relationship, and then decided that, with Bobby dead, there were only so many people he could talk to about it. "We heard that Bobby was walking out with Bess, the daughter of one of the stablemen."

"They weren't together anymore."

Miles had memory enough of his own youth to know that young love waxed and waned, but to have been walking out with a girl was very close to being betrothed. "That isn't what her grandfather thinks."

"Maybe Bess hadn't told Edgar yet. It was only last week she gave Bobby back his ribbon."

"What about Darla?"

"The kitchen girl?" Jane gave a vehement shake of her head. "I told him to stay away from her. She was no good for him and would only jeopardize his chances with someone better." She gave a little snort. "But I suppose he didn't listen. He *loved* girls, and they loved him."

Miles was even more hesitant about his next question, but he felt he had to ask it, if only because Gilbert le Gascon would. "Could one of his many women have been so upset at the loss of his favor that she killed him?"

Jane reared back, the tears abating and a look of astonishment on her face. "No! What are you saying?" But then her eyes grew thoughtful. "Besides, it was Bess who broke it off with him, not the other way around. While girls liked him, they knew better than to be jealous. He was going to do what he was going to do, and they couldn't control him."

From Miles's observations, that wasn't a recipe for a happy wife, but then, Bobby hadn't been married either. Some men managed to settle down once they found the right woman. Just look at the king, who had roamed a bit in his youth, but was entirely faithful to Eleanor from the moment of their marriage.

"And Darla?"

"I would not have said she had a murdering bone in her body, but I don't know her well." She let out a little laugh. "I'm not sure even Darla knows herself well."

"What do you mean by that?"

"She's very simple."

"Is she capable enough to murder Bobby and then convincingly report him dead a few hours later?"

"It wouldn't be like that for her. On purpose, I mean." Jane was no longer weeping, and she even managed a bit of a laugh. "She is the one person in this whole castle who could murder someone one hour and then really not remember the next."

22

Day Two

Catrin

"I am so pleased to make your acquaintance, Sir Reese! We have heard about you all our lives, and it is wonderful to finally put a face to the name." This was Princess Eleanor at her best—or maybe worst.

Despite her mourning clothes, she had worked hard to highlight her youth and beauty, both of which she had in great measure, and accentuate her charms for the only man currently in the room.

When Catrin had last been at Windsor, Eleanor had behaved similarly, shamelessly flirting with every nobleman present, whether or not she found him interesting. Catrin herself certainly thought her husband was handsome. He was also more than two decades older than Eleanor and unused to court life, even after four months in the king's service. He was looking more than a little flummoxed by Eleanor's attentions. When they'd first walked in the room, Eleanor had looked imperiously at Catrin. "It is so good to see you again, Lady Catrin." But then her eyes had gone to Rhys—and she hadn't looked away since.

Rhys was nonetheless doing his duty, taking her hand and bending over it and obligingly taking the seat beside her at the table.

They were eating this meal in the princesses' own personal dining room rather than in the upper bailey's great hall. It was a choice the girls' father and mother often made. Queen Eleanor rarely put in an appearance in any hall, preferring to enjoy her meals in the privacy of the royal apartments. The hall was far less intimate anyway, especially for the kind of gathering this meal was intended to be. It wasn't an event or a party. It was a private meal with their uncle and—apparently—their father's representatives in the form of Rhys and Catrin.

The only other person present, apart from the five sisters, was Elizabeth's nanny, Mildrith, who sat with the baby, trying to keep her entertained until the food came. Her patience was prodigious, but not endless. Eventually she gave up encouraging the little girl to wait for the main meal and instead smeared butter on a slice of bread from a platter in the middle of the table and gave it to her. There was also cheese. Elizabeth proceeded to consume both with gusto, and even Eleanor didn't object, since nobody cared to see a two-year-old unfed if it meant she was whiny. The rest were waiting for Prince Edmund, who would have been thought late if he hadn't been a prince.

In reverse birth order, the middle three girls were Mary, six; Margaret, nine; and Joan, twelve. By their clothing they were all in mourning. But they were young too, and although Alfonso had been dead only a fortnight, none of them were particularly somber.

So when Eleanor insisted that the maid open the windows, which had been draped with mourning cloths, to let in sun and light, nobody objected to that either. "We're with friends, Lenna. We're allowed a little cheer."

"Of course, my lady." The Lenna in question dropped a quick curtsey and obeyed.

One characteristic of grief, which Catrin had learned through hard experience, was that, after the initial shock, one couldn't grieve *all* the time. A person still had to rise in the morning, eat, dress oneself (or likely, be dressed, in the princesses' case). While tears could bring relief, and wandering the halls weeping and wailing felt necessary for a short while, such behavior would never bring the loved one back. *Nothing* would bring the loved one back. Even at only two weeks since Alfonso's death, there was something to be said for forgetting for a little while that he was gone. It wasn't a betrayal of Alfonso to experience a little pleasure. It would be a betrayal *not* to.

Eleanor, as the eldest and a budding copy of her mother, whether by nature or mimicry, had a mind of her own. She ordered her siblings about, something they appeared to accept without much in the way of rebellion—though the glint in Joan's eyes indicated she was, in fact, humoring her sister. Catrin caught a glance from this younger sister in the aftermath of Eleanor telling each of her siblings where they were required to sit and almost elicited a smile.

Then Prince Edmund arrived, some quarter of an hour after Rhys and Catrin. With him came the food, a long line of retainers bringing tray after tray and placing them on the table and the sideboard.

"Uncle!" Eleanor was at it again, waving her hand imperiously, so Edmund would come close and kiss her cheek. His low chuckle told Catrin he too was humoring his eldest niece.

He then greeted the other girls, particularly Mary and Margaret, with more exuberance. The prince had a family too, having made a second marriage to Blanche of Navarre, whose daughter, Joan, had just married Philippe, the heir to the throne of France. That Edmund had attended his brother's tournament in Nefyn instead of the wedding of his stepdaughter was in part testament to his loyalty to Edward and in part a product of the politics of France. Until his stepdaughter's marriage, Edmund had been the Earl of Lancaster in England *and* Count of Champagne in France, by right of his own marriage to Blanche. But with this new union, he'd been required to give up those lands to the Kingdom of France, never mind that he was stepfather-in-law to the heir to the throne.

His loyalties could now lie more with Edward, as they truly always had, than with his perfunctory allegiance to Philippe. And it had been convenient for him that Edward had asked for his presence in Wales, preempting his ability to attend the wedding in Paris. Besides, though he'd married Blanche when Joan was only a year old, she had been raised in the French court with Philippe. Such was the way, very often, of royal families, making the situation at Windsor, where the royal children rarely saw their parents, just one variation of standard practice.

Prince Edmund's place was at the head of the table, a position Eleanor didn't have to tell him to take. On Edmund's right hand sat Eleanor, then Rhys, then Elizabeth and her nanny. Joan sat to Edmund's left, followed by Catrin, Mary, and Margaret. At nine, Margaret was roughly a year and a half younger than Alfonso had been and possibly knew him best.

As everyone settled in their seats again, Eleanor pouted at her uncle, "Why haven't you brought Sir Reese to Windsor before? We know he saved your life in the Holy Land." And yet, even as she spoke, unlike before, the mischievousness of her words didn't reach her eyes. In fact there was a sadness there that had Catrin suddenly understanding the extent to which Eleanor's antics were a pretense, a covering over of her true emotions. Catrin started watching the princess more closely, with less resentment and more patience.

"Circumstances prohibited it, my dear," Edmund said mildly.

"The crusade was a long time ago, but I apologize for staying away so long," Rhys added when she turned to him with the same pout. It was a noble attempt to minimize any attention paid to him. And then, instead of responding more to Eleanor, he looked at Joan. "My lady, I was honored to have met you within a few days of your birth. You were a beautiful child, and you are beautiful now."

With the loss of Rhys's attention, Eleanor chose next to look at Catrin. "I hear you've known Sir Reese your whole life. Why did you let him get away all those years ago?"

"Eleanor." Prince Edmund's censure was quiet, but forceful. In fact, that he spoke softly gave her name more emphasis. And then to Catrin, he said, "Ignore my niece. She is not herself."

But for that reason, while Catrin had been initially shocked by Eleanor's question, she couldn't be offended or angry. Eleanor was behaving badly, but she was grieving, not to mention going out of her mind with boredom, having been shut up in Windsor Castle for some months even before Alfonso's death. Catrin knew of her discontent because she'd told her about it when Catrin had last been here, before Eleanor's parents had begun their journey to Wales.

So she answered the princess's question with honesty. "I married the man my father arranged for me to marry. I had a son, who has become a wonderful man—and who arrived at Windsor today! I had a good life, even if it wasn't the one I envisioned for myself at fifteen."

Eleanor hadn't expected a real answer, and her lips turned white at Catrin's reply. What she'd described was very close to Eleanor's own imminent situation. She too was to be given to a man she didn't know. Each of these daughters faced the exact same fate. Because she was watching Eleanor closely, Catrin also saw a single tear fall down her cheek.

Then the door opened once again, and Father Giles, the chapel priest, hurried into the room, apologizing for being late. He blessed the meal and then sat in the seat at the end of the table, directly opposite Prince Edmund. His arrival was a little disconcerting to Catrin, who'd been thinking this was a family meal (plus her and Rhys, of course). The way she talked to the girls was now going to have to be a little different. She hadn't met the priest earlier, but she'd heard all about his conversation with Rhys, and she could see in an instant from his somewhat fussy manner why he'd rubbed Rhys the wrong way.

She also didn't think she was mistaken that, as everyone joined in and began filling their plates, Father Giles kept looking daggers at Mildrith. The look was returned, full bore. It was just too bad for both of them that they were sitting next to each other.

Joan now spoke for the first time. "How is our mother and new baby brother?" From previous encounters, Catrin knew Joan to be somewhat reserved and easily overshadowed by her older sister, but she was perfectly capable of speaking her mind when she chose to. "Uncle says he's well, but ..." Her voice trailed off uncertainly.

The younger girls appeared oblivious to Joan's tension, but both Joan and Eleanor bore the exact same expression. It wasn't so much worry as ...*fear*.

That Joan and Eleanor were afraid went a long way to explaining Eleanor's excesses. These two were aware enough of the world to understand their place in it—and that of their dead brothers. The question Joan was really asking, though phrased as an innocuous *how is he?* was rooted in a far more fraught question: *what if he dies too? And what is to become of us?*

Catrin reached for Joan's hand to squeeze it. "As I'm sure your uncle has told you, baby Edward is well, with a healthy set of lungs on him. Your mother won't let him out of her sight." As soon as she made the last observation, she wished she could take it back. Each of these daughters had been let out of their mother's sight for most of their lives.

"Good." Even young Eleanor appeared relieved by the news and sat back in her chair. For the first time, she wasn't simpering or batting her eyelashes at Rhys, but gazing directly at Catrin. "We hoped that what we heard was true."

"Of course, it was true. Mary told us he would be fine and one day become king. You should have listened." This unexpected comment came from Margaret, who had been eating steadily from the moment the priest ended grace.

Rhys and Catrin exchanged a look across the table before Catrin asked, "What was that, my lady?"

Down the table, Father Giles cleared his throat. "Mary spends much of her day in prayer and has been blessed at times with visions. She knew before Edward was born that he would be a boy and that the queen and he would survive the birth. She told me that he would become king one day. Sadly, she also knew that Alfonso would not survive his illness."

Prince Edmund carefully put down the piece of bread he'd been eating. "Is that so?"

Father Giles continued, "Her grandmother has asked that she be given to the church at Amesbury, where she herself intends to retire soon. The king and queen are considering it."

Mary, meanwhile, kept her focus on her food, allowing the others to talk around her. Catrin had never thought of her as particularly quiet or reflective, and certainly hadn't known she was having predictive visions. Nor, apparently, had Prince Edmund.

Then Margaret swallowed the latest large bite of chicken. "She also knew you were coming before the rest of us did and told us why that was."

Catrin felt entirely at sea. It was not uncommon among the Welsh to have glimpses of the *Sight*. Her own grandmother claimed it. Catrin herself at times had what she thought of as special feelings, the promptings of which she had learned to follow. This was something far more momentous.

"Father thinks Alfonso was murdered." Mary spoke for the first time. "He is worried that our new brother is going to die too. He isn't so much worried about us."

23

Day Two

Justin

Justin couldn't have been more pleased by his reception at Windsor Castle. He hadn't been worried that his mother wouldn't be happy to see him, but his new stepfather was another matter. It was one thing to help out the best he could in Nefyn at Catrin's request. It was quite another to insert himself into Rhys's doings without being asked. He'd known before he'd ridden into the castle that he would face these issues immediately, since Rhys's name was on every person's tongue.

Justin's lord, Gilbert de Clare, had not been officially informed of the investigation into Alfonso's death. He knew of it only because his spies had reported that both Miles de Bohun and Vincent de Lusignan had left their lords in haste (without stopping on Clare land). Only after they'd gone had the news of Rhys and Catrin's urgent journey to Windsor reached his ears. Lord Clare had been required to guess what errand they all could be on. But given the news out of Windsor, it wasn't hard to guess why they were going.

Gilbert was one of the proudest men in England, and he had been offended that the king hadn't included one of *his* men among those he trusted to investigate his son's death. Rather than pretend he didn't know he'd been neglected, confront the king about it, or pout, he'd decided to act as if he had been asked.

So he'd sent Justin of his own accord, with the instruction to make himself indispensable. Earl Gilbert surely would be pleased at how little time it had taken. Or rather, Justin hoped he would! Sometimes it was hard to know exactly what he needed to do to keep his lord happy. Usually, he managed most of the time by doing exactly as instructed and only occasionally taking what he thought was a better path. So far, he hadn't been punished for it.

Come to think on it, what he was managing with Earl Gilbert wasn't far off from what he'd observed as the relationship between Rhys and the king. Rhys told the truth, always. He did what he thought was right, always. Few men had such courage in the face of someone who had the power of life and death over them.

It was an odd feeling, really, this sudden admiration for Rhys. Justin's father, Robert, had been a good man. Justin believed that to be true with his whole heart. But he had done whatever Earl Gilbert said, when he said it, without question. Justin hadn't been taught to question. As far as he could tell, Rhys did nothing *but* question. But then, he *was* a quaestor.

With Rhys married to Justin's mother now, they were still feeling their way with each other, not just in terms of this investigation. Though Catrin had told him outright that Rhys had no intention of trying to replace Robert, Justin remained at war with himself on the matter. On one hand, he wanted to be loyal to the dead father he'd loved. On the other, he was finding himself drawn to his mother's new husband.

Although they had never discussed it, he was quite sure his mother had loved Rhys her entire life. He wasn't entirely sure she'd ever loved Robert. He did know for certain that she'd never loved Robert the way she loved Rhys.

Some days that was hard to accept. At other times, he saw the joy in her eyes and couldn't help but feel it too. His own wife, Adele, whom he adored, had encouraged him to give Rhys the benefit of the doubt. That was easier when Rhys trusted him not only to do a man's job but a job that he himself would otherwise be doing. Justin squared his shoulders yet again, thinking in that moment—and maybe realizing for the first time—that he wanted to be a man like Rhys.

The stables were not as busy a place as one might expect for a castle as large as Windsor. At least, the stablemen were moving about in a relaxed manner, as if none of their tasks were urgent. Maybe they weren't. A horsebox had to be mucked out, but whether it was done now or an hour from now made little difference. Besides, no noblemen other than himself were currently present, so there was no need for haste—even after a dead body had been found in their storage room.

Justin went first to his own horse, hoping to learn something of the stables' habits by the care they paid to Peleus, his charger. He was almost disappointed to see a full feedbag, fresh water, and a clean stall. In truth, every horse in the stables was well-treated, which spoke of a competent stablemaster and constable.

"My lord, may I help you?"

"You're Donegal?" The man before Justin was tall and thin, red haired, and close in age to Catrin, just as Rhys had described.

"I am, my lord."

"My—" Justin paused for a moment, stumbling over what he was even to call Rhys. *Father* didn't seem entirely right, but it wasn't necessarily wrong either, especially if Justin was to elicit the responses he wanted from those he questioned. Still, it wasn't the stablemaster from whom he'd been sent to coax some truths. So he cleared his throat. "I was wondering if I might speak to your lad, Tim."

"This is about Bobby again? Sir Reese already questioned him."

"I am aware." Justin fell back on something of an imperious tone at the way Donegal didn't immediately acquiesce. And then he decided he needed to adapt to the circumstances and not allow his own pride to gain the upper hand. So he leaned closer and said in a lower tone, somewhat conspiratorially, "It's probably a waste of time, but Sir Rhys sent me. As he's my mother's new husband, I'm trying to keep the peace."

Donegal put a finger to the side of his nose. "I understand, my lord." Then he gestured towards one of the far boxes. "Dolly was feeling poorly today, and so is the lad, so I put them together."

Justin made his way down the long aisle between the numerous stalls. The ceiling stretched twenty feet above his head, grander than most stables, as well as most houses. It was lit primarily by the open doorways on each end. These let in a significant amount of light, especially at this hour of the day. Many of the stalls were empty. If the weather was good, the horses wouldn't return to the castle stables for days at a time. His horse would probably join the rest in the pasture across the Thames this afternoon, provided Justin didn't need him.

Each stall was blocked by a gate that could swing open to admit a caretaker or to allow the horse to leave. The gate in front of Dolly's box was closed, and when Justin reached it, he folded his arms along the top and leaned into them. He was very conscious of his attire, which gave him away as a knight, even though he was still in traveling clothes. He wore a sword, and that alone would ensure that Tim knew his station. Justin should have thought through this scene and the impression he would make before he arrived at it, but it was too late to retreat now.

Tim was sitting with his knees up and his back against the stall, looking dejected and weeping softly. The horse, being sensitive to human moods like many horses, gently nudged the side of his head with her nose.

"Timmy." Justin took a chance that this was what his friends called him. Among the Saxons, adding an *ee* sound at the end of a name was common practice and a sign of endearment. Really, both Bobby and Tim were at most a year younger than Justin himself, but to him they appeared years younger. He'd have to think later about why that might be.

At first Tim didn't look up, and Justin thought perhaps he'd spoken too softly. Then the boy wiped at his cheeks with the backs of his hands and glanced over. As Justin had assumed would happen, he instantly scrambled to his feet, though his eyes remained on the ground. "Pardon, my lord! I didn't realize who had come—"

"Don't fret yourself." Justin waved his hand. "I understand you've had a hard loss today. I know how that goes."

Tim looked at him, just a glance, and then gazed back until Justin realized he was waiting for an explanation or confirmation that what Justin had just said wasn't simply a platitude. Even with seeing his mother and Rhys at work, Justin had never thought about an investigation as requiring anything in particular from himself. He asked questions, and the suspects, victims, or informants answered them. In that moment, he realized that to elicit any kind of real truth out of Tim, he needed to speak to him as one man to another. That was why his mother had suggested he say that *she* was concerned about the murder. It was a shortcut to creating a bond between them.

Justin thought he had inadvertently stumbled upon something better, however, even if it required more from him. "I lost my father recently, a man I admired more than any man in the world. I also lost my closest friend during the same battle in which my father died. I can't promise that you will ever feel the way you did before Bobby's death, but you won't always feel as much pain as you do now."

He remembered the day he'd learned of his father's death as if it were yesterday. Justin himself had not been at the Battle of Llandeilo Fawr, Gilbert de Clare's humiliating defeat at the hands of the Welsh. He'd been left behind at Dinefwr Castle, which Clare had already taken, vomiting up his guts alongside a significant number of Clare's force, who'd come down with dysentery. When the news of the dreadful defeat had come, Justin had been on his knees again, retching over a bowl for the hundredth time in three days.

He'd cried then, out of shame and weakness, for giving in to his illness and for not being at his father's side when he'd needed him. Catrin had said, time and again, as often as she thought he needed to hear it, that had he gone, he may well have died too. When Justin was in his rational mind, he could see her point, but he also knew in his heart that the two of them together could have saved each other.

And then he'd learned that the son of William de Valence, also named William, had died as well, along with the three knights who guarded him. One of them, Oliver, had been Justin's closest friend. They'd been thrown together within the armies in South Wales, not only for the conflicts between King Edward and Prince Llywelyn but between Gilbert de Clare and other Marcher lords. Among these was, of course, William de Valence, Oliver's lord. Clare and Valence hated each other, but Justin had never seen any sense in hating just because others did.

Come to think on it, that trait was something else he had in common with his new stepfather. Rhys had Norman friends, despite the numerous wars and betrayals that could have created a barrier between them and him. That Vincent de Lusignan had been standing next to Rhys moments ago in Windsor's laying-out room, conversing as if all was well between them, was hardly credible.

And yet, it seemed to be. And a credit to them both that they could put their pasts aside and behave, if one could believe it, as friends. Justin didn't know all the details of their conflict, but his mother had told him about Cilmeri, and he'd seen what had happened on the field at Nefyn. Obviously, there might be a little more to the story!

That was moving far afield from the issue at hand, however, and he focused more fully on Tim's face. "I am so sorry for your loss."

Tim nodded and snuffled a bit, but he no longer had a belligerent set to his chin. "Bobby was different. He wasn't as smart as me, but he knew how to be a friend. He didn't make fun of me like some of the others. He stood up for me when the others bullied me."

Judging by the body on the table, Bobby hadn't been much bigger than Tim, but a small man could cast a long shadow if he had the right personality.

"He had secrets, though, didn't he?"

Tim's eyes dropped to his hands, which he was wringing in front of him. "I don't know what you mean."

It was a lie. Of course, it was. But it also sounded like something Tim felt he had to say, rather than what he wanted to say. He wasn't used to not telling the truth.

"Do you know what he was doing in the stables last night?"

Tim shook his head. "I would have said he was with a girl."

"Darla?" Justin knew the name from Rhys's summary of the investigation.

"It couldn't have been her, since she found him today."

"You don't think she might have killed him and then pretended to discover him afterwards?"

"Never." Tim openly scoffed. "She's a piece, but not for keeping, and she knows it. Bobby was just fooling around with her."

"Did he have enemies? Anyone who might hate him enough to murder him?"

Tim shook his head. "I don't know."

"Timmy," Justin said gently, "there must be something you can tell me. Bobby is dead. We very much want to discover who killed him. My own mother is staying in this castle right now, and I want her to be able to sleep tonight without fearing for her life."

There. He'd used what his mother had suggested.

And, as she'd suggested, it did the trick.

"He had a box." Tim blurted out the words, as if against his will.

"What box is that?"

"He kept a box of his favorite things, things he didn't want to lose or anyone else to see. We don't have much of our own, you see. Bobby had a box."

Rhys and Miles had already gone over Bobby's spot in his dormitory. They'd found nothing resembling a box such as Tim described. "Do you know where that box is?"

Tim hesitated, and then nodded, not even that reluctantly. "I'll show you. It's in the storage room."

24

Day Two

Catrin

"Mary!" Eleanor glared at her sister. "How can you say such things?"

"Why shouldn't I?" Mary gazed around at everyone's aghast faces. "You can't really be shocked. Everything I said is true. Are we really going to pretend it isn't? I want to talk about it!"

"God bless you, child," the priest began, "we have seen that God has blessed you with insight, but it would be best if you leave these things to—"

Prince Edmund made a motion with one hand, cutting him off. The servants and retainers also understood the gesture to mean they were dismissed. Everyone filed out of the room—except for Mildrith, who appeared to be making herself very small at the end of the table, indicating she very much wanted to stay but was afraid that if she called attention to herself, Prince Edmund would notice her and tell her to depart with the baby.

The priest's mouth had formed a thin line, entirely in character with what Catrin had seen of him so far. But he didn't protest again. Nor did he leave. Edmund acted as if neither the priest nor Mildrith were present and instead moved his gaze from one niece to the next.

"Mary is right, and, as you say, not for the first time. We all know it, and I, for one, do not wish to pretend to you girls—or ask you to pretend—that all is well when it isn't. Catrin and Reese are here because your parents fear your brother was murdered."

There was utter silence around the table. Even little Elizabeth seemed to understand she should keep silent and was gazing at her uncle with wide blue eyes.

Edmund continued, "And Mary is right again when it comes to your safety. While your parents love you dearly, they do not think any of you are in danger. Please believe that they would send an army to protect you if they thought you needed it or if it would make a difference."

"An army cannot stop an assassin," Margaret said. "Alfonso told me that. He read it in one of his books."

"He was correct, of course," Prince Edmund said, and Catrin didn't think she was mistaken that his eyes skated to Rhys for a moment.

Rhys *had* saved Edmund's life, as everyone knew. But that was in battle. King Edward, who'd been a prince at the time, had survived an attempt on his life by a member of the Hashashin, a highly trained group of assassins. The assassin had obtained an interview with Edward by claiming to have secret information on one of the emirs he was fighting and then attacked him with a poisoned dagger. Edward fought him off with, of all things, a stool. He was wounded in the fight, though not seriously, but because of poison on the blade that cut him, he almost died.

Catrin had never heard what happened to the assassin, in large part because she had never asked Rhys, and he'd never volunteered that bit of information. He also hadn't been a member of Edward's guard at the time. The story always seemed to end with the triumphant recovery of the prince. The world would have been a very different place for all of them if he hadn't survived.

Margaret now looked across the table to Rhys. "I overheard one of the servants saying you were better than an army, and Father really must be worried if he sent *you*."

Catrin had been focused on the platter of vegetables in front of her, but now she looked up at Rhys, who met her eyes before moving them momentarily to look at Prince Edmund. The prince might have nodded. Regardless, it was a matter of a few heartbeats before Rhys looked seriously at the little princess. One was allowed to look into the face of royalty when she was nine years old and needed to know you were speaking truthfully. Catrin hardly dared breathe, not wanting to interrupt the moment.

"My lady, I cannot speak to others' opinions of me. I do feel that if Alfonso's death was not from an illness, we need to know." He looked around the table. "I assure you I will do my utmost to find the truth."

Prince Edmund folded his arms across his chest and settled back into his chair. "Sir Reese is our best chance." Then he looked directly at Eleanor. "You admonished your sister for speaking this truth, for reasons I understand, but you fear it too, my dear."

Eleanor looked down at her plate rather than meet his gaze. "I have learned to fear it. I didn't at first. In fact, I didn't even think of it until Mary spoke up. I didn't want to. Until they found Bobby dead today, I told myself the entire notion was absurd."

"From your voice, I'm sensing you knew this lad?" Rhys asked.

"We all did," Margaret answered for her sister.

Catrin still had her eyes on Eleanor, who took advantage of the fact that everyone's attention was diverted to Margaret to put a hand to her cheek and wipe another tear—or maybe two—from her cheeks.

Meanwhile, Edmund tipped his head. "How is that?"

"We know everyone, Uncle. We hardly ever go anywhere or do anything, especially now that Alfonso's gone." As before, Margaret was very blunt. The young prince had been the center of the world for everyone at this table. He'd been the heir to the throne, and his needs and desires had taken precedence over everyone and everything else. It did not appear, however, that he'd taken advantage of that fact as much as he might have. He had free rein in the castle to do as he liked, and clearly everyone catered to him, but it hadn't spoiled him or soured his disposition, as Catrin herself had witnessed the last time she'd been here. "Lately, Bobby was responsible for replenishing the drink in our rooms, though I hear that just today Butler James found someone else to do the job properly. Bobby did anything anyone asked him. He swept the floors, he chopped wood, he served in the hall, he fetched and carried. Anything."

"We all liked him," Joan said softly. "He always had a smile on his face."

"Alfonso played with him often," Margaret continued as if Joan hadn't spoken. "He was teaching him to fight."

"Was he now?" Prince Edmund said, though Catrin wasn't certain if Margaret meant Alfonso was teaching Bobby or Bobby was teaching Alfonso.

It seemed important to be sure. "Are you saying Alfonso was teaching Bobby to use a sword?"

"Yes."

A glance at Prince Edmund showed him to be somewhat offended by the idea. But then Margaret continued. "But he said he was learning from Bobby too."

And then, maybe not at all surprisingly, given his experience in battle, Prince Edmund no longer looked concerned. Quite the opposite. He even nodded.

The priest, however, was staring down his nose at Margaret. "That's absurd." Maybe he'd intended to speak more quietly than he had, but he'd spoken loud enough for everyone at the table to hear. Even to a nine-year-old princess, his comment was rude—not to mention an offensive observation to all of them, since Alfonso was dead.

Prince Edmund's eyes narrowed as he gazed down the table at the priest. "Alfonso was only ten, but he'd carried a sword of one kind or another since he was three years old. Bobby was a man. He wouldn't have known how to use a sword, but as any man who has fought in battle knows well, men need more than just sword skills to win in combat. Possibly, the skills they developed through wrestling or fighting with their fists are even more valuable. Alfonso would have had teachers for that. But as common men who learned to fight on the streets of London understand more than most, in those times when one's life is on the line, there are no rules." Prince Edmund paused for a moment and then added softly to himself, "I learned that the hard way."

The priest didn't even look abashed, though he did bow his head to the prince. "My apologies, my lord. I didn't think."

Catrin herself was thinking quite a lot by now. She was thinking that Eleanor was closer to Bobby than she was letting on. The tears seemed to be for him, rather than for Alfonso.

"Bobby often brought me sweets from the kitchen." Mary said. "Alfonso too. We both loved honey cakes."

From across the table, Rhys's attention sharpened. "What honey cakes would those be?"

Mary shrugged. "The kitchen made them sometimes just for Alfonso and me. We love anything with honey."

"Alfonso loved honey so much that he preferred drinking mead to wine." Joan's eyes brightened. "Shall we call for some? I don't care for it myself, but it would be fitting, perhaps, to raise a glass to him." Without waiting for approval from anyone else—

even her uncle—Joan went to the door. She seemed comfortable with doing what needed to be done herself and not waiting for a servant to do it for her.

Catrin spoke to her back. "Alfonso drank mead?"

"It was all he liked." Joan opened the door, spoke to someone in the corridor, and then returned to her seat. "These last months he refused anything else."

"I think it also had less to do with liking honey so much, though he did, than with pretending to be Astolfo." This was from Eleanor, who appeared to be recovering. "He tried mead for the first time because he read about it in one of his books. In the days of Charlemagne, mead would have been all the son of the English king drank. Or so the books said." She herself looked as if that couldn't possibly be true. Catrin didn't know herself, since Saxons drank ale in quantity and for the most part turned up their noses at mead, which was the drink of the Welsh.

"Can you speak to us of when he fell ill?" Rhys's tone was very calm, but Catrin could hear in it the way his senses had sharpened.

"One moment he was fine, and the next he wasn't." Margaret also continued to be open and ready to talk. She clearly had wanted to have this conversation earlier, but none of her elders had been willing to listen. "It was too bad too, because it came on the evening of Elizabeth's birthday dinner."

Catrin was suddenly a bit puzzled. "That was twelve days before he died. I didn't realize he'd been sick that long."

Prince Edmund leaned forward. "I didn't either."

"Well, he was." Margaret shrugged. "He pretended not to be. If he was sick, then he'd have to stay inside. He hated being inside, except when he was reading. But his stomach started bothering him long before he told anyone else about it."

Edmund was gazing at Margaret with a look of concern and a bit of astonishment. Then his eyes went to Mildrith and the priest at the end of the table. "Did either of you know this?"

"No, my lord." Mildrith ducked her head. "I did not."

"Nor I." Father Giles paused. "But then, I had gone to see my sister for the first half of the month of August and didn't return until the Feast of Saint Mary." That would have been August 15th, only four days before Alfonso died.

Everyone was looking at Margaret.

"You are certain he was ill that long?" Rhys said.

"I am certain."

"What were his symptoms?"

Margaret's face held a look of relief, as if she could hardly believe they were finally paying attention to her. "He had little appetite so had to force himself to eat sometimes, and he was tired in a way that didn't feel right."

"Did he have a sense that any particular food caused it?"

"Not that he said to me."

"Why did you not tell us this earlier?" Prince Edmund was just short of glaring at his niece.

Margaret made a helpless gesture, one that made her suddenly seem far older than her nine years. "At the time, he made me promise not to tell. And then after he died, nobody asked."

Catrin put out a hand to briefly clasp Margaret's own. "And nobody was here to listen even if you did try to speak of it?"

Margaret nodded, a bit hesitantly. "I'm sorry. I should have said something in those first days, but he'd had stomach aches before that went away. Everybody does at one time or another. I'm sure we both thought that was it."

The mead arrived in the form of Miles. Prince Edmund didn't blink an eye, but then, Rhys had already told him what Miles was doing. His mouth did twitch once. For his part, Rhys stood to speak to Miles. It wasn't quite the usual protocol, but his look was intent, and his question pointed, "Where did this mead come from?"

Catrin hadn't thought to be worried about it, nor realized what exactly had sharpened Rhys's attention, until Rhys asked the question. They were here to investigate Alfonso's death, but she had been telling herself all this time that Alfonso couldn't possibly have been murdered. Rhys was clearly further along in his thinking than she.

Thankfully, Elizabeth chose that moment to stand up on her chair and jump up and down, shouting, "Honey! Honey! Honey!"

Under the shouting, Miles said, in his guise as Gilbert le Gascon. "The contents of this carafe arrived on the barge today, my lord. It has been sampled and found acceptable."

Mildrith attempted to coax Elizabeth off her chair, but the little girl was having none of it. Finally, Edmund strode over to swoop her up in his arms and cover her belly with kisses.

She laughed, as did her sisters, even Eleanor.

Catrin took the opportunity to get to her feet too and move to Rhys's side. She was in time to hear him say, "We hear that Alfonso was fond of mead. Does any remain in the castle from what he last drank?"

Miles met his eyes for a few heartbeats longer than might be normal for a servant before replying. Again, none of the girls noticed, since they were distracted by their uncle. "Hugh the cellarer seemed to think so, but he couldn't find the cask. I will find out for certain, my lord."

"Thank you."

Miles was still hesitating, his eyes flicking about the room, prompting Rhys to ask with some urgency, "Have you learned something we should know?"

"All the drink is sampled before it is circulated about the castle. My sensitive tongue, though not the primary reason I was employed, is seen to have use in that. When I decanted the mead, I offered a measure to Hugh, who tastes all the drink before it is served. He declined the opportunity, confessing that he despised the stuff and usually convinced someone else to test it instead."

"Dare I ask who that other person might have been when Alfonso was alive?" Catrin asked.

"George." Miles answered in the way she feared he would.

"Who is dead," Rhys said.

Miles lowered his voice even further. "And, occasionally, Bobby."

Rhys grimaced. "We will have to question Hugh more fully, but you should not do it."

As Miles acquiesced, Rhys retook his seat, and Miles then carried the carafe around the table to pour out a portion for everyone before retreating to the safety of one corner.

By now, the family had returned to their seats too, including Prince Edmund. It occurred to Catrin, looking into the prince's face, that he was fully aware of their conversation and had been behaving exuberantly to give them the chance to speak to each other without anyone else interfering or even noticing.

Prince Edmund raised his cup. "To Alfonso."

"To Alfonso."

As Catrin repeated his words along with everyone else, her eyes once more met Rhys's across the table. She was reasonably confident the mead in her cup wouldn't kill her. But it was terrifying, now that they were enmeshed within the royal court, to realize all the ways Alfonso might have ingested something that could.

25

Day Two

Rhys

"Investigating is new to me, Rhys." Vincent continued to insist on pronouncing Rhys's name the Welsh way, instead of the Norman *Reese*. That was clearly new to him too, so he didn't get it right every time. But even when he didn't, he managed that little trill of the *r* that meant he was trying. Rhys was almost embarrassed by how sensitive he was being. And starting to feel uncomfortable about his own behavior towards Vincent, as in maybe he needed to be more sensitive in return. Friendship was a two-way road, and this—whatever *this* was—wasn't going to work if Rhys himself wasn't a full participant. "I confess I set off from the laying-out room with something of an amused perspective. I'm not amused now."

They were meeting in the upper bailey's guesthouse common room, in a building now wholly unoccupied, since the prince had found other accommodations for Rhys and Catrin. The fire seemed like a *long* time ago—except that the room was an immediate reminder of all the questions they still hadn't asked.

While neither Justin nor Vincent were so privileged as to be staying in the upper bailey—and, of course, nor was Miles—it was still the most private spot Rhys could think of. He could have cleared the keep as before, but then the whole castle would have known that they were meeting and that their meeting was important. Instead, Rhys had done a full circuit of the perimeter of the guesthouse before Vincent had come in. Unlike the royal apartments, which were built around a central courtyard, like in a monastery cloister, the guesthouse was a stand-alone building.

"Does that mean you've discovered something?"

"I discovered nobody likes speaking to a nobleman such as I."

Rhys made a motion with his head, which was a way of saying *of course.*

Vincent scoffed under his breath. "But if you knew that already, why send me?"

"For the very reason you put forth: because you were unexpected. Catrin and I just ate a meal with the royal family! Even now she is sitting with the princesses in their solar." Her purpose was to speak to them of their parents and new baby brother, but also to provide some comfort, particularly to Eleanor. In a moment alone at the end of the meal, Eleanor had confessed that she and Bobby had been closer friends than she'd initially indicated. While the full nature of that relationship mattered less now that he was dead, it further explained her behavior that day at the meal. "I had some hope that someone would be disarmed by you."

Vincent grunted. "Well, you weren't wrong, in truth."

"So you did learn something." Rhys had already guessed things might have gone well by the way Vincent had entered the guesthouse, with his head high and eyes bright.

Vincent tipped his head. "Was this a test?"

"Don't tell me you aren't constantly testing me! I thought only to return the favor." Rhys laughed and went to a side table where he'd set the carafe and cups he'd suggested Miles leave there. "But no. I'm jesting. Truly. I needed the help."

Vincent didn't say anything in reply. Rhys didn't want to turn and see if he was angry, either at the supposed test, which genuinely hadn't been one, or the joke. The hair on the back of Rhys's neck still stood up whenever he put his back to any Norman, but he stayed in place, and this time it was he who poured wine for Vincent. Turning around, Rhys placed one of the cups in Vincent's hand, before raising his own. With a grave air, he said, "To new beginnings."

Vincent made a little *huh* sound, but repeated the words back to Rhys.

Then Rhys made an encouraging motion with his cup. "Tell me what you learned." In truth, he shouldn't have had to ask, but every conversation with Vincent seemed to hack about in the underbrush for some time before getting to the main point.

Vincent pulled out one of the less scorched chairs and sat facing backwards on it, with his arms across the rail. "There is something wrong at Windsor. I don't know what."

Rhys perched a hip on the table. "Alfonso died, so I would expect it."

"Other than that."

Rhys felt his blood run a little colder. He still didn't know how to fully trust Vincent, but he trusted his instincts. "In what way?"

"I questioned guardsman after guardsman. There are thirty here at the castle, just to keep watch on the towers and battlements, so it's a hefty task." He made another *puh* sound, like he thought Rhys had given him his own task because he knew it was hefty. Rhys couldn't tell in that moment if he resented that fact or was acknowledging it as the compliment that it was. Vincent continued. "They all knew Bobby. Most were completely bewildered as to what he might have been doing in the storage room in the stables at any hour of the night if he wasn't with a girl (which virtually to a man they posited). But two, maybe three, got a look in their eyes when his name came up—a look that told me they knew something about him or his death." He stopped, his eyes on Rhys's face. "And then I mentioned the fire in this guesthouse, and those same eyes went blank."

Rhys wet his lips. "Nobody would say more?"

"No." Vincent snorted. "That's what you meant by me being unexpected, isn't it? They were prepared to be questioned by you, but not by me, and you hoped that little bit of surprise might elicit something new.”

Rhys grinned. “So perhaps not as much of a waste of time as you thought.”

“I have those men’s names.” Vincent held out a scrap of paper where he’d written them down, and Rhys made a note of them in his little book he kept for such purposes. There was a time when he might have been able to keep all the details of an investigation in his head, but he’d learned that the mind played tricks, and he didn’t have a perfect memory. Better to write down what he could when he could.

“We’ll have to think about how to approach them. Thank you.” Rhys paused. “Though I’m not sure what the topic might be.”

“The fire, clearly. Bobby’s death, clearly.”

“Yes.” Rhys bobbed his head. “But how are they connected?”

“They occurred on the same night. Perhaps Bobby put the pitch wood on the fire, and someone killed him for it.” Vincent frowned. “That would make this a conspiracy, with many men involved. But to cover up what, exactly? Alfonso’s murder? It’s a bold move to try to kill you.”

“And an even bolder one to murder Bobby. It isn’t as if we wouldn’t notice.”

Vincent was deep in thought. “So is something else going on here someone is afraid you’ll uncover in the course of your investigation? Your wife may be right that this is about you.”

"I don't know." Rhys spread his hands wide. "Every community has its bad apples. They want what they can't have. They lie. They steal. But this feels more organized than a few bad apples."

"Spying?"

"A perennial question in a king's castle—" Before Rhys could finish that particular thought, he heard a sound outside the guesthouse. In two strides, he was at the door, and when he pulled it open with a jerk, Justin almost tumbled through the doorway.

Rhys put out a hand to grasp his wrist and hauled him upright. "Sorry. I heard you coming."

"You have ears like a sheepdog! I suppose I shouldn't be surprised."

To have both his new stepson and his old friend admiring him felt uncomfortable, so Rhys hastily changed the subject. "Do you have something for me?"

Justin held out a small box, perhaps eight inches by six, which he'd brought tucked under his arm. "According to Bobby's friend Tim, it belonged to Bobby."

"Well done." Rhys took the box and brought it over to the table.

Justin followed, somewhat warily, causing Rhys to glance at him. "What's wrong?"

"Tim wanted to talk. You would have coaxed this from him too."

Vincent guffawed. "Rhys and I just had this conversation. The more I'm with him, the more I realize his mind doesn't work the way ours does."

Rhys supposed he shouldn't be surprised that Justin, like Vincent, was wary of accolades, especially those coming from his new stepfather. But what Rhys realized too, between Justin's hesitation and Vincent's comment, was that even if both Vincent and Justin distrusted approval, they needed it. Neither was used to investigations, and if they were to continue, they needed to really believe they could help.

So he took what Vincent had said and elaborated. "I cannot be in two, never mind three, places at once. You both performed a valuable service, and I appreciate it. Besides, I'm not so sure either of you are right in thinking I could have done as well. We each bring something of ourselves, both good and bad, to these investigations. But in your cases, I think mostly good."

"Th-th-thank you." Justin's look of stunned surprise was endearing.

Vincent gave a low grunt before saying, "Shall we see what's inside?"

The three of them gathered around the table. Rhys wasn't sure what he was expecting—a few trinkets, tokens from childhood, a letter perhaps, though it was unlikely that Bobby could read. What he got was a beanbag, such as jugglers employ, a pack of papers smaller even than Rhys's book, poked through in the corner so it could be tied with a string, and a loose sketch of a man.

Rhys picked up the sketch first and showed it to the other two men. The image was a drawing in charcoal of a slender older man, bald on top with a big beard that more than made up for his small stature. He was sitting at a table, as in a hall or tavern, with a cup at his hand. It wasn't anyone Rhys knew by sight, though something about him tickled at the back of his mind, as if he *had* in fact seen him before. By the blank looks on Justin's and Vincent's faces, they didn't know him either.

The little book of papers was all in French and comprised a list of goods, mostly luxury items and some just labeled *item*. He handed it to Vincent, eyebrows raised. "What does this look like to you?"

"Someone has been smuggling rather than spying?"

"I'd say so." Justin picked up the beanbag and tossed it in one hand. "It looks like a list of movable goods."

"A list that Bobby, a kitchen boy, was keeping in a box." And Rhys explained to Justin about the three men Vincent had identified as suspicious.

Meanwhile, Vincent was flipping through the list. "It could be that Bobby was stealing from the castle stores and selling the items out the back. He'd need help, and guards are perfectly placed to help him."

Justin caught the beanbag one last time and tossed it back into the box. "Or he discovered who was really involved, and that knowledge got him killed."

26

Day Two

Catrin

"What is the significance of the beanbag?" It was Catrin's first question once the three men brought what they'd discovered to her.

They'd vacated the guesthouse common room, not because it hadn't been a good meeting place, but because it was high time the five of them consulted together, and the lower bailey's great hall was the only place they could legitimately encounter Miles without causing comment. Even so, he chose a seat a bit down the table. The intent was to imply that he wasn't a close confidant but be close enough to hear their conversation. Most of the castle workers were present this evening. Only that day, Constable Geoffrey had commissioned a bard to distract everyone from the rumors about the investigation swirling around the castle.

They couldn't talk while the bard was singing, but he had adapted his entertainment to the needs of his audience. Once most people had eaten their fill, he incited them to dance. The overall merriment provided a good cover for their little group to huddle together in the back of the hall, which, as befitting Windsor's grandeur, was long and wide, built in wood for the most part, with great wooden beams supporting the roof. It had two large fireplaces, one on either side near the dais, with chimneys that let out the smoke. These appeared to work better than most.

"We don't know," Rhys said.

"Bobby kept it for a reason," Catrin said. "It would be one thing if the box contained personal treasures, but this isn't a treasure box. And yet, these things are obviously important to him and all related to why he was killed. They have to be."

"You aren't supposed to assume, Mother," Justin chided.

"You are correct, Justin," Rhys said, "but as we gather more information, we can start putting the pieces together. I agree these items Bobby saved are important. The question before us is where they fit into the edifice we are constructing, stone by stone."

"I'd also like to know how he acquired them," Vincent said. "I see this list as very telling of … something. Is it his list? Could he really read? Or was it something he stole from someone else?"

"Which got him killed," Justin said.

Miles was staring at the image of the man, his eyes narrowed. Then he slid it back across the table. "I know him. He was at the tavern during my contest with Butler James and then at the docks the next day."

Rhys snapped his fingers. "That's it! I saw him at the tavern too. Do you know his name?"

Miles pursed his lips, thinking back. He remembered the taste and names of wines, but people's names were harder. "J-J-J—Jean?" He shook his head. "It was French, I know that. Someone will know for certain. I can inquire."

"Quietly," Rhys warned. "Keep the sketch."

"I dare not. I can describe him well enough."

Catrin picked up the beanbag and turned it over in her hands. The stitching was coming out on one side, and a bean fell out. It skittered across the table towards Justin.

He caught it and handed it back to her. "That happened to me earlier when I was tossing it."

Catrin was about to put the bean back into the bag, when she hesitated, frowning. "I don't want to make something out of nothing, but isn't this a castor bean?"

"I believe so." Rhys was the one to speak, but she could see the same thought reflected in the faces of the other men. Essentially they were saying, *yes, and what of it?*

"They are an oddly pretty bean," Vincent said with greater definitiveness. "They are common in the Holy Land, used in making castor oil. We would see them in the market."

"I have never been to the Holy Land, but their beauty is why I remembered them too. The oil has some wonderful medicinal uses, though they don't grow well in Britain." Catrin paused. "But if these are castor beans, they're poisonous in any form that isn't oil. And that's to say, *really* poisonous. Chewing as few as two or three could kill a man."

The men gazed at her.

"You didn't know?"

"We knew." Rhys's voice was low and careful, almost as if he was afraid to pursue this line of inquiry.

"What happens when they are consumed?" Miles continued to drink his ale with a steady focus that implied he had little interest in what the others were talking about. But that didn't mean he wasn't listening.

"Initial symptoms may include abdominal pain, vomiting, diarrhea, and heartburn." Vincent recited this in something of a monotone. "Inability to keep anything down or inside can lead to dehydration and ultimately the complete failure of the blood to flow through the body."

Everyone was looking at him now. Even Miles shot him a perturbed glance.

"How do you know this?" Rhys asked.

"You aren't the only one who learned something in the Holy Land, my friend. I spent some time with a healer at one point, who loved to talk. She—" He broke off, perhaps deciding he'd said too much. None of them were going to judge him for a relationship he had a decade ago, but Catrin guessed that his embarrassment and the nature of the knowledge the woman had imparted to him meant she'd been a Saracen. "This was after Rhys and I—" Vincent didn't finish that sentence either.

"—after you and I were no longer speaking, though of course, Simon and I traveled home with Prince Edmund shortly thereafter anyway." Rhys didn't make him continue.

"Those are Alfonso's symptoms." Miles speared a parsnip with his knife. "Bobby must have had these things because he murdered Alfonso."

Justin wasn't ready to concede that, and rightly so. "If Alfonso died of castor bean poisoning, and Bobby was responsible, why keep the beanbag? It implicates him."

"The smart thing would definitely have been to throw it away," Catrin said.

"Unless he thought he might have need of more beans," Vincent pointed out.

"Bobby's friend Tim implied he was smart. He could have been part of a smuggling ring. He also could have been smart enough to be involved but keep evidence against the people he was working with in case they turned on him." Justin made a motion with his head. "Smart enough to want to survive."

"Another option is the real killer planted the beanbag on him and then killed him, with the idea that we'd find it." This was also from Vincent. "With Bobby dead and the beanbag among his possessions, we would assume the investigation was over."

Rhys was rolling his eyes, but he made no attempt to stem the speculation coming from his friends' mouths.

"The only person that really could be is Tim." Justin's expression was offended, since, if so, Tim had successfully lied to him. "Otherwise, the killer would have left the beanbag in Bobby's hand. Without Tim, we would never have known about the box."

Catrin took a sip of ale, grimaced, and set down her cup. "From what you described, Tim was contrite and sad. But it's possible he got that way out of guilt at what he'd done, not just out of grief at the loss. The box could even be *his*."

Justin chewed on his lower lip. "Even were that true, the motivation is different for this murder compared to Alfonso's, isn't it?"

"If he was murdered." Rhys spoke under his breath and without force.

"Why would you say that?" Miles eyed Justin from down the table. "Murder is murder."

"If Alfonso is dead it isn't for his own sake," Justin said. "It wouldn't be because someone hated *him*. It would be because someone has a grudge against the king."

"It's hard to see how someone could avenge himself more profoundly than by killing a man's son," Miles said.

Justin nodded. "Even more, while the killer may hate the king personally, his action could also be retribution for one of the king's policies."

Catrin held her breath as her half-Norman son latched upon something about which she and Rhys had barely dared speculate.

Justin's words had Vincent frowning. "Are you suggesting that the death of Alfonso could be part of a larger whole, something more organized?"

"Such is my thought," Justin said.

"This could then include the attacks on the king's life." Miles's eyes scanned the hall, as if an assassin might leap from the tapestries at any moment.

"It could." Rhys had let the others talk, but now he shot a glance at Catrin, which she returned with a completely mild expression. They were both thinking that they knew of one such cabal already. They would not speak of it to any of the men here, however, since all of their lords were implicated in it. If it got out that the noblest lords in the March were conspiring with one another, whether to murder the king, his son, or to augment their own power, England would be torn apart.

A significant portion of Catrin thought that wouldn't be a bad thing. It still wasn't something to share even with her own son. Not yet anyway. Maybe not ever. Rhys hadn't even talked to Simon about it.

Justin was continuing the thought: "The king has pursued the policies of his predecessors, and in so doing has overtaken many peoples, not just the Welsh, I hasten to add. We've got the Irish, the Scots, the various French domains, as well as the Saxons to contend with."

"You are certainly correct that time doesn't heal all wounds," Miles said dryly, shooting a glance down the table again, this time towards Rhys, "though it apparently can heal even stubborn ones."

"You neglect to mention the many barons who also might have a grudge against the king," Vincent said into his cup. "I won't name names here."

Miles gripped his knife, half-rising to his feet. "If you are implying—"

"Nobody is implying anything." Rhys's voice was low but harsh and cut through the sudden anger on Miles's part and a momentary sulkiness on Vincent's. "Miles. Vincent. This is why we keep speculation to a minimum. We are all friends here."

"Sorry," Vincent said. "I wasn't thinking about—" He cleared his throat. "I should have thought before I spoke."

In turn, Miles let out a long sigh. "Old wounds, my friend."

"We all have them."

Catrin didn't think she was mistaken that Vincent accompanied the comment with a glance at Rhys, who now spoke again, "If nothing else, the one thing we can agree on in all this is that we have a murderer in this castle *right now,* and everyone knows it. However this investigation turns out, and whatever avenues we end up pursuing, we will seek justice for poor Bobby."

It was meant to be an ending to their speculative talk, but Vincent looked now at Justin. "You didn't finish your thought. In what way are the motivations of the two murders, if they are two murders"—he said this with another glance towards Rhys— "different?"

Justin was happy to continue. "I heard Rhys say in Nefyn that murder tends to happen for the same reasons every time: hatred, jealousy, or fear. Bobby's death is the result of fear."

Miles was rubbing his chin, calmed down enough to rejoin the conversation too. "Fear of loss, fear of consequences, fear masquerading as love. I would point out, however, that we have all known men who seemed to enjoy killing. For them, battle was almost—" here he paused to consider, "—a pleasure."

"Let's hope we aren't dealing with someone like that here," Rhys said.

"What was someone afraid of that made him kill Bobby?" Vincent asked—and then, before anyone could reply, answered his own question, "Fear of discovery, obviously."

"And we are back right where we started," Catrin said.

"Thank you, Catrin," Rhys said, "for your level head. We have more people to speak to before we are going to have any of these answers." And he proceeded to pass out tasks to each of them. Rhys, as the principal investigator, would take the papers to the constable. If the castle was missing stores, they had to start at the top to find out how and why. He would follow that information all the way to the last worker on the dock on the Thames.

Justin's quest was to trace the owner of the bean bag. Vincent was charged with inquiring among the staff about George, the dead food taster they were trying not to forget about. Catrin was to go back to Tim one more time.

That left Miles to take the names of the men in the garrison. After Rhys passed him the list under the guise of pushing the platter of bread towards him, he said, surprise in his voice, "I know these three. I was introduced to them yesterday. Their primary watch is the dockside of the castle." Off he went, losing himself in the crowd.

If the guards were involved in smuggling, being posted to the dockside as a regular duty made sense, though smart garrisoning usually meant that duties rotated. That way no one person would become complacent. Still, in a castle this large, she could see why specialties would arise. All this would be the charge of Captain Thaddeus.

"I'm glad Miles is on our side," Vincent said in an undertone, in French, as he watched the Norman lord go.

"I am too." Rhys spoke with real fervor. "He is the cleverest of all of us, I think." As soon as he spoke, he put out a hand to Vincent. "No offense meant."

"None taken, though I think it would be an even bet between the two of you. Both of you have minds that follow twisting paths. I confess to understanding Miles's better." Then he nudged Justin, who was sitting beside him. "No offense to you or your mother either."

Justin laughed. "You don't have to apologize to me. I know when I'm outmatched." But then he sobered. "Though I think you underestimate my mother." Before Catrin could protest, because she knew her limits as well, he added, "It isn't really a question at this point, though, is it? The rest of us are going to go about our business asking questions, but we are protected by our stations. Bobby wasn't. I have to think that Miles is taking on more risk than he knows."

27

Day Two
Vincent

Vincent had never told anyone, not even yet his betrothed, how he struggled with talking to people. As a result, he often came across as gruff and unforgiving. The assignment Rhys had given him of speaking to the members of the garrison had been hard for him, and he'd had to work even harder not to appear aloof and superior. Even he knew that treating those beneath one as *beneath* one was a poor way to get them to speak the truth.

And by God he was going to figure out a way to talk to these workers if it was the last thing he did. His pride was on the line. And they were just people. He'd discovered over the years that if he imagined them with frogs' heads and croaking voices, it relaxed him and made them easier to approach.

By those lights, there were a great number of frogs in the kitchen as he passed through it, even though the primary cooking for the day was over. This was preparation for tomorrow's meals.

Because of the entertainer in the great hall in the lower bailey, the upper hall had been quiet this evening anyway. In both baileys, the staff worked long hours, though he'd also noticed they came and went in shifts, just like the members of the garrison. Those whose task it was to prepare the meals earlier in the day had long since finished their duties.

He stopped a pretty frog with a pink ribbon in her hair. "I was wondering where I might find either Cook Armand or Cellarer Hugh."

"They are together in the cellar." She pointed him the way, and he went down the stairs to arrive in the midst of what was clearly a heated argument. He could feel Rhys at his shoulder saying, *Excellent!*

At the sight of Vincent, Hugh and Armand broke off and turned to look at him with identical innocent expressions. Unfortunately, Vincent hadn't caught what they had been arguing about, not even a vague sense. And then Cook Armand hastened forward. "May we help you, my lord?"

"I am here to ask about the procedures for sampling the food and drink before it is served to the royal family."

The cellar was not well-lit, but even so, Vincent couldn't have missed the flash of relief that crossed both of their faces at the topic Vincent wanted to discuss. Whatever they'd been arguing about, it hadn't been that.

"What would you like to know?" Hugh moved forward smoothly. "We are happy to assist in any way we can."

Now Vincent really knew their argument had been important. But he persevered with the initial question anyway. "Who tastes the wine before it is served?" He already knew the answer from Miles, but he wanted to hear it from the source.

"I do," Hugh said without hesitation. "Though now that new dispenser, Gilbert, has come to work, he will do it when I am busy."

"What about possible contamination that could occur between when the drink leaves the cellar to when it reaches the recipient's cup?"

"We are talking about Alfonso, I assume." That was Armand, and Vincent gave him credit for tackling the issue head on.

"Yes."

"As the heir to the throne, his food was tasted by me, as all food is, to ensure its quality, and by his official taster, George."

Vincent frowned, deciding in that instant to pretend that he didn't know anything about George's death. So far, the only person who'd mentioned it, as far as he knew, was Charles, Alfonso's tutor. "I have not met this George yet. I'm quite certain Sir Rhys has not either. Where is he?"

Armand glanced at Hugh, and they both swallowed hard. He found himself leaning forward, with perhaps a hint of menace in his posture—and tone. "What is it? What are you not telling me?"

Hugh sighed. "He's dead."

Vincent had a strong impulse to smile with satisfaction, but instead he glared at Hugh. "When?"

"Two days after Alfonso died."

Armand hastened to add, "His death had nothing to do with Alfonso's!"

"How can you be sure?"

"He was old—" Armand began.

Vincent wasn't having any of it. "*How did he die?*"

"His heart failed him," Hugh said. "That's all."

"How do you know it was his heart? Where was he when he died? I need every detail, right now, and when you're done talking with me, Sir Rhys will be asking you these questions and more."

Armand was looking stricken. Hugh, on the other hand, put his head in his hands. "We have to tell him, Armand. We know this Sir Reese. He will never believe that George died of natural causes, not so soon after Alfonso's death. He was his food taster!"

"Hugh, are you sure—"

Hugh cut him off. "No, of course, I'm not sure. He was my uncle. I loved him. But he is dead and buried and does not care what we say about him now."

Armand tried again. "Hugh—"

"George was *my* uncle." Hugh turned to look directly at Vincent. "Uncle George took his own life."

Vincent had been prepared to learn something momentous. With this news, however, he found his temper rising. "How is it possible you never mentioned this?"

Armand and Hugh began talking over one another in a confused babble, and Vincent made a motion with one hand. "Armand, tell me what happened." He might have asked Hugh, whose uncle George had been, but his face was back in his hands.

Armand obeyed, wringing his own hands all the while and practically bowed with contrition. "He loved Alfonso, you see. He'd been with him since he was weaned, and with the royal family since he was a young man. Most of us have, but George *cared* so much. He'd also lost his only son in the Welsh war two years ago and had never been the same. The loss of Alfonso was one too many."

"How did he die?"

"He hung himself in the stables."

"Are you talking about the stables in Eton or in the lower bailey where Bobby was found dead today?"

"The latter." Armand cleared his throat. "In the same storage room, in fact."

To say Vincent was aghast—and appalled, horrified, and utterly stunned—was to woefully understate how he was feeling. "Does everyone in the entire castle know about this, and they've all been keeping it a secret?"

"No! Of course not!" Though there was no *of course* about it. Armand gestured between him and Hugh. "Just us and Donegal. We were all together, having just shared a drink, when we found him."

"Where had you shared a drink that you ended up in the storage room?"

Hugh made a dismissive gesture. "We meet sometimes in Donegal's little room, just the three of us. We get along." He shrugged. "It was late in the evening, but the horses were restless. We toured the stalls with Donegal. I can't remember why he went into the storage room. Just seeing to things, I think. Then he called us over, and there George was."

"Hanging from the rafter by a rope." Armand let out a heavy sigh. "I will never forget the sight."

"Then what? You took him down and—"

"Lied," Hugh said bluntly. "We lied about how he died, so he could be buried in holy ground."

Armand coughed delicately into his fist. "The physician was well drunk by then, God be praised, so he didn't notice the marks on his neck, which we hid the best we could with the collar of his shirt."

"George definitely killed himself, my lord," Armand said.

"Cook Armand!" A woman's voice called down from the kitchen. "You are needed."

"Please excuse me, my lord, I have a kitchen to run." Armand sketched a bow and disappeared up the stairs.

That left Hugh.

Vincent felt like sighing at the sight of his contrite face. "Sir Rhys will be questioning you further. You do realize that?"

"Yes, my lord." Hugh heaved a sigh of his own. "I will tell him everything."

"What were you and Armand fighting about when I came in?"

Hugh blinked again. He had an expressive face, and Vincent could see him rearranging his thoughts. "It was an issue regarding the appropriate wine to serve with the main meal tomor-row."

"What wine did you suggest?"

Hugh made a gesture with one hand. "I don't even remem-ber."

Vincent didn't believe him, but he sensed that Hugh was done for now. He could haul him into a guard room and question him, but Vincent's years of overseeing men made him think they might do better to let him stew a while in his thoughts. "I'll leave you to your duties."

But then, once he was back in the kitchen, he sought out Armand, who was checking the quantities of spices in his jars. "What were you fighting about with Hugh when I came in?"

Like Hugh, Armand hadn't been expecting the question, and his face went completely blank before he said, "I wouldn't say we were *fighting*."

"Discussing heatedly, then."

"It was merely a question of what wine to serve with the meal tomorrow."

It was the same answer Vincent had received from Hugh. And it was a good one. Vincent just didn't think either man was exactly speaking the truth.

28

Day Two

Catrin

Vincent had managed to catch Catrin and Rhys as they were leaving the hall and told them what he'd discovered. Catrin had been keeping her husband company while he'd been keeping an eye on the constable. She'd stayed partly because she wanted to be with him, and partly not to give the impression that any of them had a mission. The questions they had to ask were not to be asked in public.

The sun had set, so most workers in the stables were done with their duties for the day. The work hours were long in the summer, filling every moment of daylight, but with the turn of the seasons, people started to think about warm fires and long nights. They had another few weeks until the equinox, but in the cool air of the early evening, even after a warm day—or maybe especially after—one could feel it coming.

Thus, Tim was to be found not in a stall with a horse, but sitting morosely with a carafe of ale on a bench against a west facing wall. Catrin hadn't known what he looked like, so she'd first had to inquire of the stablemaster, Donegal, who pointed her in the right direction with something of an exasperated air.

"I heard he gave you what you needed. What more do you want from him?"

"A man died today." Catrin was surprised by Donegal's attitude, especially to her, a lady, and it was conveyed in her voice. She didn't mean to antagonize the man, but she didn't understand his dismissiveness. Honestly, she'd felt dismissed more times since she'd come to Windsor than in all the months she'd been in Wales. Then again, England wasn't Wales, as she'd been continually reminded since her marriage to Robert at sixteen. She could be happy everyone was at least treating Rhys with respect.

Donegal was immediately contrite. As she continued to look at him, he stepped away from the horse whose hocks he'd been checking. "My apologies, madam. We've had a time of it these last weeks, as you can well imagine."

It was an opening, and one Catrin was completely willing to barge right through. "You're speaking not only of the death of Prince Alfonso, but also of George. I understand he hung himself in the storage room here."

At least he didn't deny it. Instead, he sighed. "Was it Hugh or Armand who told you?" Then he made a gesture. "Never mind. It doesn't matter. I knew that was going to come up eventually. Of course it would, what with that quaestor seeking to air everybody's dirty laundry."

Again, it was something of an attack, in this case on her husband. Catrin steeled herself not to react overtly and instead said, "What do you mean by that?"

Donegal gave a shake of his head. "Nothing. My apologies. I meant nothing by it."

Catrin refused to be put off. It was as if the stableman was wavering between the way he knew he was supposed to behave and a deep-seated anger. That was the best way she could describe it. "You did mean something by it. Do you have a grudge against Sir Rhys?"

Donegal snorted, reverting again to his less polite self. "I know his type."

"In what way?" She tried to keep her voice entirely non-committal.

"To a man like that, any answer will do. I tried—" He broke off again, looking away so she couldn't see his face.

"You tried what?" Catrin wasn't leaving until he told her what was going on or physically left. So far, he couldn't quite be rude enough to do that, and she thought he really did want to tell her what was on his mind, but was warring with himself about it.

"George was my friend, even if he was Hugh's uncle. He didn't kill himself. He would never do that. I tried to explain that to Hugh and Armand—" here he snorted again, as well he might, "—but they wouldn't listen. They were so afraid he wouldn't be buried in holy ground they covered up his murder."

This was *not* what she had been expecting to hear from Donegal. "*I* am listening."

Donegal had been standing in shadow, turned partly away from her, his hands on his hips. Now he glanced at her. And then he looked again a little longer. "You are, aren't you? Why? Why listen to me? I'm just a grieving friend. I'm not even his nephew."

"I like to think that I would have listened to you whether or not Bobby had died—or Alfonso, for that matter. Regardless, three deaths within a fortnight at Windsor Castle cannot be dismissed. Bobby was *murdered* outright. Stabbed. There's no mistaking that. We need to ask, then, if George's and Alfonso's deaths were unnatural too."

"Those deaths were all very different." Even though Catrin was listening now, Donegal was disbelieving. "A prince, an old man, a boy."

"The heir to the throne of England, his food taster, and, if others are to be believed, his friend," Catrin corrected.

"Oh." It was as if the sun had suddenly dawned in Donegal's mind. His obstreperousness was gone, replaced by an urgency and perhaps the real thought that Catrin was an ally. "I didn't see it that way."

"It's how we are seeing it," Catrin said. "Tell me about George."

Donegal swallowed once, and then acquiesced. Essentially, it was as Hugh and Armand had relayed to Vincent. George had been found in the storage room, hanging from the rafters by a rope. He was long buried, in holy ground as Armand and Hugh had said, since the three of them had agreed to keep silent about the way it had happened. George had been devastated by Alfonso's death. Donegal could agree with that, at least.

"Was there anything you saw at the scene that made you think it could be murder? Any detail you might remember? Was there anything in particular, besides that you knew him, that made you think it was murder?" She paused, thinking herself. "Was there a stool beneath him?"

Donegal rubbed his eyes. "Was that it? There was a stool, but it wasn't overturned, and it wasn't directly beneath him. I tried to tell Hugh that by covering up the way he died, he might be letting a murderer go free, but he wouldn't have it. I let it go, deciding Captain Thaddeus wasn't one to explore every option anyway, especially on my word."

"You two don't get along?"

"Not particularly. He's arrogant and sure that he's always right." Donegal instantly put out a hand. "Please don't tell him I said so."

With the promise that her husband would *not* be letting this go and would come to speak to him in the morning, Catrin moved on to tackle Tim. She no longer felt that her particular task was less important than any of the others. In fact, she was starting to feel an urgency deep in her belly that couldn't be denied. Three people *were* dead, one just today. If all three were murdered, why hadn't the killer simply left after Alfonso's death? Catrin would have thought it should have been his primary mission. And if not, what was keeping him at Windsor?

Tim was well into his cups by the time Catrin sat beside him, and for that reason she didn't stand on ceremony, but simply looked at him with sympathy in her eyes. "I'm so sorry for your loss."

He burst into tears.

Given Justin's description of his conversation with Tim, it was what she had expected to happen. He had claimed to be smarter than Bobby, but he was acting something like a simpleton—or a very smart young man riddled with guilt.

"It's time to tell me what Bobby was doing in the stables last night."

Tim shook his head back and forth multiple times, repeating, "I don't know; I don't know."

"But you know something." Catrin said this as a statement of fact. "What do you *think* he might have been doing?"

Tim looked up at her, a little blearily. "I told that other man the truth. He would have been meeting Darla."

"But he wasn't, was he? What else could he have been doing?" She paused, thinking. "Even more, who else could he have been meeting?"

Tim stared down at the cup in his hands. Catrin decided to wait, and she settled back against the wall. The silence dragged out, and she deliberately didn't fill it. She was tired anyway and closed her eyes. After a bit, once she realized she was in danger of falling asleep right there, she nudged him. "Tell me."

He startled, and then looked at her as if he'd forgotten she was there. This was the problem with trying to question someone so late in the day. Sometimes drink made a man talkative, but it could easily reach a point where he was too far gone to be coherent.

It was worth trying again, however. "You thought Bobby had been acting strangely recently, right?"

Tim blinked. "How did you know that?"

"So he had been." She nodded, feeling a momentary triumph. It had been a trick to say that, but people were dying, and she was willing to try a few tricks if it got them some answers. "Did you ask him about it?"

"He didn't want to talk to me, but I kept asking, because he would sit in the hall with this look on his face, like he was watching everyone all at the same time. He also sat with his back to the wall like a soldier. At first I thought he was excited, but then in the last few days he seemed almost afraid."

"Do you think he was afraid for his life?"

Tim gazed into Catrin's eyes for a moment, and then tears began to fall again. "I should have pressed him harder. I should have found out what was going on. And now he's dead!" The sobs began in earnest.

Catrin put her arms around him, and he wept into her shoulder. Men needed to cry too sometimes. Welshmen knew that, but these Saxons and Normans seemed to think they had to swallow all emotion down—which was also why they tried to drown their grief in ale.

"Did he mention anything, or anyone, that you can think of that could be useful in finding his killer?"

Tim's sobs lessened. His face was still in her shoulder, but he was breathing instead of crying. Then he pushed back, and a little lightness came into his voice for the first time. "He did say one thing, now that I consider it. It was about the way some of the guards would do favors if you paid them."

Catrin decided she would again behave as if she knew more than she did. "You know about that?"

Tim made a dismissive motion. "Everyone knows about that."

"What kind of favors?" Catrin didn't want to digress too much from the main point, but this was suddenly important too.

"It wouldn't be for people like me, you understand, but for the nobles who visit the castle. If a man wants a woman who isn't his wife, or a game of chance, they can arrange that."

"Does the constable know?"

Tim scoffed. "Of course he knows! It's his job to keep the guests happy. Otherwise he turns a blind eye so he doesn't have to arrange these things himself. But he takes his cut."

Catrin was working to breathe easily. "I understand." Or at least she thought she might once she brought it to Rhys. "What did Bobby think was different about it this time?"

"He'd seen one of the guards in the tavern with someone, a Frenchman he didn't like named Jehan. I didn't understand it because we all know Jehan. He's a fine fellow."

"Bobby told you all this? I thought you said you had no idea what he was doing in the storage room?"

"I don't. This was months ago, before Prince Alfonso was ill. It was just something he said when one of the guards came into the hall. Even I could see him pass something to one of the others. It looked like coins. Bobby said, *I wonder if he's been at the tavern with Jehan. I don't think that Frenchie is what he says he is. I don't like seeing Frenchies in Windsor.* Jehan's been in Windsor for years, like half the employees at the castle. That new wine dispenser Gilbert is from France. At the time, I didn't see what all the fuss was about."

"What does Jehan look like?" Catrin didn't have the sketch with her, but her heart had started to race at a possible connection. Finally.

"Big beard, thin." Tim frowned. "He's lost a lot of weight recently, now that I think about it." Then he shrugged. "I didn't understand what Bobby was talking about. I still don't! But he didn't want to explain, and he didn't ever mention it again."

29

Day Two
Justin

Earlier in the day, Tim had been easy to find. Tracking down someone who might once have owned the juggling bean bag was another task entirely, one to which Justin didn't think himself particularly suited. He understood the notion of divide and conquer, having read the works of the ancients in the original languages (more at his mother's urging than his father's, who thought reading important enough only to the point that a man wasn't entirely dependent upon his clerks and scribes).

The truth was, Justin had felt a rush of excitement when he'd elicited the location of the box from Tim, and even more when they'd opened it and understood that its contents might be important. But he was beginning to discover that there was a certain degree of tedium involved in investigating. His mother was questioning Tim again. Vincent was off to ask questions in the cellar, and here was Justin, trying to determine who might know how to juggle but had lost a beanbag. The one Bobby had kept was an unfamiliar weight in his purse, which hung from his belt.

It seemed perfectly obvious that this job would have been better left to Miles, who might already *know* who juggled.

Then again, Miles had been employed at Windsor for less than a day, so allowances had to be made. Not that his mother or Sir Rhys needed any concession from him. Their single day had brought them more information than anyone in the castle had put together in all the days since Alfonso's death. It was in Justin's mind that one more day might do it. He could be grateful that he'd arrived in time to be a part of it.

If only Justin could manage to figure out how to find a juggler.

He could ask, of course, and proceeded to do so, bending down to a likely looking fellow and posing a simple question to his table. "Do any of you juggle?"

At first the man frowned in thought, as if translating Justin's words to make sense of them, which perhaps he was. Then he gestured down the table to a young, straw-haired man at the end. "Billy does."

Billy looked up at the sound of his name. "Billy does what?"

"Juggle."

Billy wrinkled his nose. "Nah. Not like Francis."

The subsequent banter around the table revealed at least a dozen men in the hall who were decent enough jugglers to argue about who was better. The conversation at first was a bit overwhelming, and then Justin hit upon an idea that was probably on the far end of what Rhys might have had in mind when he gave Justin this task, but he thought he might be forgiven if it worked. Besides, his parents had finally left the hall. They'd sat with him for quite some time, but then when he'd moved away (casually, so as not to cause anyone to remark upon it), they'd departed together.

The very thought pulled him up short. *His parents*. He grunted to himself. He supposed he was growing used to having Rhys for a father after all.

Justin navigated over to the bard, who was at the moment taking a break. During his performance, he had spoken in both perfect French and English, alternatingly, for the entertainment of the whole of his audience in the hall. But Justin had an idea he'd seen this man before.

So, he slid onto the bench beside him and spoke in Welsh. "*Combrogi*, how is it you are so far from home? You were introduced as *David*, but I remember you as Dai ap Goronwy."

Combrogi was Welsh for *countryman*. In a single word, Justin had claimed his own Welsh heritage, which he didn't do in public very often these days. And clearly Dai didn't either. But they were in a corner of the dais, some paces from anyone who might overhear. He thought they were safe.

The man turned to look at him in a sudden movement, his eyes widening and answered in French, "It's David, my lord. My name is David."

Justin wasn't to be put off, but he acquiesced by not reverting again to Welsh. "Nobody knows your origins?"

"No, my lord, and I would prefer that nobody did."

Justin put out his hand soothingly. "I didn't mean to startle you, and I have a favor to ask. I will not betray you whether or not you perform it." He pulled out the beanbag. "I need to discover to whom this belongs. Can we find out who in this hall right now knows how to juggle?"

Dai/David immediately brightened. "A contest, perhaps?"

"That could be fun, right, to keep the merriment going?"

The constable had gone, which was why Justin's parents had left, but Captain Thaddeus had just risen from the dais. While Justin slipped back into the crowd, the bard went over to him with his request. Justin knew it was going to be all right when Thaddeus nodded immediately and clapped Dai on the shoulder. Though Justin couldn't hear well in the noisy hall, Thaddeus spoke loud enough that his voice carried. "Good idea. Well done for thinking of it. Just what we need."

Dai immediately began to quiet the crowd, which had grown over the course of the evening as everyone finished their duties for the day and the last of the workers had come inside. Then, in a commanding voice, as suited to the bard he was, he announced the beginning of the juggling contest.

What followed was a far grander event than Justin had initially envisioned, with sixteen men putting themselves forward to participate. Justin had deliberately not inserted himself into the proceedings in any way, instead moving around the margins of the room, the better to keep an eye on the contestants. But then, Dai announced that he was appointing Justin as judge, since both the garrison captain and the constable had left. Somehow, Justin was the highest-ranking nobleman left in the room.

He hadn't wanted to call that much attention to himself, but it turned out to be a convenient position from which to watch the proceedings, which were at times heated, fast and furious, with several of the men having jongleur level abilities.

Towards the end, a red-haired man arrived late and was pushed forward to participate. "Hugh has to join in! He's been hiding in his cellar too long."

With that, Justin realized this was Hugh the cellarer, who may have been speaking most recently to Vincent.

Other men protested that he should have come sooner if he wanted to join in, and were clearly relieved when the man himself put up both hands and said, "I don't have my bags anymore. Continue as you were."

Justin hadn't been introduced to Hugh yet, but he was a nobleman and the judge. He could speak to anyone he wanted, so he sidled close enough to have a conversation. "Perhaps we could find you some replacement bags. You didn't have to bow out."

"I don't care to participate." Despite his words, Hugh's eyes were intent on the contestants.

"Where did your bags go?"

"I don't know, my lord. If I did, they wouldn't be missing." His words were almost impertinent, and they would have been if not for the *my lord*. It was in keeping with Miles's description of the man.

"Is this one of them?" Justin pulled the beanbag from his purse.

At first, Hugh didn't even look, so focused was he on the contest. But then, as Justin nudged him, he glanced down.

And broke for the door.

Justin went after him.

30

Day Two

Rhys

It wasn't exactly a surprise to find that an investigation progressed faster when he had more people to work on it. It was still a relief to discover that divvying up the duties, and having different people revisit suspects and informants with new and better questions—and sometimes the same questions!—was producing better answers. In the future, he should consider how to surround himself with capable investigators when he didn't have Miles, Justin, and, of all people, Vincent helping him. Rhys assumed, perhaps incorrectly, that he would never be without Catrin again.

Please God he would always have Catrin.

For now, he reminded himself that fears of what might come were just that, *fears*, and he couldn't base his current actions on as-yet-unrealized future events. It certainly would do no good to worry about them.

For now, he had upwards of three murders to address, and that meant attempting to question Constable Pickford yet again. These events had happened on his watch. He needed to have something to say about them.

To that end, Rhys ran the constable to earth in his quarters. Immediately, Sir Geoffrey became exactly as arrogant and officious as he'd been the last time Rhys had talked to him, claiming it never occurred to him that George's death, Alfonso's, and Bobby's were related.

Listening to him, Rhys quietly seethed. He could not believe the constable hadn't known *something* was amiss in his castle. He had to know, didn't he? But Rhys himself didn't know how to get anything else out of him. He replied to every question with calm denial, platitudes, and a serene expression that Rhys was seriously interested in wiping off his face with his fist.

So it was with some interest—and something of a relief—for Rhys to walk out of the gatehouse where the constable had his quarters and see Justin dashing across the lower bailey after a tall man with reddish hair and beard who appeared to want to leave the castle in a hurry.

Spying Rhys, Justin pointed. "Stop him, Father!"

Rhys didn't have to take more than a few steps to place himself in the man's path. Then he spread his arms wide and crouched a little, waiting for the runner to come to him. He was taller than Rhys—taller than most everyone, but skinny—and Rhys didn't think it would take much to bring him down.

At the last moment, the man did try to break around Rhys, but Rhys stabbed out a hand, grasped his elbow, and spun him around so he ended up on his knees. The man was lucky Rhys hadn't put him ignominiously on his rear.

Rhys didn't often draw his sword, but now he did so and pointed it. "Stay down."

The man was bent forward, breathing hard, his hands on the ground. By now, they had drawn the attention of the guards at the gatehouse, and even Captain Thaddeus strode from the guard-room. "What's going on here? Why is Hugh on his knees? Why is your sword out, Sir Rhys? What's he done?"

Justin came huffing up. "This is Hugh the cellarer for the upper bailey. I tried to talk to him about the beanbag, but he ran."

Rhys turned to Thaddeus. "Do you have a place where we can question him?"

"Follow me." Thaddeus didn't ask for more of an explanation, simply turned on his heel and led the way back into the guardroom.

"I didn't do anything!" Hugh didn't like the way Justin took his elbow, and he tried to pull away. But there was no way out for him, not while they were inside the castle.

"Then why run?" Rhys took him by the other elbow.

Hugh was still protesting when they set him on a stool in the guardroom, now cleared of members of the garrison. It was a guardroom like any other, in this case built into the curved stone wall of the gatehouse tower. It had a wooden floor, a table and benches on which the guards could sit, supplied with a flagon of water and cups. No guard on duty would be allowed ale until his shift was over.

There was no fireplace, but in the winter a brazier would be lit in the bailey outside so the guards—and any other passersby—could warm their hands.

Captain Thaddeus had the look of a man who wasn't leaving, and he placed himself with his back to the closed door.

Rhys took a moment to confer with Justin, but spoke in Welsh, so as not to share with either Thaddeus or Hugh. "What exactly is this about?"

"Since I was looking for a juggler missing his juggling bags, I got the bard to organize a contest in the hall. Hugh is apparently a very good juggler, but he declined to participate, saying he no longer had his bags. I showed him the one we found in Bobby's box, and he ran. I gave chase, and here we are."

Pulling up a stool of his own so they were sitting close, on the same side of the table, Rhys studied the man's downturned head. Defiance had turned to desolation.

"Why did you run?"

Hugh looked up, ready with his protest. "Running isn't a crime! I didn't do anything wrong!"

That, in and of itself, had to be a lie, but it rolled off his tongue as if it were the truth.

"It made you look guilty, which is how we ended up in this room. Again, why did you run?"

By this point, given that Hugh had been asked that question three times and refused to answer, Rhys figured he was working on his story and wouldn't answer until he'd perfected it. But what came blurting out of his mouth sounded credible. "I shouldn't have. I know that now. But I was afraid. I know he's your son and is investigating Bobby's death. As is Sir Vincent, to whom I just spoke."

"That doesn't explain why a beanbag made you run."

"I recognized it as mine, and if it had something to do with the investigation, I was afraid you would accuse me of murdering Bobby when I've done nothing wrong."

"Why didn't you simply say the beanbag was yours and thank him for finding it?"

"It was as if he was pointing a finger directly at me and saying, *murderer!* I didn't want to have anything to do with it."

"Did you?" The denials had come with every breath, which made it important to ask again.

"No!" The word was ejected from Hugh's mouth. Then he moderated his tone. "No, no, I didn't."

Rhys opened his mouth to speak again but Thaddeus stepped in with a threat: "If you are protecting someone, they will know by now that we tackled you in the bailey. They will assume you are talking to us and that you will betray them. If you tell us the truth, we can protect you. If you give us nothing, we'll let you walk out the door and let your co-conspirators do with you as they wish."

Threats, especially at this stage in an interrogation, weren't Rhys's style, but he could appreciate why Thaddeus had said what he had, and for now didn't contradict him, especially because

Hugh was staring up at the garrison captain with wide, fearful eyes. "I didn't do anything! There's nothing more I can tell you."

"But you know something," Justin said softly, speaking for the first time since he'd explained things to Rhys. "You fear you know who killed Alfonso."

"No! No, I don't! I don't know anything about *that*!" Hugh gaped at the three of them. "Alfonso died of an illness. We all know that if you are here about him, you are here for no reason."

Rhys frowned. He'd been assuming that the beanbag was in the box because of the possibility of castor bean poisoning, and that Bobby had either murdered Alfonso outright or kept the beanbag because he knew who did. "Then what? *Why did the beanbag send you running?*"

"I don't know. It was instinct." Hugh collapsed, almost folding in on himself.

Rhys leaned forward too, waiting for more of an answer. But again, it didn't come. Deciding he needed to change things up, he pulled out Bobby's sketch, which he hadn't yet shown to anyone other than his fellow investigators, thinking to hold it in reserve for a situation such as this. He didn't want the news he had it to get back to the man it depicted and encourage him to run before they knew who he was.

Hugh gazed at the image, his mouth slightly open, and then he shook his head vehemently. "I've never seen that man before in my life."

He was either loyal enough, or afraid enough, of whoever this was to lie comprehensively. Rhys folded up the sketch and put it away. He'd learned over the years that some culprits needed time to come to terms with their confession. They'd been in the room for less than a quarter of an hour. They had time.

Time for some guesswork too. "We know about the smuggling. What role did the beanbag play in it? Did you use beanbags to send messages to one another?"

Hugh blinked and then looked down at his feet. "I don't know what you're talking about."

That had been a guess, but Rhys couldn't have been out in the world, doing what he'd been doing, for as long as he had and not heard of smugglers using different colored scarves, marks on a wall, even bedsheets hung in the window, to signal to their partners when it was safe to conduct their activities. In the Holy land, Saracen spies had used different colored pebbles set in key locations, like a windowsill, to facilitate their activities.

"Did you sell people too?" Justin asked.

Hugh didn't look up and spoke again to the floor. "Of course not. This is all a mistake."

Rhys eyed Hugh's downturned head. Hugh had shrunk significantly in size since he'd been arrested, and Justin's query had hunched his shoulders more, identifying what might be a key element of the illicit trade—if there was an illicit trade—on remarkably few clues. Slavery had been banned by the Church centuries ago, but young children were still sold by desperate parents, or sometimes abducted, many to become prostitutes on the streets of London.

"From whom do you take orders?" Rhys tried again. "Who are you working with? Is it one of the guards?" He was just throwing out ideas now, hoping to get a response. He thought about naming the three guardsmen Vincent had identified, but again, it was early yet, and he wasn't ready to reveal everything they'd learned, especially to a suspect.

Thaddeus, however, appeared to have had enough. He put both palms flat on the table, looming over Hugh. "Give us a name!"

But Hugh remained locked in his silence.

31

Day Two

Miles

At the conclusion of his conversation with the others, Miles had headed off on his own, towards the three guards Vincent had thought might have something to say about what was going on at Windsor. He hadn't navigated directly towards them, thinking instead to circle about the margins of the room so as to come at them from a different direction.

The three men in question were named Etienne, Francis, and Gregory. Catrin had instantly dubbed them *E, F, G,* and Miles found the monikers sticking in his head too. Etienne was the tallest with close cropped brown hair. Francis had a bushy brown beard and was of medium height. And Gregory was short and squat, though not so much from fat as strongly muscled. He was also bald.

Several of Miles's fellow workers had encouraged him to join them as he passed by, which he'd done, so he'd spent quite a long while observing the three men before he approached their table. The amusing festivities instigated by Justin had facilitated the ease of his progress. Because of them, everyone in the hall was in motion at one time or another, whether standing to get a better view, moving closer or farther from the contestants, depending on their willingness to be jostled, or simply heading out briefly to the latrine. That was because the drinking was continuing too. The ale maker would have his work cut out for him in the morning. By the time Hugh ran out of the hall, Miles had finally achieved a position at the guardsmen's table.

He'd even been invited to sit, after a fashion. As he approached, in the midst of the juggling contest, he made a motion to a spot on the end. "Do you mind? It's somewhat crowded everywhere else."

Etienne lifted his chin and dropped it. It wasn't a *no*, so Miles sat. They were guards, and he was a wine dispenser. Likely, they thought his job beneath them, or at least far less important or entertaining than theirs.

Gregory, however, pushed a cup down the table in Miles's direction, along with a carafe of ale. "Welcome to Windsor."

"Thank you." Miles poured himself a full cup. They weren't a talkative bunch, that was for certain. He didn't want to say the wrong thing, but he decided he could begin as one always began forming acquaintances, with casual questions. He started with Gregory. "This has been quite a first day. Is it always like this at Windsor?"

"Like what?" Etienne answered for Gregory without looking at Miles. The interference was an obvious attempt to stop Gregory from talking to him.

Miles wasn't going to be put off so easily. Ignoring the message, he answered the question as if it had really been one. "Kitchen boys murdered." He gestured to the crowd before them. "Juggling contests in the hall."

"No." By now, it was more than clear that Etienne was the leader amongst them. After Gregory had given Miles ale, both he and Francis had kept glancing at Etienne, each with an expression that they wanted to speak. At Etienne's repressive look, they had not done so.

And then Hugh ran for the door.

Until that moment, getting on the good side of Etienne had been Miles's sole goal for the evening. In fact, up until then, Miles had been very pleased with himself for getting this far. But once Hugh, and then Justin, disappeared through the door, it was as if a cold north wind had blown across their table. Etienne's grip around his cup was so tight his fingers were turning white.

It wasn't just Etienne either. By the demeanor of all three guards, something momentous had just happened. Anyone could see it. But although many heads turned to watch the two men go, the jugglers hadn't stopped, so within a few heartbeats, the audience was back to clapping and cheering.

Miles sorted through all the possible things he could say and realized that the situation here might not be salvageable. Hugh's action had just sped up the investigation ten-fold.

Even so, Miles was never one to avoid risk, so he pointed towards the door through which Justin had just disappeared. "You don't look too happy about that. Is the cellarer a friend of yours?"

"No friend of mine." Etienne took a sip of his ale, having managed to turn his face to marble.

Neither Francis nor Gregory was as good at controlling his expression. Gregory, in particular, glanced at Etienne in astonishment, before bending his head and focusing on the cup in front of him.

Miles shrugged. "It just didn't look good."

Etienne rose to his feet and strode away. It was enough of a signal to his friends that they followed, with no word to Miles, although he did get an apologetic glance from Gregory. A moment later, all three had disappeared through a side door that would take them down the exterior walkway to the kitchen.

Miles didn't try to follow. Nor did he see any point in waiting around in the hall. His approach hadn't gone the way he wanted, but he saw now that it was always going to be hard to ingratiate himself with the three of them to discover their secrets directly. That wasn't Justin's fault, since whatever he'd done to cause Hugh to run had been as much a surprise to him as to Miles. It was up to Reese now to determine how to proceed next, with a range of options from doing nothing to taking physical action against them. In Miles's judgment, Gregory would respond best to sweet talking, Francis to a fist to the face, and Etienne was never going to say anything, no matter what duress he experienced.

Which was how Miles ended up loitering outside the guardroom with Catrin, who related in a few succinct sentences how everybody else's evening had gone. Miles was pleased to have come close in remembering Jehan's name. When Vincent appeared a moment later, Miles convinced him to get Rhys to come out of the guardroom and confer with them.

Once everyone was up to date on the proceedings, Miles told them his idea.

"I would think it would be easier just to arrest those guards." Justin was pacing back and forth in his agitation over the events of the evening. They had retired to a storage room on the other side of the gatehouse where they wouldn't be disturbed or overheard.

"When you left the hall in pursuit of Hugh, Justin, I had no doubt that Hugh would be caught, but I was concerned that you might not wrest out of him the information we needed," Miles said. "Unfortunately, I was right. Yes, we could arrest the three guards. One of them at least might respond to being roughed up, but given that we have Hugh, they will be prepared now for interrogation. This conspiracy, whatever it really is about, is more extensive than just those three and Hugh."

"Jehan," Catrin said.

"Likely," Rhys said. "But right now, the only word against him comes from a grieving stable boy. Miles is right that arresting these men isn't enough. Without someone talking, our *proof* consists of a few pieces of paper, a picture of a man who may or may not be Jehan, and a beanbag."

"Hardly conclusive," Vincent said dryly.

Miles nodded. "Which is why you have to throw both him and me into the dungeon together. Probably you should rough me up a bit first before you do it."

Though Catrin gasped, Rhys didn't even look surprised at Miles's request. "And then what?"

"And then you allow me to break us out of prison."

32

Day Two
Vincent

Vincent punched Miles in the stomach. "You *murdered* my brother!"

Vincent had a brother, but that he was alive and well in Angoulême was entirely beside the point. In preparation for his role, he'd worked himself up to the extent that he almost believed what he was accusing Miles of doing.

Captain Thaddeus and Justin were holding Miles loosely enough that he was able to double over Vincent's fist, softening the blow, which truthfully had struck harder than Vincent had intended. He wanted to make this look authentic for Hugh, and his racing heart made it harder to pull his punches. At the same time, Vincent didn't want to hurt Miles badly enough that it interfered with the rest of their plan. Nor genuinely injure him, for that matter.

In response to the blow, Miles swore loudly and long in French.

Vincent called him a bastard and a murderer and punched him again.

As Vincent had been hitting Miles, Hugh and his two guards, none of whom were aware of the scheme, had been progressing from one gatehouse tower to the other. Now, they stopped cold in the middle of the arch, allowing Hugh to gape at the scene.

Miles glared back at him. "What are you looking at?"

Hugh's expression closed up. "Nothing."

At that point, Rhys wrapped his arm around Vincent's shoulders and made a great show of hauling him off Miles. "We have him in custody. He will feel the king's justice, never fear."

Vincent dramatically shook off Rhys's arm before pointing a forefinger at Miles. "May you burn in hell forever for what you've done!"

Perhaps that was spreading the butter on a little thick, but they needed Hugh to trust Miles quickly, and the best way to do that was to unite them against the authority Rhys represented. From the look on Hugh's face, it was working.

"Take him to the tower." Rhys tugged on Vincent's arm again, conveying fear that he would renew his attack on Miles. "Put the two prisoners together. They deserve each other."

Vincent sneered. "We can hang them together in the morning."

Except in a time of war, such quick justice would be rash and unprecedented. Hugh wouldn't necessarily know that. Hopefully, he was so scared by now he was having difficulty thinking straight.

The problem with Miles's plan was that, as plans went, it was a good one. It made sense. But it was reckless, which, truth be told, was to be expected from Miles. He was the one who had found himself a job in the castle in the first place. The key now was to mitigate certain obvious deficiencies. The first of those, which they had already addressed, was the number of people they had at their disposal. Even with Rhys, Justin, Catrin, and Vincent himself, they needed more bodies than just the four of them because they had too many places to be and couldn't be in all of them at the same time.

For starters, they'd had to include Captain Thaddeus and Constable Pickford in the plan. They couldn't lock up Hugh and Miles together and allow them to escape without telling the authorities at the castle what they were doing. Edmund's men had been recruited too, and after them, Prince Edmund himself (God forbid), because he refused to be left out.

With their first task done, that of publicly arresting Miles just as Thaddeus was moving Hugh from the guardroom, they now took the prisoners to their improvised prison. Like the kitchen, the church, and the rest of the buildings in the castle, the builders hadn't been able to dig deeply into the ground to create what the French called an *oubliette* or other such ominous cell—except in one tower.

Although originally built in wood, the Clewer Tower had been extensively remodeled after the French invasion earlier in the century, extending the defenses into the old protective ditch and creating a basement with a dirt floor. In the past, it had occasionally been used to house prisoners, but most of the time—and for the last decade—it had been merely another storage area. After inspection, Rhys had deemed it perfect for their purposes, not only because of its location near the entrance to the sally port out of the castle (accessible through a trap door), but because of the vent in the ceiling through which the guards above were able to monitor prisoners without having to descend the stairs.

The arrangement was genius, really, and not one Vincent had ever encountered before. Even better, because the room had been used for storage for many years, none of the members of the garrison knew about the vent—only Captain Thaddeus. If either prisoner had been a nobleman, or known to be (in Miles's case), they would have had to hold him in an upper story of a tower. Escape would have been difficult from there too, but the ominous nature of this particular room would put the fear of king and country into Hugh.

As Justin and Thaddeus hauled Miles towards the Clewer Tower, following after Hugh and his guards, Miles kept up the ferocity of his resistance, cursing the whole way. Some of his curses were so inventive, Vincent struggled to hold back a smile. Fortunately, Hugh was ahead of them, so he couldn't see anyone's face.

They brought the prisoners first through the guardroom, which when they escaped would be conveniently empty and contain a complete change of clothing and weapons for both. That their escape would be so easy was absurd on the face of it, but they were working from the premise that Hugh would be too fearful and overwhelmed to notice—and too grateful in the aftermath to bring up objections.

Then they dragged the prisoners (Miles kicking and screaming) down the stairs to the prison they'd prepared for them, now empty of anything that could be used to escape. They hadn't even placed pallets on the dirt floor. The room otherwise had stone walls and arrow slits for windows, which overlooked the town beyond. At this hour of the night, they let in almost no light. It would have been as forbidding a place to keep prisoners as Vincent had ever seen if he hadn't spent time in the Holy Land. If this were a Saracen cell—or a crusader one, for that matter—Miles and Hugh would have been chained to the wall.

Vincent trailed after Miles, insulting him at regular intervals loud enough for Hugh to hear, and then made sure that he was the one to gleefully slam closed the door, once they'd been tossed into the room.

Rhys, Justin, and Vincent retired to the guard room above, where Catrin had been hard at work arranging things for the arrival of their prisoners some hours from now. As they entered, she looked at Rhys and expressed a reservation that had also been lurking in the back of Vincent's mind: "I'm concerned about what happens *after* they escape. We don't even know if Hugh has somewhere to escape *to*. This could all be for nothing."

To his wife, Rhys was reassuring, though earlier Vincent had seen concern in Rhys's eyes too. "If Miles doesn't attack me, then we know he is aborting the mission. It really is up to him how far he is willing to go. It's his plan."

"Which we need to make a bit more our own," Vincent said. "Miles is wrong about who should enter the cell to be attacked. It should be me, not you."

Rhys frowned. "Why is that?"

"One nobleman is not the same as another. Yes, you are the king's quaestor, but, if you don't mind me saying, your place in Windsor's hierarchy is not as clear as mine. I share family with William de Valence. Given that, I am, in a sense, the king's family too. King Edward might not see it so clearly, but Hugh knows it the way every Englishman knows it."

"You mean I'm Welsh, so I don't count in the same way."

Vincent had tried to say that without saying it, but Rhys was well used to the subtleties of court life and saw through his hair-splitting. "Rhys—"

But Rhys made an impatient gesture. "You are right, of course." Then he laughed, and Vincent realized with some shock that he was amused—and not even cynically. "I *am* Welsh, and I don't count. Which really is quite excellent if you think about it, because then I am underestimated. Also, I can see that if Miles kills me, the response by the constable and captain here at Windsor won't be quite as immediate and comprehensive as if he kills you."

Vincent was hugely relieved to hear Rhys being so sensible. "Thus, Hugh's fear of being caught will be that much greater, as well his desire to get to safety."

"It could mean he decides Miles is too much of a liability," Catrin said. "He could insist they go their separate ways."

"We will follow Hugh, regardless," Rhys said. "I almost wish he would insist on separating because I'm worried about the danger we are putting Miles in."

"He is putting himself in danger," Vincent pointed out. "This is his idea."

Rhys made a motion with his head. "I just hope that if Hugh does decide Miles is a liability, he does as Catrin suggested. The other option might be to kill him."

33

Day Two

Miles

"We need to escape, and we need to do it sooner rather than later." Miles glanced down at Hugh, who'd gone from being a mature, confident cellarer with coin in his pocket to a man destined for the noose (or so he thought). He was not managing the transition well. Ever since they'd been tossed into this hole, he'd been huddled on the dirt floor with his arms wrapped around his knees. At times he appeared to be rocking back and forth.

Miles had been exaggerating the differences between their reactions by pacing in front of the door and occasionally shouting through the little window placed at head height. Beyond was the stone stairway that would take them to freedom. Thank goodness they weren't real prisoners, or likely the guards would have taken the torch stuck in its sconce at the top of the stairway, plunging them into total darkness.

It was time to get Hugh talking. "Why are you here?"

"I didn't do anything." The fool was continuing the story from before.

"I didn't either. That's why I'm going to be hanged in the morning." Miles rolled his eyes. "I intend to be long gone before then."

Hugh sniffed. "I don't see how that's possible."

Miles crouched in front of him. "Before I make a plan, I need to know how bad it is."

He feared Hugh was going to maintain his silence. A smart man would guess that Miles had been placed in the dungeon specifically to elicit this information, especially since Miles had been hired only that day. But Hugh wasn't terribly smart, for all that he had held a leadership role in the cellar. Likely he'd risen to the top of his potential there.

Miles let the silence drag out for a time longer. Sometimes, if one just waited, the answers came.

And at long last, they did. "There's been some smuggling at Windsor."

The cheering in the room above was completely silent, but Miles thought he could hear it anyway, or, at the very least, feel the air move as Reese raised his arms above his head in triumph.

"What kind of smuggling?" Miles prompted immediately.

"All kinds."

When he didn't add to his comment, Miles opted for another tack. "What was the beanbag for? I heard them talking about it earlier."

Another sigh. "If we dropped a red beanbag, it meant we had another supply to be picked up. A blue one came from the men on the river, to say they had goods to pass through to us."

"What kinds of goods?" Miles was relentless. If Hugh were to be believed, this smuggling had been going on right under everyone's nose.

"Anything. Wine, food, sewing supplies. Horses a few times, though that was risky."

Miles waited a few heartbeats, deliberating. "Girls?"

Hugh ducked his head. "Not often."

Or rather, *all the time.*

"How many are involved?"

This time, Hugh didn't hesitate to sell out his fellow villains, though of course he didn't realize he was selling them out. "A few of the guards, me, several stablemen who stay with the horses in the pasture, since they're closer to the Eton dock. The barn there has a secret cellar too, in case anyone comes looking at the warehouse. Shipments don't even enter the castle."

"Butler James?" Miles held his breath.

"No." Hugh gave a shake of his head to emphasize the denial.

Miles had to believe him for now. "What about Constable Pickford?"

"No! No, of course not. He is an honest man."

Miles reserved the right to an alternate opinion, especially since Tim had told them about the extra entertainment provided by certain guards, of which Pickford took a cut. Some of the girls being smuggled might have been included in that entertainment. But Hugh's response in this instance appeared genuine too.

And although Hugh hadn't fully elucidated the scope of the endeavor, the details he had given Miles were damning enough. It wasn't that goods couldn't be imported at any time from France or other countries, but they were supposed to be duly registered at the docks on the Thames and, more importantly, taxed by the royal treasury. Truthfully, much of the paperwork should have been happening in London, so someone wasn't doing their duty there either. While it seemed that straight up thievery from the castle's supplies wasn't the issue, there was something definitely rotten in the center of Windsor Castle. The king was not going to be pleased.

Then again, it was better than learning that someone had murdered his son. Miles hadn't even asked Hugh about that yet. He decided that he'd made Hugh anxious enough with his sharp questioning that the matter of Alfonso's death could wait a little longer. It was Bobby they needed to think of now.

Miles settled himself against the opposite wall, his legs stretched out in front of him. Tipping back his head, he closed his eyes. "You might want to get some sleep. I'll wake you in an hour and then we'll go."

"How?" Hugh's voice came out somewhat higher than normal.

"I am thinking on a plan."

Hugh didn't look like that made him feel any better, but he offered up, "My friends can help us if we can get to the tunnel."

Miles had to work to keep the smile off his face. He had been planning to mention the tunnel if Hugh hadn't, pretending he'd learned of it even in the short time he'd been at Windsor. Much better to have Hugh do it.

"What tunnel?"

Hugh sat up straighter, excited now. "It's a way out of the castle located right in this very tower!"

"Where does it come out?"

"In the basement of The King's Arms. One can't have men appearing willy nilly out of the grass." Hugh was rubbing his hands now.

"Isn't it guarded?"

"Of course, but everyone knows me—" He instantly deflated. "They'll know we are supposed to be imprisoned." This was perhaps the first moment Hugh realized his life as he knew it was over. He'd had a good position at Windsor Castle, which he'd thrown away for a few extra pennies in his purse.

"Don't you have friends among them? I thought you just said you did."

"None who are posted there. We didn't use the tunnel to smuggle anything. It's too public and risky."

Miles made a motion with his hand. "How many men guard it at any one time?"

"Most of the time there's just two."

"Leave them to me. What about after that? I don't know Windsor well. Is there some place we could lay low for a while, until the search for us dies down?"

"Well ..." Hugh dragged out the word, all of a sudden reluctant.

"Would we be safe there?" Miles decided he could push him a little.

"I think so. Jehan will know what to do." There was a little more firmness in Hugh's voice.

"Who is Jehan?" Reese would be punching the air again.

Hugh waved a hand. "Just a friend."

"I'd like to meet this friend."

"We have to get out of here first." Hugh glared at the door as footsteps could be heard outside it.

Miles was on his feet in an instant. Upstairs, Reese had obviously decided that the time for escape was now. "Follow my lead."

"What do I do?" Hugh scrambled upright too.

"Stay exactly where you are."

Hugh was directly opposite the door, so he could be seen through the little window. This would have been more meaningful if the person at the door really was concerned about his own safety and their status as prisoners.

"You're going to get us killed!" Hugh blurted out the words in a harsh whisper.

"Didn't you hear what Lord Vincent said? We are for the noose in the morning. We are surely dead if we stay."

That quieted Hugh immediately. "I'll do as you say. What about this guard?"

"He won't be a problem." Miles needed to keep up the charade that he didn't want to be seen, so he put his ear to the edge of the door, listening hard. It was Vincent's voice on the other side, and he was speaking loudly enough that it would have been hard not to hear him.

"I'll take care of them. Get yourself a drink in the hall."

Footsteps reverberated on the floor, indicating the guard was doing as Vincent bid him. He would know that he wasn't allowed ale in the guardroom itself. Men such as these members of the garrison had learned to obey or they didn't retain their positions for long, not with King Edward needing men to fight in his wars.

Miles set himself to one side of the door. The plan had been for Reese to come and say the exact same thing. That it was Vincent didn't change anything as far as Miles knew. Hugh was wringing his hands, still standing where Miles had put him. His fear was so genuine, Miles had a moment where he thought they really were escaping.

Then the bar came off the door, and it opened. Vincent took one step into the room, and Miles attacked, slamming his shoulder into the oaken door and trapping Vincent between the door and the frame. As Vincent struggled, Miles grabbed the front of his tunic and swung him into the room—and got a good whack to the face for his troubles.

Miles retaliated, causing Vincent to stagger backwards, hit the wall, and slump to the floor as if stunned. Miles pulled Vincent's own dagger from the sheath at his waist and stabbed him with it. The amount of blood was startling as it sprayed the wall and started soaking into the dirt floor.

"What did you do! You didn't have to kill him!" Hugh had allowed Miles to do all the work, having not moved from where Miles had told him to stand. Of course, everything had happened so quickly that Hugh hadn't had time to do more than gasp. But now he pulled on Miles's shoulder. "We have to go!"

Miles was back on his feet in an instant, still with the dagger in his hand. Hugh reared back, and Miles realized he must look a sight, with his face red from exertion and from Vincent's blow and blood on his clothing.

"You're right. We have to get out of here. We don't have much time."

Racing up the stairs, they found the guardroom empty, as promised, though loud voices came from somewhere beyond its walls. Miles recognized Catrin's voice, talking rapidly in a mix of Welsh, English, and French to the point that Miles couldn't understand more than one word in three—even knowing all three languages to one degree or another. The guard spoke in such a way as to imply he was trying to get a word in edgewise, but Catrin kept talking over him.

Then their voices began moving away, Catrin doing her job to distract the guard.

Miles didn't wait around to listen for more. Going straight to a trunk set against one wall, he opened it to reveal a complete change of clothing for both of them, including tunics, cloaks, and helmets, which identified them as members of Windsor's garrison.

Miles ripped off his shirt and wiped at his face with it, at the same time licking wine from his lips. He could only be thankful and relieved that Hugh was exhausted and so out of his mind with fear that he wasn't noticing all the little things that weren't quite right about this escape. He was a wine steward himself, after all.

Catrin had come up with this final element, which was meant to have been put into use by Reese. It was Reese who was supposed to have opened the door to their cell and been stabbed by Miles, puncturing the wine skin held to Reese's side by a cloth tied around his body.

That it had been Vincent who'd been the victim instead was a little disconcerting, but the further down this path Miles went, the more obvious it became that everything was as Reese had intended. Miles hoped he hadn't hurt Vincent badly. He didn't know him as well as he knew Reese, even though they'd all been together in the Holy Land. Reese would have understood immediately that Miles needed to become a bit more physical than they had initially envisioned to make the ruse believable.

This wasn't the time to worry about Vincent's feelings, however. Besides, his own belly was still aching from Vincent's earlier punches, and he wasn't looking forward to the fat lip he'd have in the morning.

Miles and Hugh hastily stripped off all their clothes and dressed as members of the garrison, discarding the old (and in Miles's case, wine-spattered) clothing in the same trunk. They found knives in a cupboard, though not swords, since neither man should have knowledge of the use of one—and anyway, such valuable weapons weren't kept casually in a guardroom. Even Hugh might realize something was amiss then.

Miles had dropped Vincent's knife on his body, telling Hugh out loud that he wouldn't keep Vincent's dagger and risk being caught with it. The real truth was that he didn't want Jehan, if they really were to meet him, to take it from him and find even a trace of wine on it. Miles had hustled Hugh out of the cell so quickly so he couldn't check to make sure Vincent was really dead. But all Hugh kept saying was *so much blood*.

There *had* been a great deal of wine sprayed about. Catrin had outdone herself. Miles allowed himself the stray thought that he hadn't had friends like these since the Holy Land, and it was probably no coincidence that Reese figured prominently in both places.

Hugh was already lifting the trap door as Miles reached him, and he motioned to him to hurry. The secret passage was accessed from the main level, tucked into a forgotten corner of the castle (though with the round tower, it wasn't exactly a *corner*, and not exactly *forgotten* either). Like the tower, the tunnel had been constructed as part of the remodeling done after the French attack. Coarse chalk blocks formed the walls, and the arches above the long stairway down into the earth were impressive, giving Miles hope they wouldn't collapse any time soon. At the base, the passage turned sharply and continued to its outlet beyond the castle.

Miles grabbed a lantern left on a table for them and followed Hugh down the steps.

34

Day Two

Rhys

Now that it was said and done, Rhys could admit that Vincent had been right to think it would be better if he were the one to enter the cell. Vincent was a higher-ranking nobleman. For Miles/Gilbert to have the temerity to murder him would mean more to Hugh. In addition, by taking on that particular task himself, Vincent had left Rhys free to pursue this investigation. At this moment, that meant being ready at the exit to the tunnel out of the castle.

Before they had gone their separate ways, however, Rhys had pulled Vincent aside one more time.

At first, Vincent's tone had been full of exasperation. "You don't have to mother me, Rhys. I know what I'm doing."

"I'm not questioning the wisdom of this choice anymore. It's just—" There, Rhys had paused, frustrated with himself for what he was struggling to say, wishing he could be more elegant and casual about it. "If something happens to one of us, I don't want to have left anything unsaid. You have been open with me. You've apologized to me. And I have failed to meet you even halfway. I'm sorry."

Vincent had wrinkled his nose in distaste. "I have no idea what you're talking about."

"I hated you for so long, obvious from the battle at Nefyn, I'm sure. When you apologized to me, I was not only surprised but undone. And the truth is, your ability to apologize exposed my own role in our estrangement, if that's even the proper word for it. I didn't have to chastise you all those years ago in a public square. I was full of myself and my own righteousness, and I'm sorry."

He had paused then, watching Vincent's face for any sign that what he was saying meant something to him. It meant something to Rhys. And then he'd decided that he might as well spend all his pennies in one go. There might never be a better time. "I have already apologized to Simon for not letting him know I was alive after Cilmeri. I will not apologize for serving Prince Llywelyn, as my father did before me. But even though we weren't friends anymore, I didn't have to leave London the way I did, in the night, without a backward glance, though I assure you that I did look back. It wasn't fair to all of you. It wasn't worthy of this cross I wear on my back."

Once Rhys stopped speaking, Vincent had gazed at him for a long moment. And then he'd laughed. "Do you read minds?" Rhys had been somewhat bewildered by the question, since obviously he didn't, but then Vincent had laughed again and stuck out his hand to Rhys. "The older a man grows, the more mistakes he makes. The key is to learn from them. Perhaps, in the future, we can give the other the benefit of the doubt before we decide to condemn."

Rhys had been listening through the vent above the prison while Hugh had explained to Miles how the conspiracy worked. He was pleased that he'd been close in at least one of his guesses, that the beanbag had been a way to send a message. If Hugh had kept his head, he could have simply smiled and thanked Justin for its return. But he'd panicked, and here they were.

Perhaps Hugh wasn't really as cowed and fearful as he appeared, but if so, he was an excellent mummer. What's more, it was hard to see what he might be gaining by lying to Miles. It would be far better to say nothing than to implicate anyone else in his schemes.

Thaddeus had been listening too when Hugh had identified the guards as his co-conspirators. He'd wanted to arrest them immediately. Prince Edmund himself had not only supported Rhys in his insistence that they wait, but reiterated that Rhys had complete authority in this investigation. Woe betide the man who went his own way. Rhys very much hoped he wasn't making a mistake.

Edmund hadn't even had to be that forceful, thankfully, and Thaddeus had seen the wisdom of letting all the players continue as they were until they had this Jehan, whoever he was, in custody. They hadn't publicized the sketch up until now, and once Miles and Hugh had been arrested, Rhys had stopped pursuing any other aspect of the investigation. He wanted nothing to jeopardize what Miles was trying to accomplish. He certainly didn't want to scare off any of the culprits, and that included the three guards. Miles had been afraid he'd already done it, but Thaddeus reported they were behaving as if nothing was amiss. One had come on duty as scheduled, and the others were in the barracks.

Which left Rhys and Justin in *The King's Arms*, waiting for Miles and Hugh to appear from the cellar. Before, when Rhys had first seen Tom overseeing Miles's challenge with Butler James, he hadn't known that the king actually owned the establishment.

"Hello, old friend!" Rhys lounged in the doorway of Tom's little room where he kept the inn's accounts. Tom could read and write because Rhys had taught him. Vincent, at the time, had told him he had no respect for rank, which had been mostly true. Probably he would still say the same.

"My God, man!" Tom was on his feet in an instant, dwarfing Rhys as usual, both in length and breadth. "They said *that Welsh quaestor Reese* was here, but I hardly dared believe it, thinking it had to be a different one. I should have known that wherever Lord Miles went, you wouldn't be far behind." Then he made a motion with his hand. "Pardon. I mean Gilbert le Gascon."

Miles hadn't confessed outright to Rhys that Tom had been in on the deception from the start, and Rhys wouldn't have gone so far as to suggest the contest had been rigged in Miles's favor, but he wouldn't put the possibility past the two of them either. Miles was too irreverent and Tom too pragmatic to let a pesky thing like honesty get in the way of what needed to be done.

"You should know by now there is only one Rhys." That came from Justin, standing at his stepfather's right shoulder.

Rhys quickly made the introductions, prompting something of a bow from Tom. "I should call you both *my lord*. Forgive my familiarity."

"You probably should, at least in public," Rhys admitted, "particularly in the next hour." And he explained what was going to be transpiring in his cellar.

"Do the guards down there know?" Tom asked.

"You may have noticed Captain Thaddeus coming through here earlier, so the answer to that is *yes*. One will be absent and the other conveniently asleep with his head down on the table when the door from the tunnel opens."

"And then what?"

"And then we let our fugitives walk out the door and down the road to wherever life takes them."

Tom's look was entirely disillusioned. "You can't expect me to believe that."

"At this juncture, the less you know, the better. Once all this is over, I will come back and explain more to you. I promise."

Tom openly scoffed. "Where have I heard that before?"

His words stopped Rhys in his tracks. "Have you heard that before from me?"

"My apologies, my lord." He gave Rhys another little bow, but this time one that was entirely ironic. "I wasn't referring to you."

Rhys grunted. "Am I to gather they aren't exactly forthcoming up at the castle?"

Tom put up both hands. "You didn't hear it from me. But when a man died in my inn six months ago, Thaddeus came to investigate, after which I never heard another word about it."

"Who was the dead man?"

"Not someone I knew well. I'd seen him around in the weeks before."

"How did he die?"

"See!" Tom threw up his hands in evident frustration. "These are the kinds of questions an investigator asks. Not Thaddeus, he took away the body and never came back."

"So how *did* the man die?" Justin asked.

"He was stabbed."

Rhys and Justin shared a meaningful look.

"What?" Tom looked from one man to the other.

"You may have heard that a servant at the castle died today too. He was also stabbed."

"If murder is to be committed, it is one of the most common methods," Tom said.

Rhys acknowledged that was true. "What happened with your man?"

"I have no idea other than that we found him dead in the stables one morning."

Rhys didn't know if he should get excited or not. Thaddeus himself hadn't said a word about the murder, but the simple fact that both men had been stabbed should have been enough for him to at least mention it to Rhys. Then again, as Tom pointed out, Thaddeus himself wasn't an investigator.

"Do you see Thaddeus in here often?"

"Certainly. It's his job to inspect the tunnel, and he'll have a cup or two of ale most evenings."

On impulse, Rhys pulled out the sketch. "Do you recognize him?"

"Indeed. That's Jehan."

Justin let out a sharp breath, prompting Tom to turn to him. "Is this important?"

"It may be," Justin said. "Does he drink with anyone in particular?"

"Oh sure." Tom gestured to the sketch. "Captain Thaddeus for one."

It was as if someone had just dumped a bucket of cold water over Rhys's head.

Justin's mouth fell open. "But he said nothing when we showed Hugh the picture right in front of him!"

"No, he didn't." Rhys's stomach was in a knot.

"Maybe he didn't get a clear view of it." Justin was frowning as he puzzled it out. "Maybe he doesn't know—"

Rhys cut him off with a gesture. "I'm worried too, but we have no means to address this now. We are out of time." He tipped his head towards the entrance to the cellar. "Miles is still our best chance to get to him."

Upon Tom's arrival in the common room, various patrons hailed him, indicating he was quite popular. No surprise, to Rhys's mind. They made way for them, giving them a table near the door, with an easy view down the corridor to the cellar stairs. Before sitting, Rhys had a look around the room and asked Tom if Jehan was present.

"No, though he was earlier." Tom sat on a stool, unaware of the turmoil inside Rhys, or at least not asking about it. "I'm quite sure I don't understand what you're doing. They'll see you."

"That's exactly the point," Justin said.

"Oh." Tom's eyes grew thoughtful as he settled himself. Rhys might have let him figure it out for himself, but Justin eagerly stepped in.

"If Hugh decides to walk out the front door, we are happy to pretend we don't see him, but the idea is to push him even more towards trusting Miles and assuage any second thoughts he might be having by now about taking him to Jehan. They'll get to the corridor, look towards the common room, see Sir Rhys and me, and then go out the back."

"Where Lady Catrin and Prince Edmund will be waiting to follow them." Tom nodded.

"I still think I should be out there while Mother is in here with you," Justin said to Rhys as an aside.

"It would look a little odd to see you holding onto the prince's arm, though, don't you think?" Rhys accepted the cup Tom placed in front of him, and then blinked to see that it contained mead, not ale.

He stared at the drink for a moment—long enough, in fact, for Tom to hesitate in the act of pouring a second cup for Justin. "Don't you drink it still?"

"Yes, of course I do. But I wouldn't have thought you served mead here."

"It comes up the river every now and again, and I lay in a batch. I know Butler James ordered it with some regularity."

"For Prince Alfonso," Justin said.

Tom had been about to drink from his cup, and he set it down without tasting it. "You tell me truly?"

"Yes." Rhys looked at him carefully. "Does that mean something to you?"

"I don't know." Tom was looking extremely thoughtful now.

"Tell me. Please."

"A bit ago, one of my maids shared a drink with that boy Bobby who was killed today. She was quite ill afterwards and said it was the mead."

Rhys sat up straighter. "Can I speak to the maid?"

"She cleans the guest rooms. She'll be here in the morning." He tipped his head, listening to the bells chiming midnight. "It is time to close up."

Here in the town, people stayed up later and slept later than in a village—and by the raucousness ongoing in the inn, some might never sleep at all.

"They're here." Justin nudged Rhys's elbow, his head tipped slightly towards the back of the inn.

They all knew enough not to look at Miles and Hugh directly, just keep track of them out of the corner of their eyes. Rhys hadn't been able to catch Hugh looking towards the common room, but since they remained in the corridor for hardly more than three heartbeats before turning towards the back, they may have always intended to go that way. With the inn closing, they needed to depart anyway, and the flood of patrons would provide them cover.

As Rhys stood, he looked hard at Tom. "We need to speak to that maid of yours as soon as possible."

"I'll send her to the castle when she comes in."

Justin was on his feet too. "And, hopefully, by then we'll know a great deal more about most everything than we do right now."

35

Day Two

Catrin

Catrin had been sure that Rhys was going to want to leave her behind. If she'd been in charge, *she* might have left herself behind. She understood that he wanted to be protective.

But he had admitted that he needed more rather than fewer helpers in this moment, and she would be safe with the prince, whom she also could hardly believe Rhys had allowed to participate. Then again, he was the king's brother. He said he wanted to be involved, made a forceful argument that this was what he'd come to Windsor *for,* and somehow, Rhys had given way.

"I can see why Rhys has been so successful in enlisting able men—and women—" Prince Edmund shot her an amused glance as he spoke, "—to assist him in these investigations. For once, it feels like I'm *doing* something. It is only in battle that I get that feeling otherwise."

That was a telling comment if she'd ever heard one, and perhaps went a long way towards explaining the behavior of King Edward too. He wanted to *feel* something. Once a man had been to war, it was hard to feel anything outside of it. She didn't think Edmund was fully aware of how revealing his words had been. But it seemed, as had been her experience since she'd joined the queen's retinue, that the very nature of her ambivalent status invited confidences.

Edmund certainly didn't look like the Earl of Lancaster and a prince of England tonight. Although his cloth was still fine, he wore no sword, only a knife at his waist, and was clothed in a cloak and tunic as befitting the wealthy merchant he was pretending to be. He even wore a large hat with a wide brim.

Three members of his personal guard, men whom Rhys's friend Simon Boydell had formerly led, were ranged throughout the yard and street. One was dressed as a stableman, another wore clothing similar to the prince's, and the last had merrily (with Catrin's help), adorned himself in rags and dirt to appear a beggar. Two more had been sent to the other side of the river hours ago, once they'd learned that some of the activities to which Hugh had alluded were centered on the Eton side of the Thames. The last two of the seven with whom Edmund had ridden from Bangor were still at the castle, to help with the aftermath of Vincent's supposed death.

Catrin and Edmund, meanwhile, had planted themselves near the stables with Edmund's false stableman. To all appearances, they were discussing the disposition of a horse. She hoped, from the outside, all seemed perfectly unremarkable.

The question before them now was what *unremarkable* behavior meant. As Miles and Hugh walked out the back of the inn, was it *unremarkable* to glance casually towards them and away again? Surely it would be less usual not to look at all.

So Catrin looked, noting the way Miles grabbed Hugh's elbow to hurry him out of the yard. The moment they disappeared, Catrin and Edmund set off at a fast walk to follow. Their pace slowed as soon as they reached the street, affecting the casual stroll of lovers in the late evening, never mind that it was after midnight, so really, lovers should be in bed by now.

The inn's common room was emptying out the front door, along with the common rooms of the four or five other similar establishments in Windsor. Windsor had its own charter from the king, granting the townspeople a certain degree of autonomy, and since then the town had grown to a population of several thousand, not even including the residents of the castle.

Catrin and Edmund joined the throng, as did Rhys a moment later, coming right up behind them. "Where are they?"

"They turned towards the river," Catrin said.

Rhys squeezed her shoulder once and then was gone. Edmund tipped his head to the left, just slightly, sending a message to one of his men, who went down a nearby alley. The beggar was limping along on the other side of the street, and he picked up his pace, only to slow again in the moment before he followed after Miles and Hugh.

"They are good men. Simon trained them well." Edmund sighed. "I do miss him."

"I understand that it was your idea to send him to the king."

Edmund shot her a look that could have been sardonic. It was dark, and his hat shaded his face from the torches that lit the streets, so she might have been mistaken. Then he said simply, "My brother needed him. Little did I know he would get Rhys in the bargain. It hardly seems fair."

"Perhaps you can borrow them every now and again," Catrin said. "Like this week."

Edmund let out a low laugh. "I'm not sure this counts, but I will keep it in mind, madam."

As they approached the river, they slowed and then halted. The point of the two of them being a couple was that they could loiter without calling attention to themselves in a way that a single man could not. Catrin still felt out of place, since the inn's patrons had dispersed quickly, once the common rooms were closed, and there were only a handful of people in sight. Miles and Hugh were halfway across the bridge that spanned the Thames, heading to the village of Eton on the other side.

"That bridge makes a regrettable chokepoint," Edmund said. "Whoever leads this group is clever."

"So is Rhys. That's why he sent two of your men ahead." Catrin eyed Windsor's dock directly to their right, where even now a half-dozen cargo boats and barges were moored, ready to be unloaded or to continue their journey in the morning. The Thames was a thriving commercial pathway, navigable all the way to London to the east and past Oxford, even as far as Radcot, to the west.

At the same time, by building warehouses on the Eton side of the Thames, merchants avoided having to accommodate Windsor's guild (although the king's taxes remained another matter). Eton, as a town, was thriving in its own way, occupying the land between the Baldwin and Windsor bridges on the main road from London. Behind the commercial area at their docks, off the high street, were the second stables associated with the castle, ready to accommodate any overflow. Catrin's own horse should be spending the night there.

"You don't have to defend him to me, my dear. I know well his worth."

"Why don't you pretend to be drunk?" Catrin was a little wary at making so fraught a suggestion.

However, the prince immediately began to weave on his feet, to the point that she had to struggle to hold him upright. In that haphazard fashion, they traversed the bridge after Miles and Hugh, and were in time to see them turn into the second warehouse downriver from the bridge. It was similar in size to a prosperous farmer's barn, built in wood, with large doors that faced the street, though Miles and Hugh entered through what in a castle would have been called a wicket gate.

The warehouse was unfortified—or so it appeared from their perspective. Once Miles and Hugh disappeared inside, the street was completely quiet but for Catrin and Edmund.

A horse whickered in the stables, and Edmund tugged her in that direction, a mere fifty feet farther on. "We can watch from there."

"How do we let Rhys know where we are?"

"Leave that to my men." He flicked out with his fingers again as a signal to those of his men who'd been watching all along from the shadows. "I can assure you with utmost confidence that we have never once been out of their sight."

36

Day Three
Miles

Miles was initially disappointed that he and Hugh were being made to cool their heels in the center of a cavernous warehouse. A long table took up the center of the floor. Numerous small boxes and crates were stacked on it, as if someone was in the midst of packing for departure. One box looked like the kind used to store ledgers, and his hands itched to open it. He quelled the desire, not wanting to give himself away to Hugh.

Then the door to a far room opened to reveal a man who was a good likeness of the fellow in Bobby's sketch, though even thinner, his eyes a little sunken. He looked … ill. He entered the room holding a carafe with a wide mouth, which he set in on the table.

Five men entered with him. Three were men Miles didn't recognize, but one was Etienne, of the three castle guardsmen to whom Miles had spoken earlier that evening. Gregory and Francis were not in evidence, more's the pity. Gregory might have been made an ally.

The last was Captain Thaddeus.

In that moment, Miles acknowledged that they—and he, in particular—had made a huge mistake. He just didn't know what to do about it, how big it was, or if things were still salvageable.

For his part, Hugh gaped at Thaddeus. "What-what-what are you doing here?"

"Cleaning up your mess."

"But-but-but—?"

Thaddeus might have rolled his eyes at Hugh. He then conducted a thorough search of both of them, stripping them of their newly acquired weapons. The rest of the men ranged themselves around the room, just far enough apart so Miles couldn't watch them all.

When Thaddeus stepped back, he gestured to Miles and spoke in English, which Miles as Gilbert was not supposed to understand. "This is the man I was telling you about, Jehan. He is working for the king's quaestor."

Despite the fraught situation, Miles allowed himself a moment of relief. Thaddeus didn't know who Miles really was. That might be his only saving grace.

Hugh had initially protested the loss of his knife, and now he sat, disbelieving, in the chair in which Thaddeus had placed him. He even tried to defend Miles, "This is my friend, Gilbert! I was going to be hanged in the morning, and he helped me escape. Jehan, you have to believe me!"

"I don't, actually." Jehan put a hand on Hugh's shoulder and spoke in a gentle voice, in English with a light French accent. "He did not help you. He used you to get to me. I'm sorry, friend." A dagger appeared in his hand, and he thrust it up under Hugh's ribs into his heart. Hugh slumped off the chair and, a moment later, was bleeding out on the floor.

None of the other men, seemingly Jehan's to a man, twitched an eyebrow. That is, except for Captain Thaddeus, who gaped in a very similar manner to poor, dead Hugh. "What have you done?"

"Unlike you, I am actually cleaning up the mess."

The murder had happened so quickly, Miles hadn't been able to do anything about it. Jehan was such a small man, one whom some might see as weak, that he could see why Hugh hadn't seen death coming.

Thaddeus stared at Hugh's body and then looked back to Jehan. "It was *you*! You murdered Bobby."

"And George, if you must know." Jehan's expression showed no remorse. Rather, he appeared pleased with himself, and this admission had been thrown out casually, as if two murders, three now with Hugh, were of no importance.

What's more, Jehan had murdered Hugh in front of Miles and Thaddeus, and then confessed to two other murders. That he had done so could only mean that he did not expect to have to pay for any of these crimes. Either he was leaving England immediately or Miles and Thaddeus were walking dead men. Or both.

Likely both.

Thaddeus didn't know it yet. "George died when his heart gave out."

"No," Jehan's voice was all patience, "I strangled him and then made it look as if he hanged himself in the stables. But then someone covered it up. Hugh, I'm thinking, the imbecile." He poked the body with the toe of his boot. "Maybe I shouldn't have killed him so quickly."

"Why kill any of them?" Thaddeus remained aghast.

"Do you really not know?" Jehan seemed happy to talk. Maybe he'd felt himself surrounded by fools for so long that he relished the opportunity. "I couldn't risk being discovered. First George started asking questions, and then that kitchen boy came snooping around. We've had a good thing going here for a long time, haven't we, Thaddeus?"

Thaddeus nodded dumbly.

Miles's intent in coming with Hugh had been to reach the headquarters of the smuggling operation, learn its details, and ingratiate himself. He'd assumed that would take some hours. Instead it had taken a matter of a single conversation—except for the part about ingratiating himself, which clearly was a complete nonstarter.

Having faced Miles again, Jehan's lips twisted into something that might have been a rueful smile. "Last night, I thought I could save the situation. Clearly I cannot. Not here, anyway." Without turning around, he added, "And what of you, Thaddeus? You can stay and face the king's justice, or you can take the ship with me. Your choice."

"A ship ... to where? Where are you going?" Thaddeus was not recovering.

Miles found it hard to believe he hadn't known until now who he was in bed with, but maybe, to him and Hugh, they'd simply been involved in a little smuggling, and this ruthless side of Jehan was new to them. He had apparently kept the knowledge he was working with Thaddeus from Hugh. Clearly, Thaddeus hadn't realized he was a cold-blooded killer. For Miles's part, he understood now, if he hadn't before, that Jehan was very good at what he did.

"To France."

"You're from France?" Thaddeus was continuing to think slowly. "I mean, *France,* not Gascony?"

"Of course, I'm from France." Jehan finally removed his gaze from Miles's face and turned to look at Thaddeus, who gaped back for a count of three before backing away through the doorway that led to the docks. It wasn't clear to Miles what decision Thaddeus was making. And maybe it didn't matter because, after he left, Jehan jerked his head at two of his men, one of whom was Etienne, who went after him. That left Miles with Jehan and still too many opponents. The odds were hardly better than before.

In truth, Miles didn't much care what happened to Thaddeus. He had been very slow himself in encompassing the scope of Jehan's project.

Jehan was back to watching Miles's face. "Does Sir Reese know where you are?"

Miles didn't answer. And since he'd spoken in English, Jehan didn't seem to expect it, instead talking to himself: "If Reese does know, where is he? Why hasn't he come storming in here to rescue you? Are you somehow investigating on your own?" He gave a quick shake of his head. "You couldn't be. Thaddeus assured me your escape was planned. So where is everyone? What is really happening here?"

Miles looked steadily back. He couldn't answer that question, because he didn't know. He was plenty intimidated by the position he was in, and by Jehan, but he was determined not to show it. The best thing he could think to do was keep Jehan talking as long as possible, on the chance that a rescue really might be forthcoming. So he asked a question of his own, in French, of course: "Am I to understand that you serve the King of France?"

"I *served*—" Jehan emphasized the word, replying finally in the same language, his native tongue, "—King Louis. When he died, his son Philippe proved to be a worthy successor."

Miles knew in that moment Jehan intended for him to die. That didn't mean Miles himself wasn't determined to live as long as he possibly could, by whatever means necessary. He'd been in sticky situations before. His friends were coming. He knew it. He just had to stay alive until they arrived.

"If you served Louis first, you must have arrived in England as early as 1270. That would be about six months before Louis died."

Jehan accepted Miles's guess with a nod. "The king had not yet left on crusade, though we knew he was going. He died there."

If Jehan had been English, *the king* would have meant Edward, but Miles knew he meant Louis. Either way, they both sailed for Tunis in the summer of 1270. Louis arrived first, at some point contracting dysentery when it swept through his army, and died at the end of August, only a few days after Edward himself (who was not a king yet anyway) arrived. That would be fourteen years ago, nearly to the day.

"I must be going now before your friends really do come to rescue you. If they're coming." He canted his head towards the carafe. "The question now is how are *you* going to go? Quick or slow?" He held up the knife. "Your choice. Either way, even were your friends to come, they will not be able to save you."

Miles stared. He'd assumed this was the end for him, but he had hoped to go down fighting.

"Why give me a choice?"

"I was at the inn when you bested the butler. You like drinking games." Jehan smiled gently, as if this choice was doing Miles some kind of favor.

"What's in the carafe?"

"Mead, with a heavy dose of castor bean in a potion of my own devising. The honey hides the taste exceptionally well. Never fear, it will work quickly."

"Is this how you killed Alfonso?" Miles saw no reason not to confront the issue head on and was impressed that his voice didn't shake.

Jehan kept up that supercilious smile. "It's perhaps fitting that you will die the same way he did."

Then his men closed in, and Miles was forced to make a choice. He chose the mead.

And drank.

37

Day Three

Rhys

One of Edmund's guardsmen, this one named Henri, found Rhys and Justin loitering on the Windsor side of the bridge, at the corner of a closed bootmaker's shop, and told them where Catrin and Edmund were waiting.

"What about the rogue stablemen Hugh mentioned?"

Henri shook his head. "Two boys watch the horses there. Since we began our watch, they did not stir from within the stables except to use the latrine."

Rhys blew out a breath at the news, relieved at least to know his wife and the prince were safe. He waved a hand in the air, summoning Prince Edmund's remaining men, Raoul and Edgar, neither of whom had yet crossed the bridge. Soon, the five of them were huddled together in the shadows.

"How many men in the warehouse?"

"We watched for two hours. In that time, we saw six men. It was dark and they wore hoods as they went in and out, so no faces were ever visible."

"Run back to Captain Thaddeus, if you will, and let him know we need more men if we are going to enter that warehouse. I fear to go in after Miles with just enough men to get us all killed."

But one of the other guardsmen, Raoul, grabbed Henri's arm before he could leave. "Captain Thaddeus was amongst those out tonight. I saw him not a half-hour ago."

"At the warehouse?"

Raoul winced. "On the bridge."

"That isn't what we agreed." Rhys had never worked with Raoul before, but he had ridden with him from Caernarfon. After such a journey, he knew him well enough to believe what he said. "After speaking to the guards in the cellar, he said he would return to the castle and await my call."

"I assure you, he is not there now."

"He *has* betrayed us," Justin voice was remarkably matter-of-fact, "as we feared."

"And Miles might pay for my mistake with his life." Rhys swung around to look back at the castle. Unfortunately, Thaddeus's defection also meant Rhys had a dearth of people he could call upon.

Rhys and Justin had left the castle before the discovery of Vincent's body, which was supposed to have been managed by Captain Thaddeus and the last two of Prince Edmund's personal guard, who were to have kept it to themselves and spirited Vincent to Rhys and Catrin's quarters in the queen's rooms. Vincent had to stay hidden so as not to give the deception away to any allies Hugh—or Jehan—might have inside the castle. Rhys hadn't known one of these might be Captain Thaddeus himself.

Rhys made an instant decision. Pointing to Raoul, he said, "Find Tom at *The King's Arms* and tell him I need any men he can muster immediately. We will do what we can with what we have."

"Where will you be?"

"At the Eton stables." Rhys didn't tell him that he himself might not be there when they got there. The knot in his belly was tightening, and he forced himself to take a deep breath to clear his mind. A man shouldn't live his whole life by what his gut told him, but sometimes, listening to it might just save his life. Or his friend's. He'd learned to listen when it told him to hurry.

The four remaining men started across the bridge, Edmund's men at the front and back, guardsmen as always, and Justin matching Rhys stride for stride. "You didn't send me away."

Rhys glanced at him. "Why would I?"

"I could have been your errand boy. That's, in fact, what I thought I was."

"I may need you for a little more than that. Besides, your mother would murder *me* if I didn't keep an eye on you."

Justin smirked. "That's the exact same thing she said to me, though with a different emphasis."

When they reached the stables, Edmund must have been looking for them because he was right there to greet them. "Catrin is here too. Miles and Hugh have been in the warehouse across the way for a quarter of an hour." He paused. "I'm worried."

"According to your man Raoul, Captain Thaddeus is not where he's supposed to be, which would be at the castle, waiting for my signal to come with his men. In fact, I suspect that his men are entirely unaware of what is transpiring in the town right now."

"Because he's involved." Catrin stepped out of the darkness, flanked by Edmund's last two men, Jon and Robert. "That means he has known since we conceived of this plan what might happen, and Miles is in real danger. We can't wait. We have to go in now."

It was what Rhys had thought too, but to have her say the words out loud lent a certainty to what hadn't yet become a real plan. "*We* will be doing no such thing. I will enter the warehouse immediately. The rest of you wait here for Tom and his men."

"Don't be absurd," Prince Edmund said. "Catrin will stay here with Jon. She is entirely capable of relating the situation to those who come. The six of us remaining will enter the warehouse together and rescue Miles, if such a thing is possible. We can't wait."

Catrin nodded. "I'll be fine, Rhys." Jon had been dressed as the beggar, and thus tonight had carried fewer weapons, none of them large.

Rhys gripped his wife's hand, finding himself filled with love for her, for Justin, for Miles, and even, God help him, for Vincent. He knew now that he had purpose, a calling even, that in his own small way might make the world better. Just because his current aims aligned with the crown of England didn't make them wrong.

Rhys and Justin hadn't disguised themselves at the inn, since the point was to scare Hugh out the back door and into taking Miles to his safe haven. Thus, they had worn their swords at their waists. Since he was pretending to be a merchant, Prince Edmund wasn't wearing a sword, but a wicked dagger appeared in one hand. The prince and Rhys had fought in the Holy Land together, and while they were a dozen years older than they had been then, and by no means young, Rhys didn't argue. Anyway, the prince was right. Entering the warehouse alone could have been a suicide mission. He'd known it when he'd suggested it and suggested it anyway. The three guardsmen who were coming with them also produced weapons, though again, since they were in turn meant to be two stablemen and a merchant, none were carrying swords either.

Six against six, if that was how many Jehan had, were terrible odds, but at this point they had to go in.

Justin gripped the hilt of his sword, now bare in his hand, and hefted it. "Lead on, Father. We will follow you."

38

Day Three

Vincent

Vincent hadn't ever been one to stay behind, not fifteen years ago, not five years ago, and certainly not now. His friends, and by now he really was feeling that he could call Miles and Rhys *friends*, were outside the castle risking their lives, and he was stuck in a bedchamber in the castle.

He might have convinced himself that to leave was entirely foolhardy if Prince Edmund's two men, Geoff and Ham, hadn't reported Captain Thaddeus missing. Constable Pickford had assured them that all was well, but with Thaddeus's absence he had been unable to prevent the news of Vincent's supposed death from spreading through the castle like wildfire. It was another death in a string of deaths, and he had his hands full managing the uproar.

Rhys had given Vincent strict instructions to stay out of sight, and he wasn't normally one to defy orders, but somehow, it was the easiest thing in the world to borrow a set of clothing from Geoff and leave the shelter of Rhys and Catrin's room. Besides, the idea that he would sit out the end of the investigation had been absurd from the start. He told himself that Rhys hadn't really assumed it.

"The castle is closed by order of the constable." Vincent hadn't attempted to exit by the main gate nor follow the same path as Miles and Hugh out of the castle, figuring that would be the hardest to get through. Instead, they'd gone to the postern gate by which food and drink were brought into the kitchens. The door could be opened only from the inside. Once through, they would not be able to get back in that way.

So be it.

"We are leaving now," Geoff had taken charge of their escape. "Our lord is outside the castle, and therefore we must be as well."

"Your lord—"

"Prince Edmund," Vincent put in, impatient with the delay and forgetting for a moment that he didn't command the same respect in this guise, since the whole point was not to be recognized as a lord, and especially not as Vincent de Lusignan, the man who'd been murdered earlier that evening.

The guard still looked uncertain, but he had three men glaring at him, all wearing Prince Edmund's colors, and he could not gainsay them for more than a few breaths.

They were through the door in a manner of moments, and Vincent allowed himself to feel pleased to have successfully navigated that small obstacle. It was a way to not think quite yet about the much larger one coming up.

Geoff and Ham were used to following the orders of their betters, but they hadn't liked the idea of sitting out this final act any more than Vincent. Vincent wasn't entirely sure what he was trying to accomplish, other than providing three more men to augment Rhys's pitifully small force. He just had this terrible feeling that it had been a mistake to include Captain Thaddeus in this scheme. That he'd left without telling Geoff and Ham had to mean he was up to no good. If it turned out otherwise, Vincent would apologize for maligning him unnecessarily, even if only in his own head.

Windsor's docks were deserted at this hour of the night. It had been nearing midnight when Miles had escaped. The silence in the streets told Vincent that the taverns and inns had closed. On one hand, that made any motion, including theirs, obvious to a watcher. On the other hand, it made it easier for them to watch.

Fortunately, as Prince Edmund's men, they would never be questioned as to their right to be anywhere. The issue was where Miles and Hugh had got to—and if Rhys and his hodge-podge collection of helpers had successfully followed them.

Vincent supposed Miles and Hugh could have found horses and ridden out of Windsor by now, which would have made following them a little difficult. Rhys had left horses at the inn in case of such an eventuality, and if that was the path his friends had taken, then Vincent wouldn't be doing them much good still in Windsor. In that eventuality, he could go back to the castle by the front gate.

But he didn't think that was what was happening here. The smuggling had been taking place along the river, and it made sense that whatever secret—or possibly not-so-secret—lair to which Hugh had taken Miles was located along the river too. Hugh had mentioned a warehouse.

So they crept along, trying both to be quiet and also to appear like they knew where they were going and what they were doing.

"I see nothing and nobody," Ham said in a gruff whisper. He was shorter than the others, burly, and older as well. Truthfully, Vincent had been pleased that he himself had fit easily into Geoff's clothing, since Geoff was a decade younger and not fighting a thickening around the midsection like Vincent.

"Nor I, but we've only just started."

As they passed each darkened warehouse, Vincent sent one of the men around it for a cursory inspection, on the off chance of finding someone lurking in the shadows. These warehouses numbered a dozen, ranging in size from that of a barn to hardly more than a hut. Vincent knew nothing about shipping, beyond the general, but he imagined that the size of the warehouse depended upon the size and quantity of the materials being brought in and out.

Having passed without incident the first four warehouses, all locked up tightly, Vincent took the men along a narrow path between two buildings and fetched up on the dock itself, which stretched a full hundred yards downstream from the bridge.

And then, at long last, Vincent felt, more than saw, movement. It wasn't taking place, as he'd expected, on the Windsor side of the river, but opposite, at the Eton docks. At first, he just heard multiple sets of footsteps echoing hollowly on wooden boards, and then was able to follow the light of a bobbing lantern, visible through the mist that was settling on the river.

The keeper of that lantern could have been a watchman or the king's taxman looking for smugglers. But Vincent held still anyway, putting up a hand to stop the others from moving or speaking. Geoff had already noticed the light, and Ham walked a single pace farther before falling still.

Night and water carried sound like at no other time, and through the mist came the unmistakable words, "Jehan sends his regards," followed by a grunt and a splash.

Another man said, "*Au revoir*, Hugh," after which was another splash.

Vincent's throat constricted. He'd just heard two bodies going into the river. If the second was Hugh, then the first had to have been Miles. His companions had heard it too, and beside him, Geoff's sword suddenly appeared in his hand, as if he could leap the Thames and gut the men opposite.

Vincent wanted to do the same, but if Miles had just been stabbed and was one of the dead bodies in the river, giving their location away wouldn't bring those responsible to justice.

But then the man who'd bid Hugh adieu asked his companion, "What about the Gascon?"

"Leave him. He isn't dead yet, and we don't want him thrashing about in the water calling attention to himself. He's fine where he is."

A mix of hope and terror had Vincent's heart pounding loudly in his ears, but instead of freezing him in his tracks, he found his legs taking him towards a dinghy moored at the end of the dock.

As he reached it, he heard more footsteps, from multiple additional men, and then a third voice, this one more gruff than the other two. "Are we ready?"

"They're both in the river, *chef.*"

"*Bien,*" came the reply. "*Allons-y.*"

Footsteps and grunts, not to mention movement, on the opposite bank indicated that a number of men, beyond the three who'd spoken, had boarded a boat and pushed off from the Eton dock.

Vincent could have chosen to cross the river to the warehouse, but he decided to trust that Rhys was on his way. They'd all been caught on the hop by Thaddeus's betrayal, but Jehan was getting away. Vincent couldn't countenance it.

None of them were watermen, so getting into their boat quietly was a challenge. They did the best they could, hoping that the villains on the other side of the river were making enough noise themselves to cover any other.

With Vincent in the bow to keep watch, Ham untied the mooring rope and settled himself at the oars beside Geoff. They began to row downstream after Jehan and his men.

39

Day Three

Rhys

Though they hadn't known it when they'd started, a quarter of an hour was too long to have left Miles alone, and Rhys cursed himself for his complacency. He'd thought he'd known what he was doing. He'd been wrong. And Miles might already be dead because of it.

The quiet in the warehouse was difficult to credit. Rhys hadn't wanted to come in through the main door, so he'd tried two others which were locked before Justin discovered several loose boards halfway down the alley that ran along one side. All the while they were searching, Rhys could hear voices that sounded like they were coming from the dock, but he couldn't make out the words. He was all for leaping out and surprising them, but even six men—which was a far cry better than one or three—were not enough to ensure the evening wouldn't end in the death of the king's brother. He couldn't trade Edmund for Miles.

"Well done." Prince Edmund patted Justin on the shoulder as he followed Rhys through the newly created hole in the wall, leaving Justin gaping at him. In truth, it was every knight's dream to come to the attention of the prince.

They found themselves faced with pallets of wool, strapped into large bundles with thick ropes. Wool would not have been the item Rhys would have figured Jehan would primarily be importing—or smuggling. But as he passed among the stacks, he realized these bundles were old, musty, and dusty, from some other year's shearing, now having sat too long in the warehouse. They were a front, in other words, something to show a taxman if one ever came to the warehouse, since likely Jehan had paid taxes on them as he should have. These were to be trotted out for inspection only if the bribes he'd paid had proved insufficient.

Rhys wasn't here to address tax evasion, however, and he hustled twenty feet until he reached the large central area of the warehouse, now completely devoid of people.

Justin veered off with two of Edmund's men towards the six-foot-wide doorway that led to the docks. He sent the other men through it before turning back himself to Edmund and Rhys. "Someone has just rowed away. I can hear the oars hitting the water."

"How many men?" Prince Edmund asked.

"I can't tell from here. Ten? It's at least a half-dozen."

Rhys, meanwhile, had crouched to the floor, tentatively reaching a hand to a pool of dark liquid. He didn't have to sniff it to know it was blood. On the table next to him was a carafe, which he did sniff, causing his brow to furrow. "Mead."

Fear coursed through him. Someone had bled a great deal. *And someone had drunk a carafe of mead.* But the warehouse was empty. He hated to think that Miles was captive and dying on the boat that had just floated away while they had been dithering about the safest way to enter the warehouse.

He pointed to his stepson. "Find us a boat, Justin. We'll have to go after them—"

He cut off the rest of what he was going to say at the sound of hammering. It didn't sound so much like a hammer on wood, but like someone was banging two blocks together. Prince Edmund sprinted towards a door to a room located in a corner of the warehouse, walled off from the rest of the wide-open building. Rhys followed, also at a run, and by the time he came through the doorway, the prince was using his dagger to saw at the ropes that bound Miles's hands behind his back and his feet at the ankles. Otherwise, he was curled up on the floor in a pool of vomit.

Miles was alive. And angry. It had been he who'd been banging a scrap of wood on the leg of a small table by which he was lying.

Rhys stared at him. "You drank the mead."

"Of course I drank it! A slow death seemed preferable to an immediate one."

"What was in the carafe?"

"Jehan claimed it was loaded with castor bean." Out came a string of profanity to rival what Miles had shouted back at the castle before he was locked up.

Justin arrived at Rhys's shoulder. "What happened? He's alive?"

"For now," Rhys said grimly. "Go get your mother—"

"She's here."

Rhys stepped out of the doorway to see a dozen men, a variety of weapons in hand, spreading out about the room, joining Edmund's men, who'd been canvassing for threats.

Catrin ran to Rhys and flung her arms around his neck. "I was so worried!"

"Worry about Miles, not me." And he explained about the poisoned mead.

With the addition of Catrin, the little room was crowded. As Justin blocked the doorway to anyone else coming inside, Catrin lifted her skirts to avoid the vomit and crouched beside Miles. "Can you stand?"

"I'm seeing double."

"How long was the mead in your stomach?"

"As little time as I could manage. I had to wait until they'd gone, though, before I vomited."

"How did you manage to vomit with your hands tied behind your back?" Rhys asked.

Miles was well enough to give him a sardonic look. "When you've won as many drinking games as I have, you learn how."

Even amidst the anxiety, frustration, and fear, Justin was aghast. "You cheat, you mean!"

A laugh swept among them, begun by Miles. But then he choked a little, sobering them all. "I drank it because Hugh was murdered before my eyes. Jehan did actually give me a choice: I could go the same way as Hugh or I could drink the mead, which he said would be appropriate since that's how he murdered Alfonso." His voice dropped to nothing at these last words, meant only for their ears.

Edmund had given way to Catrin, but he remained close enough to grip Miles's arm. "That's what he said? His exact words?"

"Exact enough, my lord. I'm sorry."

Rhys found himself barely reacting to the revelation. By this point, it was what he'd assumed.

"Do we believe him?" Edmund said.

"We have no reason not to," Rhys said. "It makes sense."

"What about the other boys, John and Henry?" Catrin asked.

"We will have to ask Jehan when we find him." Rhys's tone was grim.

"This must stay among the five of us, though," Edmund said, confirming what Miles had known instinctively, in speaking Jehan's words so softly. "My men, and certainly Tom's men, know only that we are after smugglers. They cannot know more. Not yet. Maybe not ever."

"There will be rumors given that Miles is so ill," Justin said.

"We can deal with rumors."

With Rhys on one side and the prince himself on the other, they got Miles up and out of the room.

Catrin followed, a worried expression on her face. "He needs an emetic. We'll see what the physician has in his stores. And then milk."

"I haven't drunk milk since I was an infant." It was some relief to hear Miles speak in an outraged voice, given the effort it had taken to get him upright.

"You need to vomit more, to the point of turning your insides out. Elder, if the physician has it, will encourage that. Drinking milk afterwards helps to prevent some poisons from being absorbed into the body. I don't know how it works or if it will with castor beans. I'm hoping you got most of it up before it was too late."

"Me too." Rhys gazed at his friend, who was looking so white as to be almost translucent.

His friend.

Miles nodded vigorously for someone at death's door. "Me too."

40

Day Three

Vincent

The men in the other boat were French, which was deeply troubling to Vincent. He had been born in Lusignan, one of many sons and a much younger one to boot. William de Valence hadn't been an eldest son either, but he had done very well for himself in England in the retinue of the English kings. Under William's patronage, Vincent had too, though of course not rising to become the Earl of Pembroke.

Nonetheless, he knew France. He knew the rivalries and in-fighting among all the lordships, all of whom were under increasing pressure, and had been for decades, from the King of France to submit entirely to his rule. For some years, despite an overt peace, King Edward had been fighting a rearguard action to maintain hold of his lands in Gascony and Aquitaine, the English crown having already lost both Normandy and Brittany to France earlier in the century.

He knew that a Frenchman such as Jehan should not be murdering Englishmen, no matter how treacherous, and dumping their remains in the Thames.

On a positive note, while Vincent had only two companions with him, they were both soldiers, men to be relied upon. Jehan had more companions than that. Vincent could hear them talking ahead in the other boat. These undoubtedly were, to a man, cruel and ruthless, given their easy acceptance of murder. But they were not soldiers, nor disciplined in the way of the royal guard. And they didn't know Vincent was coming.

He was praying that was the case, anyway.

And then he got lucky, because Jehan hadn't decided to float down the Thames all the way to London, some twenty miles away, but only to the docks at Old Windsor, where the palace of the Saxon kings had been. In fact, if Jehan had walked out the main gate of Windsor Castle and ridden here instead of rowing, it would have been a matter of traveling some three miles.

Given the loss of royal patronage, Old Windsor was not nearly as prosperous as it had once been, but it still had its church, dedicated to Saints Andrew and Peter, and, more importantly for Jehan's purposes, its old dock. The warehouses here were much older and more weathered, but still standing. Vincent had been forced to allow Jehan and his boat to get well ahead of them, in order to keep the fact that they were following a secret. It seemed to have worked, because Jehan was making no attempt to hide his presence. The warehouse was lit with several torches, enough for Vincent to make out the shape of it clearly, even through the mist.

They'd been keeping to the center of the river where the current was fastest, and it took longer than Vincent would have liked to find a place to pull their boat out of the water downstream from the dock. He and his men then backtracked over land to the town and then through it to the warehouse. Having slipped around to the dockside of the building, the three of them hid behind a stack of crates. In so doing, Vincent and his companions were able to watch the single guard Jehan had left on watch saunter down to the end of the dock to relieve himself into the water.

Vincent thought it pretty bold of Jehan to have a second warehouse within a stone's throw of the old kings' palace, which had become a hunting lodge for the new king. But then, he'd set up shop right under the battlements of the current Windsor Castle, so nothing appeared to be beyond him. In fact, Vincent was starting to think Jehan was far cleverer than any one of them, including Rhys or Miles.

Even intelligent men couldn't plan for everything, however.

If Jehan's men hadn't been so careless with their talk on Eton's dock—along with dropping two bodies in the river—Vincent wouldn't have known to follow them in the first place. It was another reminder that, while Jehan might be clever, the men with him were less so. That wasn't unusual, of course. Rare was it for a leader to tolerate brilliance in his subordinates. The risk of one of them deciding they wanted to be the leader instead was too great.

Even as the thought crossed Vincent's mind, he frowned as he realized that *Rhys,* for all that he was the apparent leader of their motley crew, had no trouble allowing those who worked with him to have their own ideas. In fact, he encouraged it. It was something to consider at another time when they weren't chasing down a murderer.

"Do I kill him?" Ham asked in a voice so low it was barely even a whisper.

"Disable him if you can. We are not Jehan."

Ham circled around behind the guard, a move made easier by the thickening mist. While Geoff and Vincent watched, Ham came up behind the man, clapped a hand over his mouth and tried to render him unconscious with an arm around his neck.

Unfortunately, the guard had heard him an instant before he grabbed him. That heartbeat was enough time to foil the initial attempt. He made a noise as if he was going to call a warning, at which point Geoff leapt forward and slid his knife under his chin. Then he and Ham carefully lowered the dead guard to the dock.

"Sorry, my lord," Ham said to Vincent as he approached. "Do we put him in the river?"

"No. As I said, we are not Jehan. This man was a smuggler and who knows what else, but I think I recognize him as one of the guards from Windsor."

So instead, they picked up the body and manhandled him behind the crates.

"How many more, do you think?" Geoff asked.

"I dare not guess."

Before leaving their little boat, Vincent and his companions had removed their surcoats identifying them as Edmund's men. Now, Vincent had the foresight to keep the cap the watcher had been wearing, along with his jacket. In the dark, Vincent had hope that his silhouette would be similar enough to the dead man's to give him a few moments' leeway before his identity was discovered.

Then they approached the warehouse. They'd talked on the dock, but now Vincent didn't want to risk speaking a single word, not even a grunt, and they communicated by hand signals. Fortunately, all men in the royal guards were taught the same signals, further confirmed now that Simon, who'd led Edmund's men for years, was the captain of King Edward's personal guard.

Vincent knew these signals too, simply by association, and they worked out that Geoff would go to the right, while Ham went to the left. They would disable, or kill if they had to, any watchers they found. Rhys wouldn't thank them for leaving him nobody to question, but sometimes it couldn't be helped.

While Ham and Geoff were doing that, Vincent, who was roughly the same size and build as the man they'd killed, and now wearing his clothing, went through the door. They were only three men, and grossly outnumbered, but sometimes, necessity meant taking risks worthy of Miles de Bohun.

Vincent came upon his first guard just inside the door. It seemed he might have been guarding it, but as he was sitting on a low stool, with his head on his arms as they rested on a crate, he wasn't doing a very good job of it. Vincent wrapped an arm around his throat, rendering him unconscious, as Ham had failed to do to the first guard. It was quick and quiet and didn't get blood on him. He'd heard of men strong enough to stab a man through the spine at the base of the neck, or even through the ear, both effective only when one had a significant strength and size advantage over one's opponent, as well as a really sharp dagger. Vincent was strong, but he was out of practice with killing.

As he might have expected from a derelict warehouse on the docks, the building was empty of goods—though not crates and boxes. There were dozens of them, on shelves, stacked on top of each other, and scattered randomly across the floor as if the previous owner of the warehouse had walked out one day without a backwards glance. Though Vincent had never given a moment's consideration to shipping on the Thames until that day, he was surprised the boxes and crates hadn't been scavenged by the villagers. But maybe they all knew Jehan and wouldn't invade a warehouse he owned.

As silently as he could, Vincent made his way towards the center of the building, following a long stack of crates until it ended in an open space, perhaps fifteen feet on a side, with a long table, stools, benches, and one proper chair on the far side, facing Vincent. The table showed the remains of a meal served cold but augmented by plenty of wine. The chair was occupied by a man, who was hunched over a ledger, a single candle lighting his workspace. He looked remarkably like the man in Bobby's sketch.

"So you've finally come, have you?" He spoke before he looked up. "What took you so long?"

Vincent stayed in place, uncertain how to respond.

Then the man at the table motioned with one hand and said, "Come into the light so I can see your face."

Vincent deliberated for a count of five and then stepped out of the shadows.

The other man let out a laugh. "Ah. Earl William's man, is it? Vincent de Lusignan, who is obviously not dead. Thaddeus spoke the truth. Perhaps I shouldn't have killed him so soon either." He spoke these last words under his breath, perhaps not meant really for Vincent to hear, just before he sat back in the chair and downed a full goblet of wine in one go.

If nothing else, the pause gave Vincent time to think. He hadn't actually had a plan beyond this point. He didn't know where the rest of Jehan's men were. The warehouse was deserted but for the two of them. Rather than answer, since he wasn't good at talking to people anyway, he drew his sword. He was starting to worry as to where Geoff and Ham had got to. Truthfully, with the table between them, it would take some doing to capture the other man. "You appear to have been expecting me."

"I was expecting someone." He gestured to the food before them. "We had a nice meal while we waited. Help yourself."

"Is that why you stopped here?" Vincent just managed not to clear his throat and give away that he was nervous. "You wanted a meal while you waited to surrender?"

"It seems I wasn't looking forward to crossing the Channel as much as I thought." His manner was mocking and superior, similar, in fact to King Edward's manner when he questioned someone who'd displeased him. "I'll have you know that the Gascon you sent with Hugh is dead."

He didn't know that Vincent had overheard the conversation on the Eton dock. Vincent decided he wouldn't believe Miles was dead until he saw the body with his own eyes. "He has always been able to take care of himself."

"You would not think so if you drank what he did."

Vincent wanted nothing more than to wipe the smirk off the other man's face. "His name is Miles de Bohun, uncle to the Earl of Hereford."

"And I am Jehan, though from your expression you already knew that." Jehan rose to his feet, having drained a second cup of wine, just as a far door banged against the wall. A moment later, two men brought a struggling Geoff into the warehouse.

"This is all you brought with you? One man? Where is that Welsh quaestor I've heard so much about? If I'd known he was this bad at his job, I would have worried less." Jehan laughed once more. "You were a fool to follow me, Vincent de Lusignan. And now you're a dead fool. I seem to be surrounded by them."

41

Day Three
Rhys

Rhys had sent Catrin and Tom's men back to the castle with Miles, while Rhys, Justin, Prince Edmund and the five members of his guard boarded a boat moored to the dock. It proved to be riverworthy, with two sets of oars, which speeded their progress down the Thames. Rhys stood in the prow with Edmund and Justin, peering through the mist for any sign of Jehan and his men. They were still woefully behind, getting worse with every moment that passed. If Miles died, it would be Rhys's fault. Catching Jehan, though necessary now, wouldn't even begin to make up for it.

And then, out of the corner of his eye, Rhys sensed more than saw motion on the bank to his right.

"It's Ham." Edmund blurted out the name, and then immediately hushed himself.

"Your eyes are better than mine, my lord," Rhys said.

Hastily, the oarsmen steered their boat out of the current towards the dock. Ham reached out a hand for the mooring rope. "Hurry! Geoff and Lord Vincent are inside."

"How many men does Jehan have?" Rhys asked.

"At least four. Two are guards from the castle. Two I don't recognize. We killed one already."

"We enter in force." Between one heartbeat and the next, Prince Edmund took charge, putting on the mantle of military commander. "We'll split into three groups. Stick together."

Rhys and Justin were put with Ham and sent around to a side door Ham had found. The others would go in through the front and back doors. Rhys didn't object to the plan, nor the fact that the prince intended to lead it. He'd been worried about Miles, and now he didn't think he should be any less worried about Vincent, not with the cold-blooded way Jehan had murdered George, Bobby, Hugh, and maybe Thaddeus, if Miles was correct about the order of events.

Once through the door, they found themselves in a cavernous space, similar in size to the warehouse on the dock at Windsor. The door they'd come through was exposed to the room, but it was also dark where they were standing, with the only lights in the center of the warehouse. There, men stood around a table.

"What do we do with them, *chef*?" The speaker was half-turned away from Rhys and held Geoff's arms. They were talking to the same slender man from Bobby's sketch. At long last: *Jehan.* Vincent was facing Jehan and was also held by two guards. His sword and dagger were on the table in front of him rather than in their sheaths at his waist.

"Dump them in the river like the others." Jehan touched the handle of the sword. "It's a shame to waste such lovely work, but these should go in with him."

"Vincent." Sword in hand, Prince Edmund stepped out of the darkness behind Vincent, who reacted to hearing his name with impressive efficiency, dropping to the ground as if his legs had just been cut out from under him. His guards were so surprised to find themselves holding Vincent's entire weight that they banged into one another and let go of him in the process. In almost the same breath, Geoff scraped his boot down the inside of one of his guard's knees.

At that point, the rest of Edmund's men converged on the villains. For his part, Jehan grabbed Vincent's sword and backed away from the table, holding off Prince Edmund with it, both hands on the hilt.

"Don't kill him, my lord!" Rhys bounded forward, Justin at his side. "We need him to talk."

The prince put out a hand. "I'm aware, Reese. But you stay back. He's mine."

Jehan's attention immediately diverted to Rhys. "So you're the quaestor everyone's been talking about." He made a few threatening moves with the sword, which he held determinedly in front of him. For now, despite his slender arms, his wrists appeared strong enough to wield it. But also by now, all four of his men were on the ground, two bleeding profusely because they'd fought back, and two more with their hands clasped behind their heads. "What took you so long?"

He wanted to talk, heaven knew why, but Rhys was willing to oblige. "It took a long time to see you for who you really were."

Jehan preened. That's the best way Rhys could describe it. "A man like me is always underestimated." It seemed Rhys was being thrown a bone, like Jehan felt he could be magnanimous now that he was caught. "I serve my king, as you do yours."

"Geoff," Prince Edmund said. "Take these men outside. Make sure we have everyone."

"Yes, my lord."

Edmund wanted to be alone with Jehan to ask his questions. Thus, Rhys, Vincent, Justin, and Edmund waited in silence for the rest of Edmund's men, all seven of them, to get the four guards out the door. They'd be marched back to Windsor over land rather than rowed in a boat.

"You don't deny your role in Alfonso's death?" Prince Edmund's voice was soft, but Rhys recognized the fury within it.

"Why would I deny it?" Jehan sounded nothing more or less than proud of what he'd done. He also appeared to like the sound of his own voice. "You wouldn't be here if you didn't already know the truth. Yes, I poisoned the prince with castor bean in his mead."

"Why?" It was almost as if the question was wrenched from Edmund against his will.

"England is too strong. Too powerful. Louis knew to fear Edward even before he was crowned king. How better to bring a strong king to his knees than to deprive him of his heir?"

"Does King Philippe know you're here now?"

"Of course." All of a sudden, Jehan seemed to accept that he had nowhere to go. He flipped the sword and offered it hilt out to Vincent. "You've won." Both hands came up. "I will not fight you."

Edmund gestured that Vincent should take his sword back. The prince was gripping his own so tightly Rhys thought there was an even chance he would run Jehan through right there and then.

By the expression on Jehan's face, he had no notion of Edmund's rage, or if he did, derived only amusement from it. He was so relaxed, he pulled out one of the chairs at the table and sat, to the point of pouring himself a cup of wine before gesturing to the table in general. "Help yourself."

Prince Edmund didn't move. "Tell us exactly what you have done. All of it."

"Happy to." Jehan lifted his cup, as if giving homage to Edmund. "I spent over ten years working my way into the good graces of the retainers of Edward's children. Buy a man a drink every now and then, and he'll tell you his life story. Some might even do anything for you and call you friend."

If Rhys had eaten anything in the last eight hours, he would have vomited it up.

"How many?" Edmund's voice revealed that he felt as sick as Rhys.

"Not Henry. He was a sickly boy. I saw no reason to take any risk with him. I knew he wouldn't live to inherit the throne. But John. And Alfonso, of course."

"How?" This was from Justin and came out almost a wail.

"Alfonso loved mead. He was the only one who drank it. But if not mead, I would have found another method."

"Why castor beans?" Edmund said.

"I discovered them in the Holy Land." And then, at Prince Edmund's disbelieving look, he scoffed. "Yes, I was there too, though before your time. A wise woman taught me how to process the beans to extract the poison without killing myself. And then I was sent here. The most difficult part was not to kill too quickly."

"Why now?" Edmund was so focused Rhys thought he might have forgotten anyone else was in the room. "You could have murdered Alfonso at any time."

"You mistake me entirely." Now Jehan's expression turned pitying. "This isn't about killing children. It's about undermining King Edward's rule. He conquers a whole kingdom," here he gestured to Rhys, "and then produces a second son named after him, only to have his beloved heir die unexpectedly shortly thereafter? What pain he must be in! When he learns the truth, he will know deep in his soul how weak he is and how strong France is. What's more, every day for the rest of his life, he will live in fear that at any moment, this last son will be taken from him too, leaving him a king with no heir. He will know that his life's work will end in failure. There are others, you see, like me, here in England, waiting to fulfill their missions."

"King Philippe." Edmund's face was entirely gray. "You truly work for Philippe?"

Jehan's face lit. "Isn't he your stepdaughter's new father-in-law?"

Edmund swallowed hard. It was impossible not to respond in some way to Jehan's gloating and chortling.

The Frenchman continued, "Weren't Joan and Philippe married three days before Alfonso died? How appropriate."

"I don't—" Edmund shook his head.

Jehan leaned forward. "No, you don't, do you? *France* is the most powerful kingdom in Christendom. *France* has God's favor. If not, how else could I have survived this long to do as much damage to Edward's world as I have? All I did was bring about the death of two boys. A life's work for two deaths. Who would believe it? And yet, it shows the power one well-placed man can wield." His eyes were alight with triumph.

That Philippe's marriage to Joan could be in any way related to Alfonso's death had rendered Edmund speechless. Rhys didn't necessarily believe it, but he was determined, if not desperate, to puncture Jehan's surety and spoke for the first time since the questioning began. "The castor beans were how we found you. They were in the beanbags you used to communicate amongst your smuggling crew. Why get involved in smuggling? Why risk your position for such small gain?"

"Those bags weren't even mine." For the first time, Jehan looked discomfited and lifted one shoulder in a half-shrug. "The money was good, and it put men in my debt, men who would do things for me when it counted."

"Why not leave once the job was over? Why did you wait?"

Jehan snorted now, his confidence returning. "I wanted you to find me. I wanted Edward to know."

For the first time, Jehan wasn't speaking the truth. Rhys was sure of it—as sure, in fact, as he'd ever been of anything. "That isn't the real reason. You're dying."

"We are all dying, a little bit every day."

"But you are dying faster. You have the look of a man who used to be heavyset and has lost a great deal of weight recently. One of my informants commented on it too."

"It doesn't matter."

"What matters is that you failed in the end." This was from Vincent. "Baby Edward lives."

"He's an infant. Infants die all the time without my help. Besides," Jehan shrugged again, "I left a parting gift up at the castle. It's too late to stop, if that's what you're hoping."

"What did you do—" Edmund took a step forward, and then went all the way to Jehan, who had started to tremble to the point of almost falling out of his chair. The prince caught him with one hand, a firm grip on his upper arm, and righted him. Then Edmund looked over at Rhys, who'd moved closer too. "What's going on?"

Jehan managed a dismissive wave with one hand. "Hemlock this time. It works faster."

Rhys crouched before him, watching his eyes, which were dilated. The end was coming too fast. They weren't done. "Why?"

"Your prince asked that before. Didn't my answer satisfy?"

Rhys gave a shake of his head. "Why kill yourself?"

"When the evening began, I thought it might be enjoyable to be put on trial. It was important for everyone to know what I'd done. But then I decided I didn't want to put myself through that, not when I had so little time left anyway. This way is better. King Edward will know, and he will *suffer*. That's enough."

Rhys had him by the arm now too, and he could feel the poison taking hold. "Tell us what you did at the castle!"

Jehan tried to push his hand away. "I knew after this morning that it might end this way. You brushed off the fire in the guesthouse like a crumb from your sleeve, as if a threat to your life could be shrugged off as nothing. I didn't expect that. I thought you would be like all the others. It was then I prepared the tincture, in case it came to this." Jehan's smile was a rictus of pain. "I've been dying a while. Let me go."

Edmund spun around to point at Justin. "Bring this news to your mother. We have no horses, so you'll need to run. Go!" He looked back to Jehan who had started to convulse. "We are out of time."

Before Justin had gone three steps, however, the door to the warehouse swung open. It was Geoff, looking panicked. "I'm sorry, my lord. I don't know what's happening to them! It's like they're dying right in front of us, and we barely touched them."

"He talked, and fools that we are, we listened." Edmund growled down at Jehan. "May you roast in hell for all eternity!"

"You need not worry about that." Jehan made one more motion with his hand. "It's a certainty."

42

Day Three
Catrin

The young women came to Catrin while she was sitting at Miles's bedside. He was sleeping in the bed that Edmund had ordered prepared for her and Rhys after the fire in the guesthouse. By this point, with dawn on its way, she wasn't going to be using it. Miles was far from out of danger, according to the physician, a man whom Catrin still didn't particularly like. She didn't think he knew more about castor bean poisoning than she did, but she did think he was right in this instance. Miles had developed a fever, was disoriented and had a quick pulse and rapid breathing. His pupils were also dilated. Though initially Catrin had made him vomit, since then, every so often he'd roll over and vomit over the side of the bed on his own.

In other words, he wasn't getting out of that bed any time soon.

"I'm Agnes." The first girl stopped just inside the doorway, taken aback perhaps at the sight of Miles in the bed. "I work for

Tom the innkeeper. He sent me the moment I came in." She gestured to the girl beside her. "This is Jane, Bobby's cousin."

Catrin glanced at Miles, who hadn't stirred, and then guided Agnes and Jane to a nearby sitting area. She thought she already knew most of what was important, namely that Jehan had murdered Alfonso with castor bean in his mead and Bobby in the stables afterwards, but since they were here, she thought to question them anyway. "Both of you knew Bobby well?"

Agnes had taken the seat Catrin offered. "I loved him—not to marry, you understand, but he was fun."

"He was always *fun*," Jane put in.

"The innkeeper said you shared a drink of mead with him and were sick afterwards?"

"Vile stuff." Agnes shuddered. "Give me a good ale any day over that."

"Did Bobby drink the mead too?"

"Just a sip. He had to taste it for the prince, but he hated it just like the rest of us."

"Bobby never became ill?"

It was Jane this time who shook her head. "He always said he had an iron stomach."

Agnes shrugged. "At least that day the honey cakes were good."

Catrin straightened in her chair. Margaret had mentioned honey cakes at the meal yesterday. "What honey cakes are those?"

Agnes gestured to Jane. "Jane started making them a few months ago from a recipe a friend of hers gave her. The spices are unlike any we can get locally."

Fear curled in Catrin's belly. "Spices?"

"He said they came from the east." Agnes's eyes were alight at the memory of this delicious treat. "Come to think on it, Bobby didn't eat those either."

"What friend would this be? Is he special to you?"

Jane laughed. "Oh no. Not in the way you're thinking. He's old enough to be my father." She waggled her head. "He is always buying drinks for one man or another in the tavern, and he knows food."

"He comes in most nights," Agnes supplied. "He's been around for years."

Catrin sat for a moment, looking at the girls, who gazed back at her innocently. Then she reached into her purse where she'd been keeping Bobby's sketch since Rhys had given it to her in the stables before he entered the warehouse on the Eton docks, not wanting it confiscated if he himself were caught.

At the sight of the man depicted, Agnes squeaked a little, and Jane smiled sadly. "Bobby drew that, didn't he?"

"Yes. We found it among his things."

Jane and Agnes both nodded. "That's Jehan."

Catrin couldn't be surprised. "How often do you make these honey cakes?"

"Every so often." Jane was completely unaware of the momentous news she'd imparted. "In fact, one of the maids brought a packet for me from Jehan last night, so I could make them first thing this morning.”

All of a sudden, Catrin’s heart was in her throat. “Where are these cakes now?”

“I sent them to the princesses’ table.” Jane gave Agnes a dark look. “I was going to bring them myself, but Agnes made me come here.”

“Has anyone eaten any?” Catrin was on her feet. “Before you sent them off, I mean.”

Agnes pouted. “Jane wouldn’t let me.”

Catrin bolted from the room and ran flat out through the corridors to the princesses’ dining room. All she could think was that one or more of the princesses would have risen early and be merrily breakfasting on the honey cakes.

Except they hadn’t, and they weren’t.

Catrin arrived breathless in the room to find Mildrith alone, standing before the sideboard, loading up a plate for herself. Catrin’s eyes went immediately to the tray of cakes, given pride of place in the middle of the dishes.

“Did you eat one yet?” Catrin pointed to an empty spot on the edge where one might have been.

Mildrith gaped at her a bit, but answered easily enough. “No.”

Catrin let out a breath. “So that’s all the cakes there ever were? It looks like one is missing.”

An expression that looked like guilt crossed Mildrith's face, and Catrin grasped her wrist. "Where is it?" She made no effort to keep the urgency out of her voice.

"I gave it to Charlie."

"Who is Charlie?" Catrin was just restraining herself from shaking the woman.

"Our pet mouse." Mildrith pointed to the floor underneath the sideboard.

Catrin bent down to see a tiny mouse lying next to a honey cake. She scooped up both and dropped them into a covered dish that until a moment before had contained scrambled eggs, which found a home on a different tray.

All the while, Mildrith looked on, astounded. "What is going on?"

"The honey has gone bad." It was all Catrin could think to say on such short notice.

"Honey doesn't go bad—"

But Catrin was already out the door, the tray of honey cakes in one hand, and the covered dish with its now-dead mouse in the other.

43

Day Three
Catrin

At long last, Miles opened his eyes, took in Catrin's face, and then managed a genuine smile. "I'm alive."

"You are."

"When I saw your face, I thought I might be in heaven. But then I told myself I was wrong since it was unlikely to be my final destination. By the same token, I couldn't be in hell, since you're here."

It was so like Miles to be witty at the edge of death, Catrin couldn't help responding with something of a smile herself. "It's your own fault you're still alive. You vomited up the mead before we arrived."

"I did, didn't I?" He closed his eyes again.

Catrin clasped her hands before her lips and studied Miles's face. In repose, he looked younger than his true age, even being so ill. "I'm glad you're going to live."

"Me too." He winced as he tried to scootch himself further up the bed.

Catrin helped him adjust his pillows so he was propped more upright. He hadn't vomited in the last hour, which she took to be a good sign. Then she helped him drink some wine. He was exhausted by the time he'd drunk three sips, which was all she would give him.

Once she'd settled herself back in her chair, she found him studying her face. "What is it?"

"You have something to ask me."

"Do I?"

"Don't play dumb with me, Catrin. You've been wanting to speak to me about something since Nefyn, and it isn't about Alfonso or this investigation. You might as well tell me what it is."

Catrin thought about saying something witty in return but swallowed it down. "This isn't really the time."

"Isn't it? When would be better?" Miles was well enough to raise his eyebrows as he waited.

"You're still at death's door—"

He cut her off. "Just on the stoop."

Yesterday, a lifetime ago, she and Rhys had decided not to speak of Miles's possible treason. But that had been before the fire in the guesthouse and everything that happened after. He was right that before they went any further down this road towards friendship, she had to know what kind of man Miles really was. She knew already that his foremost guiding principle was what was best for his family. He cared about his friends, but his moral center pointed to Humphrey, and then the king, and then maybe God, in that order.

Mindful of the constant threat of eavesdroppers, Catrin checked the corridor and then closed the door. Pulling a stool close to the bed, so they were only two feet from each other, she said, "Why did you conspire with that carpenter who went missing in Nefyn to sabotage the viewing stand? It is in my mind, and the king agrees, that we can include it as another attempt on his life."

Miles blinked. "That's what this is about? That's what you think?"

She spread her hands wide. "You were seen in the graveyard with the carpenter."

"Does the king know what you suspect?"

"No."

"Reese could tell you that I quite like graveyards as meeting places." Miles then eased out a long breath. "Perhaps the king should have appointed you spymaster instead of your husband."

Catrin looked sternly at him. "That would be Simon, not Rhys, as you well know."

"Right. I forgot." Miles winked knowingly.

Catrin waited.

"This isn't what you think, though I give you full marks for getting this far. I knew Adam because he worked on several of my nephew's castles before being enlisted for the king's works. He agreed to keep his ears and eyes open to anything untoward among the men he encountered. We met in the graveyard in Nefyn in the hopes of keeping our arrangement secret."

"Adam was seen leaving the viewing stand in the early hours of the morning before its collapse."

"I cannot speak to that since I did not meet with him again. If he discovered the sabotage, he did not report it to me. Please believe I would have said something if I'd known!" Miles appeared to drift for a moment, before blinking and continuing his explanation. "In retrospect, I find it likely that the person who sabotaged the stand may have been watching too. He would have been concerned about discovery. When I heard Adam had gone missing, I was worried that he and I had been seen—as you now say we were. My fear was that talking to me may have got him killed. Unfortunately, given what you say, now I'm sure of it."

"We believed the carpenter was the one who sabotaged the viewing stand, likely on behalf of someone else," Catrin said. "If you say he is innocent, then we still have no answers there."

"Adam was working for me. If he hadn't been, he would still be alive."

"We don't know he's dead. We never found a body."

Miles gave her a sardonic look.

Catrin respected the way Miles was taking responsibility for Adam, even though the real culprit would be the one who killed him (if he was, indeed, dead). Rhys, as spymaster (despite Catrin denying it just now), was in exactly the same position in this regard as Miles. It was fully possible that men and women were going to die on his watch. That he was doing the king's bidding was not an excuse.

But still, Miles didn't need to carry that burden. "You serve your nephew and your king as best you can. You have to give Adam the same agency that you give yourself. He made his choices. It's likely he paid for them, but if Rhys dies in the service of the king, would the king feel guilt? I suspect not, because he would have been doing what was necessary."

Miles looked up at the ceiling. "Such is war. Just because it hasn't been declared and great armies have not been marshaled makes no difference."

Catrin nodded. "If nothing else, we've learned that here."

Miles turned his head to look at her. "Are you going to tell me who saw me?"

Catrin didn't have to answer, not even with a denial, because footsteps echoed in the corridor outside, and the door to the room was flung open, revealing the anxious faces of Rhys, Vincent, Justin, and Prince Edmund.

Catrin leapt to her feet to greet them, but all the men looked past her to Miles.

"You're alive!" Rhys strode to the bedside and accepted the hand Miles offered.

"So it seems."

Rhys looked back to the prince. "How is it everyone is well?"

"I do not know." Edmund moved into the room and sat heavily in a chair against the wall. "Could Jehan have been lying?"

"Lying about what?" Catrin asked.

"About the danger to the princesses," Rhys said.

"You caught him, then?"

"Him and all his men, all of whom are dead," Rhys said. "In his last words to us, he claimed he had set in motion one final act of treachery, one we were too late to stop."

"He spoke the truth, my lord, except for the ability to stop it." Catrin went to the side table and pulled off the cloth she'd used to cover the honey cakes. Then she lifted the lid of the dish to show them the dead mouse. "Charlie was his name. The princesses will be sad their friend is dead."

"But they are alive." Prince Edmund seemed to fold in on himself, and he put his head in his hands.

Rhys then related what had happened since she'd departed the warehouse with Miles, concluding with a further elaboration of Jehan's last threat. None of the others interrupted the recitation, though Vincent kept glancing into the corridor to make sure they were alone.

"Meanwhile, Jehan himself is dead," Rhys's tone was utterly flat, "along with all of his men because he poisoned them himself."

"So it's over." Miles eased back into his pillows.

"It is over." Edmund's head came up, his eyes brighter than before. "As it turns out, Jehan's death is a gift. Suddenly I find myself grateful."

"I don't understand, my lord." Vincent had finally closed the door and now stood with his back to it.

"We have the ability to deny him his last wish."

A silence settled on the room as Prince Edmund rose and went to the window to look out at the dawn. Everyone waited for him to speak again.

"I've been thinking on this since we left Wales. My brother sent us here to find the truth. He thinks he wants it. He doesn't. And even though we know it now, we cannot give it to him. In fact, we cannot tell anyone the true story of what transpired in the night, especially not my brother."

Justin put up a tentative hand. "You're really suggesting we allow the king to think God has forsaken him?"

The prince turned around to face them. "It is better than the truth. God's favor can be won back."

Everyone stared, first at the prince's face and then at the floor. It was Catrin who managed to speak next. "How are we to keep what happened here a secret?"

"We will do it because we have to." Prince Edmund was more certain than Catrin had ever seen him—or seen anyone. "Think back. Is anyone left alive besides the six of us in this room who knows the whole truth?"

"Miles *is* lying here at death's door, thanks to Jehan, my lord," Catrin said softly. "He was poisoned with castor beans. We have the carafe. The physician knows it, as does most of the castle by now."

"As I said, I am not at death's door, Catrin. My stomach is lined with lead, just like Bobby's." Miles was trying to inject humor into the situation, but nobody laughed.

Prince Edmund was unmoved. "What does it matter that Jehan poisoned Miles? He isn't dead, is he? And he isn't going to die. We were after smugglers, and all the smugglers are dead. Was anyone besides us, who is not dead, party to Jehan's confession—either the one to Miles or the one before he died?"

Slowly the others shook their heads. Only Miles spoke aloud, "Not on my part."

Prince Edmund nodded. "We will empty the warehouse in Eton, and I will send my men back to the one in Old Windsor to burn it, the bodies, and every hint of evidence, to the ground." He gestured to the side table. "That includes those cakes."

"You are right, my lord." Despite his illness, Miles was the most composed of any of them. "It is what must be done."

Rhys wet his lips. "Are you really asking me—a man trusted because I'm always honest—to lie to the king?" And then he drew in a breath at Edmund's continued impassive expression. "Yes, you are asking exactly that."

Edmund looked from one companion to another, his gaze landing last on Catrin. "For ten years, the king gave free rein to a spy from the French court who murdered his children. Surely you must see that he must never know this truth?"

Up until that moment, Catrin hadn't known how to answer, but she answered in the only way possible in this moment. "I do."

"Prince Edmund is right." Vincent's hands were on his hips. He was newly transformed into a better man, but he, like the other Marcher lords in the room, including Catrin's son, was eminently practical and conditioned to obey his betters as a matter of course. "We are fortunate that Jehan disguised his true purpose in a smuggling ring."

Again, Edmund's eyes went to Rhys, who slowly began to nod. "We can put out that our presence at Windsor was always about rooting out a few bad apples, that we never suspected Alfonso had been murdered at all, but that his death was an excuse to investigate. We will turn what we said at the very beginning, and what everyone assumed was true, on its head."

"I would never question Prince Edmund's wisdom," Justin was growing more mature by the heartbeat, "but will anyone believe such an elaborate story?"

"Yes." Catrin reached for her husband's hand. She didn't know if he could do what Prince Edmund was asking, and the only way he was going to be able to go through with it was if she stood firm beside him. "They will believe it because they want to."

Historical Note

Paladin is rooted in historical fact: three weeks after King Edward's Arthurian-esque tournament in Nefyn, intended to celebrate his triumphant conquest of Wales, his eldest living son, Alfonso, died of an unspecified illness. Always a healthy child, unlike his elder brother Henry, the death was unexpected and without explanation, since he had already survived the usual childhood diseases that killed so many children before the age of five. His death is recorded on August 19, 1284.

King Edward and Queen Eleanor didn't hear the news until three days after Alfonso's death, on August 22nd, the day they left Caernarfon with their retinue. Thus, they did not attend the funeral at Westminster Abbey, nor, in fact, change their traveling plans whatsoever.

With Alfonso's death, they were left with five living daughters … and baby Edward, born in April at Caernarfon and still on tour with his parents.

History doesn't record that Edward sent anyone to investigate Alfonso's death, but it is interesting to note that his death was the last of the premature deaths of Edward and Eleanor's children. After two decades of tragedy, starting with the death of their first daughter twenty years earlier, every one of Edward and Eleanor's six remaining children survived to adulthood.

    As a further note, as readers of my other books will attest, I love tunnels. The one used by Hugh and Miles still exists, hidden beneath a trap door in what is now known as the Curfew Tower.

About the Author

With over a million books sold to date, Sarah Woodbury is the author of more than forty novels, all set in medieval Wales. Although an anthropologist by training, and then a full-time homeschooling mom for twenty years, she began writing fiction when the stories in her head overflowed and demanded that she let them out. While her ancestry is Welsh, she only visited Wales for the first time at university. She has been in love with the country, language, and people ever since. She even convinced her husband to give all four of their children Welsh names.

Sarah is a member of the Historical Novelists Fiction Cooperative (HFAC), the Historical Novel Society (HNS), and Novelists, Inc. (NINC).

She makes her home in Oregon.

www.sarahwoodbury.com